Arrows, Bones
&
Stones

The shadow of a child soldier

Because escape is only the beginning...

donna white

Donna White

For Angela

Also by Donna White

Bullets, Blood and Stones:
the journey of a child soldier

(Book I in the Stones Trilogy)

Information for this story was obtained through
interviews with former child soldiers from Joseph
Kony's Lord's Resistance Army in Uganda. In
certain cases, incidents, characters, locations, and
timelines have been changed for dramatic purposes.
Certain characters may be composites,
or entirely fictitious.

The story of *Sesota* and *Walukaga* are taken in part
from Rosetta Baskerville's, *The King of the Snakes
and Other Folk-lore Stories from Uganda*, London,
The Sheldon Press, Northumberland Avenue, W.C.
2 New York and Toronto; The Macmillan Co.
Kampala; The Uganda Bookshop. 1922.

Cover design by H. Leighton Dickson

PRAISE FOR
ARROWS, BONES AND STONES:
THE SHADOW OF A CHILD SOLDIER

"*Arrows, Bones and Stones* compellingly reveals the struggle faced by those trying to overcome childhood trauma. For youth abducted and forced to fight as child soldiers, escape is not the end of the story, but just the beginning. The shadow of their past haunts them, and the physical scars and psychological wounds cut deep. But even in the darkest hour, there is always the promise of new light. Yes, this is a story of despair, guilt, and shame, but it's also one of resilience and hope."

- **Patrick Reed**, Director/Producer, *Fight Like Soldiers, Die Like Children*

"In this second installment in the trilogy, Charlie, Fire, and Sam, provide us with the necessary human contexts to the plight of girl child soldiers but also the harsh reality of losing a loved one at a young age. The gripping tale reminds us that even in the midst of inhumanity, we all have the ability to be hopeful, and have the will to survive. An incredibly well written book! I can't wait for the next one."

> - **Michel Chikwanine,** former child soldier and author of *Child Soldier: When Boys and Girls are Used in War*

Part I

Chapter 1

A fallen branch cannot bear fruit on its own.
~ African proverb

It had been seven nights since he had danced in the rain. Seven nights since he had left his gun on the ground and felt the thrill of freedom as each raindrop washed over him. Each step he took, each mile he covered, each night he spent walking under the cover of darkness brought him farther and farther away from the army. It calmed his heart and erased his trepidation. For once he felt alive.

Until he came to the school.

It was like any school in Uganda. A long brick building, a stand of brush on one side, and a large field on the other. A field worn from years of football, *bolingo*, and *kakopi kakopi*—childish games forgotten until now.

But the school was empty and the field was bare except for a solitary pump set on a cement base.

Charlie smiled. He saw the faded images of

years past: wrestling with his friends on the red clay ground, tumbling over each other, pitting himself against them—a playful game that left them glowing with sweat and panting for breath.

He stared at the yellowed walls of the school, and then the vision came. Fast, fierce, overpowering. Stronger than reality.

He pushed his fists to his ears and tried to silence the gunfire blasts that echoed in his head. It was no use; the noise deafened him. He shut his eyes tight, but the images of the dead bodies, shredded with bullet holes, burned into his eyelids. He smelled the bitter metallic breath of spent guns and the acrid stench of singed flesh.

He fell to the ground and moaned as he rocked back and forth. The noise invaded the jungle, quieting the birds, stilling the leaves. He saw the shadowed images of the women and children who stood before him and heard a voice that commanded his attention.

"Now applaud the work of the Lord Resistance Army."

He opened his eyes and drew his hand across his face, wiping the tears away. A bee flew past: a soft buzzing drone that pushed the deafening sounds of the gun blasts away. It landed on a golden sunflower, and the images of the bodies faded. A cricket called across the field and waited for a reply.

The air filled with the afternoon heat and a gentle, cool breeze blew across Charlie's bare back.

He sat up and drew in a long, deep breath, then took off his shoe, adjusting the leaves and grass he had stuffed inside to hold his feet in the oversized Nike runners, blue with stains of dark red. He slipped his foot back in, and pursing his lips in deep concentration, retied the lace: crisscross, under and pull, crisscross, under and pull. He stood and arched his back, then walked across the field toward the school that lay at the end of the clearing. He chided himself for taking such a risk in exposing himself but quickly dismissed the thought. Something here demanded his presence.

He walked into a classroom and stopped and stared. It was as if he had stepped into a strange dream—once lived and almost forgotten. It had been two years since he'd gone to school. Two years since he had been forced to leave his village. He was twelve years old now. Too old to be a little ka-boy. Too young to be haunted by such memories.

He scanned the room. The desks were upturned and the benches lay on their sides, but the beginnings of a lesson were still visible on the blackboard. He took a piece of chalk from the ledge and drew a picture of a mud hut, adding a grass roof and an open door. Next, he drew a stick figure of a small ka-boy with his foot aimed at a soccer ball. After he returned the chalk to the ledge, he stood back and stared at his work. He tilted his head to one side, then the other, but the long thin line of his lips remained the same.

Then he saw the blood, sprayed across the blackboard, dried and dark. The classroom faded and came back into focus. This time he saw a teacher standing in the doorway, blocking the way. He heard a voice deep inside his head.

"Take your gun and your evil out of here!" the teacher demanded.

Charlie peered past his brigade leader, a teenager who stood just a head taller than he did, through the doorway into the classroom full of students.

"Our evil? And what evil could that be?" the teenage soldier replied. He walked into the classroom and aimed his gun at the teacher. "You are the one who is evil. We come to free our country. And you," he said, shoving the gun into the man's chest, "you dare to seek the protection of the Uganda People Defence Force? You dare to take the side of our government? Our enemy? Only a coward would do that!"

The soldier pulled the trigger, and the teacher dropped to the ground. The children screamed.

"Shut up!" the teenager yelled. "Shut up!" He

*marched into the room, knocking the desks and
benches onto the floor "Out! Now!"*

The children ran out the door.

Charlie blinked and the images faded. He took
a book from the floor and opened its cover. He ran
his fingers over its burnt edges and the words and
symbols spread across the smudged pages. He read
one word, then another. "If a boy has th . . ." He
stopped and tried again. "Th-i-rr . . ." He tried the
next word and the next, but the words were foreign
to him; he couldn't read them. The book slipped
from his hands.

He crossed the room and picked up a striped
flag that lay ripped and discarded in the corner.
Shaking the dust off, he stood on his tiptoes, took
two tacks from the bulletin board, and pinned the
flag to the wall. He ran his fingers over the silk,
touching each of the colors while he remembered:
*black for the people, yellow for the sun, red for the
blood of brotherhood that makes us one.* He stepped
back and stared. His face was hard, offering no
emotion.

*"Bring them here!" a voice shouted across the
schoolyard.*

*Charlie looked at the window on the opposite
side of the classroom. Large trees and bush
surrounded this side of the school, offering cover,
protection. He walked to the window and looked*

right, then left.

A young soldier stepped out from the bush. "You got everyone in that room?"

"Yes. They are gone," Charlie said.

"Good. I will patrol here. You bring up all the straggler."

Charlie turned and walked out the door.

A big crowd of men, women, and children had massed in the schoolyard. Faint sobs and anguished cries were heard as fathers and mothers searched for their children.

A general, three stars sewn on the epaulets of his uniform, stood on top of a jeep and lifted a megaphone to his mouth. He bellowed, "We have heard you think our gun are rusty. We have come to show you this is not true." The man grinned. "But now you will learn to applaud the work of the Lord Resistance Army!"

The air was filled with screams as the soldiers walked through the crowd, singling out the men, pulling their wives and children from their grasp, and forcing them to lie facedown in a row on the ground. Soon the older boys from the crowd were herded together and made to do the same. Sons searched for fathers; fathers lay still, not daring to move.

The general yelled again. "That is not enough. Gather more!"

9

The screams grew louder and louder as the soldiers pulled several women from the crowd and forced them to lie on the ground with the men and boys. A soldier dragged a woman, very young and very pregnant, across the field.

"This is not the season for killing pregnant women," the general said calmly into the megaphone. "Let her go."

The soldier released the woman. She collapsed to the ground and held her belly. Her eyes were wide. Her breaths came to her in short, quick gasps as tears streamed down her face.

Charlie forced himself to walk toward the row of men and women and boys. His gun strap lay balanced over his shoulder, weighing him down. He spaced himself between two of his fellow soldiers and aimed his gun. He looked up at the general and waited for the signal.

"Now look, you mother and sister. Do not cry, do not be coward, or you will join your husband and father, mother and daughter, son and brother." The general stared down at the line of soldiers and nodded.

A riot of bullets tore through the air.

"Again!" the general shouted. "Again!"

And then it was quiet. The blasts echoed across the field and fell silent on the dead bodies lying in a long, long row.

Charlie hoisted his rifle over his shoulder and followed the troop into the bush. He closed his eyes and allowed the trees to surround him. But it was no use. The images of the corpses were engraved in his mind.

The same voice bellowed over the megaphone: "Now, mother and sister, applaud the work of the LRA."

Faint clapping followed them into the bush.

Charlie blinked and the classroom came into focus. He walked out the door and into the schoolyard. "No!" he moaned. The images, the sounds, and the smells could not be his. They belonged to someone else. Someone deranged. Someone evil.

He stared at the scars on his wrists left by the ropes that had held him captive, that had dug deep and bit into his skin. He began to shake, and then he realized the truth. *No, this boy who held the gun* was *me. This boy who obeyed the commander was me. This boy who killed those men and women* was *me. Oicho Charlie, son of Oicho Moses and Olarobo Margaret of the Acholi tribe. The same tribe of the vicious warlord Joseph Kony, who stole children from their parent and forced them to kill or be killed.*

He fell to the ground and sobbed.

Chapter 2

When the music changes, so does the dance.
~ African proverb

Charlie raised his head from the ground and looked up across the field. The day was nearing its end; the sky surrounded the setting sun with a multitude of pinks, purples, and reds. A lone bird cawed, flew over the field, and nestled in a tree nearby.

Charlie tried to push himself up from the ground. It was futile. His body would not listen. Every muscle and every nerve had locked into place, refusing to take orders from a mind filled with disbelief, disgust, and despair.

Charlie took a deep breath, then let it escape in

a heavy sigh. It was much too risky to stay out in the open—he would have to get back into the bush. He had been in the field too long. He pushed himself onto his knees and then to his feet. Stumbling, he took a few steps into the dense growth of the surrounding trees.

Instantly, all knowledge he had learned in the bush with the LRA became second nature. Charlie crouched below the level of the scrub and peered into the forest ahead of him. The faint outline of a path, perhaps no longer in use, lay ahead. He became wishful; maybe it led to an abandoned hut, left by a family who had fled to a refugee camp long ago—a hut that offered some shelter and a place to rest.

Charlie followed the path, paying careful attention to any signs that hinted at recent use: a broken branch, an upturned stone standing beside its empty hollow, or grasses bent in one direction, trodden under the feet of a passerby. He looked quickly from branch to ground and ground to branch, and expertly moved in a way that could not be heard by nearby ears, or detected by a soldier or hunter skilled in tracking prey.

He walked a short distance down the path until he was a few feet from a clearing, then crouched on his hands and knees and stared into the open space. A charred hut, its roof bare, stood in the center, with an upturned grain house near its side. A couple of broken wooden chairs lay discarded on the ground.

He stood and walked toward the hut and looked inside. A thin mattress, thrown across the room, leaned against the wall. A blanket lay at the other end of the hut, covered with a thin layer of dirt.

Charlie drew in a quick breath, cocked his head, and listened. A faint rustle of branches and leaves sounded just outside the hut. He tensed. Any unusual noise, any stray movement, was a threat. Cautiously, he crept inside and leaned against the inner wall.

He held his breath until he stood in absolute silence and waited. The rustling sound drew closer until it stopped just outside of the wall. He heard scratching on the clay ground and a soft *kuuUU- kuuUU- KUUUK*. He exhaled and smiled. A flurry of feathers and wings appeared as a chicken flew up into the hut and nestled into a large bowl placed on the top of the wall.

Charlie laughed.

"You are a beautiful girl, yes." He gently stroked the bird's warm feathers and listened to its soft clucks as it drew its head under its breast.

"What have you got here just?" He reached into the bowl and pulled out an egg and smiled again. He broke the shell and gulped it down; its warm, soft liquid slid down his throat and settled into his stomach.

He picked up the blanket, shook the dust from it, and wrapped it around his shoulders. Then he laid the mattress on the ground and looked out into the yard. He relaxed, feeling his body give up all its fears and trepidations.

"Charlie! Come! The day has been filled with work and other busyness. It is time to stop. Come sit here beside your grandfather."

Charlie looked out the hut door as his kwaro *patted the ground beside him.*

"Can you tell the Sesota story, Grandfather? Ojone? *Please?"*

"But I told it to you last night," the old man replied.

"And the night before, and the night before that . . ." Charlie's father chimed in as he sat across from Charlie. Charlie sat beside his grandfather and tucked his knees underneath his chin.

"But it is a good story. And it is my birthday. I am now eight year, and I can do as I please. I will start."

"No, no. It is mine to tell. It is my honor as your kwaro. *And no matter how old you are, I will always be older." He cleared his throat. "Now listen. Once there was a beautiful village called Kalungu that sat beside the Great Lake." Charlie's grandfather smiled, revealing a somewhat toothless*

grin. *"Now you close your eyes, and I will create the picture in your mind."*

Charlie squeezed his eyes shut.

"It was a peaceful place and the children were happy there. All the house were surrounded by many grove of banana tree, and the fruit tree were so laden with pawpaw and lemon and guava that all of their branch would bend down to the children upstretched arm, begging to be picked.

"But it was not always like this for—"

"A big snake called Sesota . . ." Charlie said, opening his eyes and looking up at his grandfather.

"Lived on the hillside and came down every day to the village . . ." his grandfather continued.

"And caught people and ate them up!" Charlie twisted his body like a snake and snapped his teeth shut with a mischievous grin.

"And every day this happened . . ."

"Until all the people of Kalungu ran away, leaving the village alone and empty."

Charlie jumped and scurried behind the hut, then peeked around the wall.

His grandfather continued. *"The king was not happy with this, so he asked all the chief if they knew anyone who would be brave enough to kill the great snake. The chief thought and thought and searched and searched for someone, but no one was brave enough to go to Kalungu and kill the great snake, Sesota—"*

"But there was one man," Charlie interrupted again, "a poor peasant man called Waswa, who told the king he would kill Sesota."

Charlie's grandfather patted the ground beside him, and Charlie returned to his seat.

"The king brought him many spear and big hunting knife, but Waswa turned his back on the weapon, telling the king that the only thing he needed was . . ."

"A large water pot and some blue bead and some brass and ivory bracelet and a ring," Charlie said with a quick nod.

"After the king gave all these thing to him, Waswa began his journey with his little ka-son who carried the water pot with the brass and bracelet and ring inside. While they walked, Waswa played his reed pipe and his son sang this song."

Charlie's father reached across and took his hand. They joined with his grandfather and sang:

"Sesota, Sesota, the king of the snake,
Beautiful present I bring.
The king of Uganda has sent me today,
With bracelet and bead and a ring."

"Now as you know," his grandfather continued, "snake adore the sound of music, and as Sesota heard them approaching he sang back to them."

The grandfather lowered his voice and sang:
"I am Sesota, the king of the snake:
Two bold intruder I see.
But if they bring me the gift of a king,
They will be welcomed by me."
Charlie grinned at his father, then turned his
attention to his kwaro.

"When Waswa and his son came to the village,
they sat near a deserted house where the boy put
down the water pot and hid. All the while, Waswa
played his pipe and waited and waited. Finally, the
snake slithered down the hillside and along the
village road until it came to the house and looked
into the water pot to see the present. This was when
Waswa sang another verse of his song:

"Sesota, Sesota, the king of the snake,
Enter this water pot here.
The king of Uganda has sent you a bed,
On which you shall sleep for a year.

"Sesota slithered into the water pot, coiling his
body around and around until the tip of his tail
tickled both his tiny nostril. All the while, Waswa
played his pipe very softly and slowly:

"Sesota, Sesota, Sesota, Sesota, Sesota . . .

"The great snake closed one eye, then the
other, and fell fast asleep.

"Quickly and quietly, without making even the
sound of a mouse scampering in the tall grass, the

*young boy crept up and put the lid on the water pot
and tied it down. Waswa picked up the pot, and they
walked back to see the king. Along the way they
sang this song:*

"Sesota, Sesota, the king of the snake,
Sleep on the bed of a king.
Beat all the drum, play all the harp,
Dance and make merry and sing.

*"And that is exactly what happened. Every
person in the village ran out of their house until the
street were filled with singing and dancing and
beating drum and playing harp because the great
snake that had eaten so many people had been
caught.*

*"And then the king ordered a bonfire to be
built, and they burned Sesota the great snake. The
king put both his arm around Waswa and beamed.
'The village of Kalungu is now yours, and you shall
be chief, and your children and their children will
rule this village for all time, and they shall be called
Wakalungu.'"*

*Grandfather grinned and patted Charlie on the
back.*

"Is the story true, Grandfather?"

*"Of course it is true. Why would you ask such a
thing? You only have to go to the village of Kalungu
and ask Waswa children. They will say it is as true
as you are you."*

"But where is Kalungu, kwaro*? I have not heard of this village."*

"Eeh? My ka-boy, it is where the sky rest on the earth and the earth hold the sky in her arm."

"But where is that?"

"Eeh? You ask too many question, Charlie. If I were to tell you all I know, you would think yourself wise, and wisdom only find it home in the old. And I am very old."

Charlie closed his eyes and held tightly onto the memory. It had been a long time since he had allowed his mind to wander back and see such good things. He laid his head down and enjoyed the slight comfort of the mattress as it cushioned him from the hard ground. He detached himself from the sounds that kept him awake—the wind and the crickets and the leaves—until he found himself in a world where he was dancing around and around a pot left to burn on a fire, singing, "Sesota, Sesota . . ."

Chapter 3

There can be no peace without understanding.
~ Senegalese proverb

Charlie sat bolt upright and stared into the darkness. The chicken that had been roosting contentedly in the washbasin gave an indignant squawk and flew out of the hut. Charlie hurried to the edge of the doorway and peered into the yard. It was still and quiet. Nothing moved. He darted out of the entrance and hugged the wall until he was at the back of the hut, facing the outer bush. Glancing to each side, he ran the short distance until he was well into the cover of the trees. He leaped onto the thick trunk of a tree and hugged the smooth bark with the sides of his shoes and the palms of his hands, and then climbed to its top, stopping in the dense foliage.

Slowly and silently, he turned toward the yard and crouched behind the leaves, looking down. Within seconds, a teenage boy walked into the clearing. Charlie noted the bow held firmly in his hand and the quiver of arrows slung over his shoulder. The boy was joined by another, and then another, until the yard was filled with a group of a dozen or more, each wielding a weapon. Some, like the first boy, brandished bows and arrows, while others carried machetes or thick clubs with darkened tops.

The first boy turned and faced the group. One hand directed half of them into the bush to the right, while a quick tilt of the head sent the others hurrying into the brush near the tree where Charlie sat, hidden.

Charlie narrowed his eyes and stared at the boys as they crept cautiously into the jungle.

What is this? he thought, mouthing the words.

An arrow whizzed past his ear and landed in the branch near his head.

"If you are thinking I am a clumsy shot with the bow, you are wrong. Come down and explain yourself. If you do not, the next arrow will find itself in your heart."

Charlie climbed down the tree. He raised both arms and stood quietly, eyeing the arrow strung in the bow, aimed directly at his chest.

"What are you doing, spying on us?"

"I am not spying on you," Charlie said, lowering his arms.

"Then why were you up in that tree? A bit late for a ka-boy to be out hunting, yes? Will not your *maa* be worried her son is out late late after his *cawa marac*? You should be safely tucked into your blanket, with your *maa* kiss on your cheek now that it is past your bedtime."

Charlie glared.

The teen drew closer to him and bent down to examine his face. He stood easily a foot taller than Charlie. From the hint of stubble on his chin, Charlie guessed he was well past his sixteenth year. "I have not seen you before. I have not seen you in the village or the refugee camp. You do not belong here, spying on us. Is that what you are? A spy? A spy sent by Kony?"

The boy whistled and the sound carried out into the bush like evening birdsong. In less than a minute, the rest of the group rejoined them, and a dozen pairs of eyes glared at Charlie. Some of the teens eagerly aimed their machetes and arrows at him, while a few others simply looked at him and smirked. Charlie dropped his gaze to the ground.

"Anyone know this boy? Is he from your village, Peter?"

A boy with arms as long as his legs eyed Charlie up and down. "No. Do not know him, Jonasan."

"How about you, Michael Jackson? You ever see him?"

Charlie looked up to see a boy whose nose was as flat as his forehead.

"No."

Jonasan kicked the back of Charlie's legs and forced him to his knees. "Tie his arm, Peter," he said, tossing a rope to the boy.

Peter yanked Charlie's arms behind him and began to bind the rope around Charlie's small wrists. "He has got the rope burn."

"Eeh?" Jonasan said, stepping in closer.

"See. The mark of the rope, here on his wrist. They go deep, too." Peter ran his fingers over the pink scars.

Jonasan walked around Charlie, looking at his back, his legs, and finally, his face. "When were you taken by Kony?"

Charlie pressed his lips together and remained absolutely still.

"Do not deny it. Only kid from the LRA have scar like that on their wrist. Where are you from? Answer the question, ka-boy."

Charlie closed his eyes. His head dropped to his chest.

"Answer me!" Jonasan kicked him in the back. He fell and didn't move.

"Tie him. And do it tight."

Peter finished wrapping the rope around Charlie's wrists and yanked it tight. Charlie clenched his teeth as he stiffened in fear.

When the rope was secure, Jonasan grabbed Charlie by his hair, lifted him up, and set him back on his knees. "Now, ka-boy, if you do not want to tell us these thing, it will be very easy for us to form our own answer. Right now, I am saying to myself you are with the LRA, because you do not deny it. And right now, I think you are here, sent by Kony, to spy on our camp and see what sort of protection the government has given to us."

Jonasan tilted Charlie's head back and stared until Charlie opened his eyes. For a few seconds they held each other's gaze. A little tear formed in Charlie's eye and rolled off his face.

The hard lines around Jonasan's mouth softened. He released his grip and walked toward the boys. "But there is the chance you have escaped and must put many mile between you and the LRA." He stood in front of Charlie and looked down at him. "So what is it, ka-boy?"

Charlie lifted his head and looked directly at the commander of the group. He inhaled a long breath. His words came out in a forced whisper.

"My name are Oicho Charlie. I escaped from the LRA seven night ago."

Jonasan nodded. "Okay, Charlie. Now the giraffe has come to the watering hole. Tell us where you are from."

"Padibe."

"And how long ago were you captured?"

"Two year."

The boys looked at each other, then stared at Charlie.

"That is enough time for Kony to warp your mind and turn you against us. We have seen it happen when our many brother and sister came to raid our village. We could not recognize them for the evil that took over their mind." Jonasan jerked Charlie's chin up. "The thing is, ka-boy, we cannot trust you." Jonasan turned to Peter. "Take him to the barrack and hand him over to the government army. Michael Jackson, you go with him. And do not take your eye off him. Ever. Not until he is safe in the hand of the UPDF."

Peter jerked the rope and forced Charlie to his feet. Michael Jackson tapped Charlie's chest with his machete, then used the weapon to point the way.

"My machet is sharp sharp," Michael Jackson said. "The machet of the Arrow Boy is always sharp."

Charlie headed out of the clearing and stepped

onto the path, only to find his way blocked. A teenage boy who had not been with the group when they arrived stepped forward and looked from the rope to Charlie, then to Michael Jackson and Peter. "What is this?" he asked.

"The boy escaped from the LRA a week ago. We are taking him to the UPDF," Peter said.

"Is this so?" The teenager stepped closer to Charlie and studied his face, staring long and hard into his eyes. He circled Charlie and bent down until they were almost nose to nose. Charlie felt the boy's hot breath on his face—long and steady, like the beat of a war drum. Finally, he spoke. "I know him. He was with Otti Lagony when they lined us up at the school."

Peter blinked. His eyes widened. "Are you sure, Naboth?"

Naboth forced each word out slowly. "I am sure. I know this face. He stood above me and my father at Atiak. He ran the bullet over us as we lay face into the ground."

Naboth grabbed the rope from Peter and yanked it, dragging Charlie behind him. The teen's steps were staggered and uneven. He stopped in front of Jonasan and the rest of the boys and shoved Charlie to the ground.

Naboth took the end of the rope and formed a loop.

"This boy was one of Otti soldier at Atiak. I know the face. He fired upon my father and me. He killed my father. He is the one. He is the one who filled my leg with bullet and left me a useless beggar boy."

Naboth wrapped the end of the rope around the base of the loop and yanked it tight. He grabbed Charlie by the hair and shook him.

Jonasan rushed to Naboth and seized the rope. "You cannot hang the boy, Naboth. Maybe he did kill your *wora*, maybe he is a soldier from the LRA, but you cannot hang him. Let Peter and Michael Jackson take him to the UPDF and they will deal with him."

Naboth pushed Jonasan and grabbed the rope from his grasp. He glared at Charlie. "Were you with Otti when he came to Atiak and killed many of the people of my village?"

Charlie's head fell until his chin lay flat against his chest.

"Did you hold the gun and fire all the bullet?"

Charlie closed his eyes.

"See? He does not deny it!"

Naboth grabbed Charlie by the neck and shook him. "Did you?"

The explosive din of a thousand bullets firing resounded in Charlie's mind.

"Did you?"

He saw the images of the still bodies and the pools of blood.

"Answer me!"

He could smell the acrid odor of bullets and the wasted stench of death. He gasped as he fought for breath. Falling flat to the ground, he clutched his ears.

Now applaud the work of the LRA!

Naboth thrust the rope over Charlie's head and pulled it tightly around his neck. With a quick jerk, he dragged Charlie to the base of a tree. He threw the end of the rope over a branch and yanked. Charlie rose until his toes barely touched the ground. His arms lay still at his side, limp and lifeless. He looked at his faded blue Nike shoes, splattered with dried blood.

"Here is what I think of the LRA," Naboth said. He pulled the rope until Charlie dangled in the air. A terrible gurgling noise came from Charlie's throat as the rope tightened around his neck.

A girl's voice shouted, "Put him down!"

Naboth yanked the rope. Charlie rose farther into the air.

The girl's voice grew louder. "I said, put him down!"

The rope slid over the branch, and Charlie collapsed to the ground. He heard the faint sound of scattering footfalls while gentle hands pulled the rope from his neck. Charlie looked up into the darkest eyes he had ever seen. Two eyes, surrounded by white diamonds painted on a dark face. He closed his eyes and lost himself in a tunnel of darkness, devoid of sight, sound, and touch.

Chapter 4

A man who uses force is afraid of reasoning.
~ Akan proverb

Patches of sunlight flickered across the floor of the hut, touching Charlie's face with brief, warm caresses. He heard the soft *croo-doo-doo* from a laughing dove as it pushed away the last of the night with its morning song. He opened his eyes and focused on the partially thatched roof above his head.

The chicken sat contentedly in the bowl on the top of the mud wall, staring down at him. Charlie let out a long sigh.

"Hello, again." His words came out rough and grating. He reached for his throat, feeling the raw and bruised skin that the rope had left behind.

A whiff of smoke drifted into the hut and drew Charlie's gaze out the door. A girl, wearing a floppy white hat and a long white dress, sat crouched over a fire. Wrapped tightly to her back in a colorful shawl, a young child lay sleeping, rocking gently with its mother's busy preparations.

"It is a good thing you are not on night watch with the chop-chop," the girl said, looking into the pot as she stirred. "Or the LRA may be giving you your second hanging for your deaf ear and closed eye. The rooster crowed long ago, and you did not stir with all my coming and going."

Charlie walked out the door and stood by the fire. His mouth watered as he breathed in the sweet aroma that drifted up to him from the pot. He swallowed and looked away.

The girl poured a thick brown liquid from the pot into a cup and passed it to Charlie. He took a step back and lowered his head.

"Eeh? It is unkind to refuse a gift. Here. Drink. Your body is in need of it."

Charlie hesitated, then took the cup from the girl's upstretched arms. Deep brown eyes, encircled by white diamonds, stared back at him. She smiled briefly, taking Charlie by surprise. He gazed at her hands and noted their size: small, only slightly bigger than his.

He gulped the warm liquid down. The coarse mixture rubbed against his raw throat like sand before it rested contentedly in his stomach.

"Here, you must take more." The girl refilled the cup.

"*Apwoyo matek*. Thank you."

"And what is the name your parent gave you?"

"Oicho Charlie." He gulped the rest of the liquid down and passed it back to her.

"Oicho Charlie, I am by the name of Fire." She patted the ground beside her. "Come and sit. You must tell me what angered the Arrow Boy so much that they were ready to kill you. And no, I do not want your thank. The spirit did not want you dead. That is the only reason I came. No other."

Charlie sat beside Fire with his hands resting in his lap. He was silent.

"If you do not want to tell me this, then you must start at the beginning. Or near to it. Tell me, when did you escape from the chop-chop?"

Again Charlie answered with silence.

"You do not need to pretend with me," she said. "I know what you are."

Charlie startled at the girl's choice of words: "what you are," not "who you are." He avoided her gaze and stared at the two sacks beside her. One lay open, exposing a small bag of rice, a knife wrapped in an old cloth, a couple of oranges, and the ends of a rope. The second bag, made from thick black cloth, lay closed, a rope securing its top.

At last he spoke. "It has been seven night," he

33

said.

Fire nodded. "And you have been running since?"

"Yes."

"And what brigade were you in?"

"What brigade?"

"Yes, were you with Gilva, Sinia . . .?"

"I was in the Stockree brigade. It was the one that raided my village. But we were always under the command of Otti."

"Not Kony?"

"No."

"You were never under Kony command?"

"No."

Fire untied her child from her back, lowered the top of her dress, and brought her child to her breast. She rocked back and forth.

"And where are your parent, Charlie?"

"They are both dead."

"By the LRA?"

Charlie paused. "Yes," he finally said. The word caught tight in his throat. Hearing it made it real and true.

"And how long were you with the LRA?"

"A year and more."

"You were with the LRA for that long, and you were under Otti command? Were you part of the Atiak massacre, then?"

Charlie dropped his head to his chest.

"That is why the Arrow Boy wanted to kill you. I cannot put blame on them. Over three hundred people were killed that day."

"I know," Charlie said quietly. He stood and stared at Fire briefly. He felt an emptiness that a lifetime of tears could never fill. He turned his back to Fire and walked away.

"It was not your fault," Fire said.

Charlie stopped. "Not my fault? What do you mean by that? I pulled the trigger. I swept my gun over and over those people. It was my bullet and my gun. I had a choice. My life or the life of three hundred? Not a hard choice to make."

"Oh, but it is, Charlie. And no one know of the choice that had to be made *kit kwo ma ilum*."

"*Kit kwo ma ilum*? Life in the bush?"

"Yes. There was the life in the bush, and now there is *kit kwo ma gang*, the life at home."

"But I do not have a home, and I do not know if I will ever have one."

"You will. All the spirit have protected you. They will show you your home."

"And what make you think I deserve a home? Or want a home?"

"Because everyone . . ." Fire stopped.

Half a dozen boys walked out of the bush. Charlie studied their faces, but he didn't recognize them from the past night. Their weapons, however, were the same: bows and arrows, machetes, and clubs. An older teen, a rifle slung over his shoulder and taking the lead, stopped in front of Fire and stared at her and Charlie.

Charlie glanced at the teen, then at Fire. She calmly took her sleeping child from her breast and wrapped him to her back, tightening the sash with a doubled knot.

"We have heard of the chop-chop boy who bring his evil to our village," the teen said as he rubbed his hand over his gun and smiled. "Come now, ka-boy. Come now or we will do our job here."

"He is staying with me, Nikisisa," Fire said. "Go. You and your ka-boy are not welcome here."

Nikisisa nodded at a boy who now stood behind Charlie. The boy grabbed Charlie from behind, lifted him, and wrapped his arm around his neck. He squeezed, blocking Charlie's airway until Charlie's face turned red and his eyes bulged. Charlie struggled and tried to pry the boy's arm away. It was no use; his grip was strong.

Nikisisa rammed his rifle into Charlie's gut. "We do not fear your foolish witchcraft, Fire," he said. "The boy is ours. He must answer for his killing."

Fire looked at the teen with calm indifference.

She reached into her sack and pulled out a rope to which several goat horns and bones were attached. She stood and shook the rope. The horns and bones rattled, sending an ominous sound into the yard. All of the boys, except Nikisisa and the one holding Charlie, took a few steps back.

"You are foolish with your concoction and bone, Fire. I do not fear you."

"Oh, but you should, Nikisisa," Fire said, glancing at the gun.

Fire shook the rope harder, and the horns and bones rattled more loudly. She moaned—a long, soft moan that bounced off the trees and filled the clearing. She closed her eyes, then opened them to reveal two white orbs. Charlie shivered.

"Stop your stupidness!" Nikisisa yelled at Fire. The boy dragged Charlie toward the path.

Fire jumped in front of Nikisisa and held her arms out, rattling the rope around and around in wide circles.

"Ooo-maaarrr-aah!" she moaned. *"Ooo-maaarrr-aah!"*

Nikisisa pushed Fire aside with his gun and followed the boy as he dragged Charlie toward the pathway.

"You say you do not fear me, but you should, Nikisisa. I have told the spirit to curse you."

Nikisisa pointed his gun at Fire. "Maybe you

have some people believing you and all of that stupid witchcraft. But I know who you are, Fire. A fake. And I am tired of you controlling the mind of all these boy, making them believe you have these power." He shoved the gun into her chest.

"Your gun has no power over me," Fire said calmly.

"You have no control over me or this gun."

Nikisisa pulled the trigger. Charlie froze. Nothing happened.

Again and again Nikisisa pulled back on the action. Nothing happened.

"See, Nikisisa? The spirit protect me. You are cursed and your gun is useless."

The boy holding Charlie stared wide-eyed at Nikisisa for a second, threw Charlie to the ground, and ran. The rest of the boys followed close on his heels.

Nikisisa glared at Fire, dropped his gun, and walked away.

Fire took Charlie's hand and helped him stand. "Come. There is some cassava that is needing the harvest. You can help."

Chapter 5

The axe forgets what the tree remembers.
~ African proverb

Charlie sat cross-legged on the ground beside the fire and rested Nikisisa's gun on his lap. He opened the bolt action and peered into the clip, then pushed down on the bullets. The bullets stayed tight and refused to lift into the chamber. He peered closer into the chamber and smiled.

"Yes, that would do it," he whispered.

He pulled a knife out of Fire's bag, and with careful precision, inserted the blade into the clip and found the piece of metal that was bent. He twisted the knife, reinserted it, and twisted it again, then looked at it from each side. The bent piece of metal at the top of the clip was now flat and straight. The bullets wouldn't have any trouble getting into the chamber now. "I un-cursed the gun," he said, putting it on the ground.

Fire shredded a large leaf into a pot of boiling water.

"So how did you know the gun would not work?" he asked.

"Because I told Anansi to jinx it."

"You asked Anansi? The trickster god? You did no such thing, and you know it. You knew the gun would not work. How?"

Fire lifted a spoon from the pot and sniffed at the green liquid.

"I have been honest with you. Why can you not be honest with me? I do not believe that witchcraft stuff, and neither do you. Your act is good, but you are too smart to believe in it."

"Too smart?"

"Yes. You knew about me at Atiak. You knew about all the brigade. And you knew the gun was jammed. How did you know?"

Fire took another leaf and ripped it in half.

"And you told me that what happened at Atiak was not my fault, and that no one know of the choice I had to make in the bush. How do you know all this?"

Fire continued to rip the leaf into smaller pieces.

"Fine. If you are going to be quiet, I can be quiet too."

Charlie sat and looked at Fire, then to the burning logs, and back to her again. Finally, he spoke. "If you were taken by the LRA, why can you not say it just?"

Fire glanced at Charlie and sighed. "Because when you are a girl, there is more to lose."

Charlie paused. An image of a familiar face came to his mind. A girl. A very beautiful girl. Dark skin, the color of a saw-wing as the sun cast its evening glow upon its ebony feathers. And eyes. Eyes that looked upon you and made you feel that all was good and right with the world.

"You are very pretty, Deborah."

"You are being silly, Charlie. You are only eleven year. A young boy should never be so bold to tell a girl she is pretty. You have been long long from your maa *and have forgotten the manner."*

"But you are, and what is the harm in telling you that? If you are, then I must say you are."

Charlie raked the coals while Deborah turned the corn. A young girl, with her child wrapped to her back, walked to the fire and held out a large leaf. Charlie made note of the two small boys following her and gave her six cobs. Without saying a word, she turned and walked away.

"Do you think I will be as beautiful as Giona?"

41

Deborah said, pointing her chin in the girl's direction.

"Will be as beautiful as Giona? You already are more beautiful."

Deborah took a cob of the blackened corn and passed it to Charlie. She took a cob for herself and sat on an upturned pail and took a bite. They watched Giona make her way back to her hut and pass the cobs to her family: one to each child, three to her husband, and one for herself.

Charlie stared at Fire. The small white diamonds painted around her eyes didn't mask her beauty. She removed her hat and wrapped a scarf around her head, covering her cropped hair. Quickly, Charlie lowered his gaze, but not before he had come to his conclusion: Fire was far more beautiful than Giona or Deborah. She would have been the cause of many fights within the army. A lot of the commanders would have wanted her for a wife. Even Kony would have wanted to add her to his group of wives. And what Kony wanted, he got.

Charlie inhaled in the steam that rose from the pot. Now what is Deborah cooking up today? *he asked himself as he added some more wood to the fire and stirred the pot. He took pleasure in breathing in the spicy smell. He looked up as she stepped out of the bush carrying several large sticks.*

"Careful with that. Stir it slow slow. You do not want to break the husk from the grain," Deborah said.

Charlie's eyes widened. He dropped the spoon into the fire.

"Careful!" she shouted.

Charlie retrieved the spoon and continued to stir, slowly, keeping his gaze on the pot. He closed his eyes, trying to shake the image away, but he couldn't. Two huge scars now covered Deborah's cheeks. Dried scabs of blood left two darkened lines, running from her nose to her earlobes.

Charlie wanted to tell her she was still more beautiful than Giona, that the scars her knife left behind in her attempt to destroy her beauty couldn't hide it, but he didn't.

"Eeh, I am not going to be letting you stay here if you are not going to do the work," Fire said, interrupting Charlie's thoughts. "I am sure you have peeled the cassava before. Grab a knife there and get to work."

Charlie took a root and sliced into the thick skin.

"No no. Not like that. Be careful. You are taking much of the food away. Take small small slice of the peel."

He readjusted his knife and carefully sliced a thin piece of the brownish-orange skin away. The

two worked in silence until the pot was filled and
Fire covered the African potatoes with water.
Charlie placed the pot on the fire and covered it
with a lid.

"Have you been here for long?" he asked,
returning to his seat by the fire.

"Almost four month. Shortly after Maisha was
born."

"And you have been here, all alone. No one to
share your day with?"

"Maisha is my joy," Fire said, patting her child
tied to her back. "He keep me happy and busy."

"But there is no one else here. You are not
lonely?"

"No."

"What about the Arrow Boy? Do you keep
their company sometime?"

"No. Only when they are wanting to know
thing. The weather, the mood of the spirit, a way of
healing. But that is all."

"There is no one else?"

"There are some who have chosen to stay here,
including all the family of the Arrow Boy, while the
rest have gone to the refugee camp. Their hut are
scattered here and there. They feel they must stay to
protect their land. Other have returned because they
have seen the disease that grow in the camp, that
take the old and the infant because they are too

weak to fight. But no, I am not lonely. It is me and Maisha just. And it is better this way."

She stirred the pot, took a sip from the spoon, and smacked her lips. "They come here, the women, the men, the Arrow Boy, to find out many thing: when the rain will come, when is the time to plant the seed. But most, they come for the medicine, for the healing." She crushed a dried leaf, stirred it into the pot, and took another sip. "Hmm, that will do."

"But the Arrow Boy—they fear you. Why?"

"Because they should. That is why." Fire poured the green liquid from the pot into a cup. "Now stop asking question and drink this. It will soothe your throat."

Charlie sniffed the steam that rose from the cup and wrinkled his nose. He took a slow sip of the hot tea and closed his eyes as he swallowed, allowing it to coat his throat. He gulped it down and set the cup on the ground.

The sound of footfalls came from the bush. Charlie and Fire glanced at each other and then looked toward the path. Three of the Arrow Boys appeared. Jonason led the way, while Naboth and Peter followed. Naboth glared at Charlie, his eyes still filled with hate and the desire for revenge. He held his fists tightly to his sides.

They stood over Charlie and Fire. Peter stepped beside Naboth, ready to intervene if necessary.

Jonason was the first to speak. "This war has brought out great evil in us. I am embarrassed to say that I cannot find forgiveness like my mother tell me to search for. It is hard hard for me. And it is much harder for Naboth. How can you forgive someone who has taken so much away from you?"

Charlie looked briefly at Fire, then stared at the ground.

"We formed our group to fight the LRA. Each of us has lost someone to this war. And each of us seek revenge. I am here to tell you that you need to go. Your life is not safe here. I have told all the boy to give you one day to leave. If you do not, more like Nikisisa will come, and I cannot promise you any protection."

The boys turned and started to walk away. Charlie watched Naboth's uneven gait as he limped toward the bush. He looked at the scars of mismatched flesh and the pockmarks on his legs.

Fire called out. "You told me your brother was taken when you were a younger boy. Is that right, Naboth?"

"Yes." He stopped and faced Fire. "They took Samson when he was fifteen. I was young. They did not take me."

"And is he still alive?"

"I do not know."

"Do you want him to be alive?"

"Of course I do. What kind of question is that?"

"Then you would want Samson to do anything to keep himself alive, yes?"

"Yes."

"But when you are under the LRA, it is always your life or someone else. You know that. We have seen it during the raid. We have heard the story from those who have escaped and then returned."

Naboth limped toward Fire and stared down at her. "But I would hope that my brother never believed his life was more valuable than so many other."

"Do you? Would you be able to make that choice? I hope you will never have to."

Naboth spat on the ground at Charlie's feet and walked away.

Chapter 6

Hold a true friend with both hands.
~ African proverb

The horizon gave up its last light as the sun hid itself in the trees. A troop of vervet monkeys, tired from scampering and leaping in the canopy, now sat quietly, nestled closely in pairs or small groups, grooming each other and nursing their young. A pair of grey plantain-eater birds called out to each other, their voices mimicking the laughter of old friends enjoying a well-worn joke.

Charlie finished his bowl of cassava and licked the remnants from his fingers.

"Apwoyo matek," he said. The words of gratitude now became words of farewell. He walked toward the bush, stopped, turned around, looked at

Fire, and smiled. "Your secret is safe with me, Fire. I will not tell anyone. But I am hoping one thing for you: that someday you will come to know who you are and where you belong. I can see it, and I am not that clever. I am surprised you cannot."

She continued to stir a pot on the coals. She did not look up.

"I am sorry, Fire. I am. Perhaps someday you will find out who you can trust." He paused. *"Apwoyo matek,"* he repeated. He turned and walked into the forest.

The bush enclosed Charlie, hiding him from Fire's sight. He forced himself to walk forward, but it felt like he was being pulled back. He stopped, turned, and looked toward the hut. He smelled the smoke from the fire as it drifted through the bush toward him, its smoky fingers wrapping around him, as if trying to pull him back to the hut, to Fire. But he knew he had to press on. It was best for everyone. He returned his gaze to the jungle floor and walked.

A thick tree stood in his path. He jumped onto its trunk, grasped the sides with his hands and the edges of his shoes, then scrambled to its top. He took in his surroundings. The clearing near the school lay ahead of him, while behind him he could glimpse the small yard of Fire's home. He would have to head toward the setting sun if he were to have any hope of staying away from people.

Charlie released his grip on the tree and carefully slid down the trunk. His ears became attuned to the sounds of the night. In the dense forest, even the best of eyes can't always see what lies ahead.

Charlie stopped. He heard the faint snap of a branch, some footfalls, and the swish of a machete as it hacked at a branch. He scrambled back to the top of the tree and looked down. A group of Arrow Boys, perhaps twenty or more, were walking in single file through the bush toward Fire's yard.

A boy said quietly, "I do not know why we are coming here. It will lead to no good. The girl is evil and has control of the spirit. It is better that we stay away."

"Hmph," another boy scoffed. "You fear her? She is nothing but a fake."

"You will see when she curse us and make us mad as a mongoose that bite the mamba."

The boys stopped their conversation. They had reached the edge of the yard that surrounded Fire's hut.

Silently, Charlie climbed to the very top of the tree, where the tip was thin and spindly, and pushed his weight forward until the end bent and touched a neighboring tree nearer to the yard. He jumped onto the second treetop and hung on to the tip, bending it forward until it brought him closer to another tree, giving him a better view. He looked down. In the distance was the group of boys surrounding Fire. Charlie noted the position of their weapons, hung nonchalantly over their shoulders or resting on the ground beside their feet. They weren't a threat. For now. He decided to wait and see.

He made his way down the tree and crept through the bush. When he came to the back of the hut, he crouched down and listened.

It was Jonasan who was speaking. "We must find out now now, Fire. We have heard a rumor just that Kony is nearby. You must talk to the spirit and tell us where he is."

"I told you before," she said. "Kony magic is strong. I have tried to listen to the spirit that talk to him, but they will only speak to Kony. They are evil evil spirit."

"Hmph!" Jonasan snorted. "I am starting to think, Fire, that you are making up the excuse. Perhaps it is because you are a liar and you do not know the witchcraft."

Charlie heard the thud of a machete striking the trunk of a tree.

"I will try again. Perhaps I can speak to Banganda. Maybe he has finally grown disgusted with Kony way and has left him."

Charlie heard the rustling of Fire's bag opening

and the rattle of bones and horns. She began to moan and chant. Her ominous voice sent its tendrils around the boys, into the trees, and up into the night sky. The hairs on the back of Charlie's neck rose and an icy chill traveled up his spine.

"Bannn-gann-daaa! Bannn-gann-daaa!" she moaned again and again.

He heard the sound of the charms hitting the ground. Fire's moaning and chanting ceased, and the jungle was quiet.

Minutes passed as Charlie imagined Fire examining the position of the bones and horns, trying to read a message, trying to figure out what Banganda was telling her.

"No," she finally said. "No, Banganda is refusing to speak to me. His allegiance is still with Kony. I am sorry."

A familiar voice responded. It was Naboth. "You lie, Fire. You are not a witch doctor. Any *lajok* would be able to talk to the spirit and tell us where Kony is right now."

"Then you do not understand the way of the spirit. They select who they will speak to. I do not choose them—they must choose me."

"I say you are a fake, Fire. I say that you know where Kony is but you are not telling us. Why is that? Why is it that every time we ask you to find out where Kony is, you cannot tell us? Is it because you are in allegiance with him? Are you one of his spy? That would explain so much. Why you came here alone. Why you stay here, alone."

"No. I am not one of Kony spy. You know that is not true."

Charlie detected a slight quiver in Fire's voice.

"I say we string you up. If you are a spy, then we are rid of you. If you are not, then what does it matter? It mean one less whore just."

Charlie stood and leaned forward.

"What do you think, Arrow Boy? We have put up with this long enough. Tale of spirit, prediction of rain that does not fall, and medicine that give no cure. It has all been lie!"

Fire's baby screamed. Charlie used all of his resolve to hold himself back.

"No! You must understand! If the spirit had told me where Kony is, then I would tell you. I have lost those I loved in this war too! If I could help, I would!"

Maisha's screams grew louder.

"No!" Fire yelled. "Give me back my child!"

Charlie couldn't stand it any longer. He rushed from behind the hut and ran into the midst of the group. Naboth held Fire's baby with one hand and shook his fist at her with the other. The baby's screams grew louder and louder until they drowned out the angry shouts and accusations. Fire grabbed for Maisha, but two boys held her arms and pulled her back.

The Arrow Boys closed in around them and shook their weapons.

"Stop it!" Charlie shouted. "Stop it!" The noise subsided as everyone looked at him. He took a deep breath. "I can bring you to Kony. If that is what you want, I can show you where he is." He paused. "But it is stupid of you to want to find him. You really do not know what wait for you there, do you?"

Fire rushed at Naboth and grabbed Maisha. She clutched the baby close to her chest as he buried his face into her neck and sobbed. Tears coursed down her cheek and landed on the boy's black hair.

Naboth glared. "We have had enough attack on our village to know what we are up against, ka-boy."

"Yes, an attack on your village by some of the LRA, not the whole army. Not the rocket launcher or all of the commander and all of the men and the boy under them. No, you do not know what you are facing."

"Then tell us," Jonasan said.

Naboth stepped between Jonasan and Charlie. "Why should we listen to him? He is one of Kony kid. You cannot trust him." He turned to Charlie. "Go. You were told you are not welcome here. Go!"

"No." Jonasan rested his hand on Naboth's

shoulder. "We need this information. We have no choice. And," he said as he turned to Charlie, "I think we can trust him. Tell us, Charlie. Tell us what you know."

Charlie nodded. "I will. And you will listen."

Charlie and Fire sat as Maisha's sobs now diminished to tiny whimpers. Fire caressed his head and rubbed his back. The Arrow Boys enclosed them in a circle.

"I walked for seven night after I escaped. But I traveled at night just. During the day I found a safe place to sleep, sometime tied to a high branch in a tree or in the thick bush away from any sign of people. The going was slow slow. I am sure if you walk the distance by daylight it would take less than three day."

"Three day, but in what direction?" Jonasan asked.

"In the direction that the sun rise in the morning."

"In the east?"

"Yes, but not fully east. Between the east and where you can see the Great Bear shine in the northern sky in the night."

"And if our group were to travel for three day, what would we see? How many soldier, how many gun?"

"At least four hundred soldier, maybe five or

six."

The Arrow Boys glanced at each other, their eyes wide with disbelief.

"Six hundred?" Naboth shook his head.

"Yes, that is what I have seen gather before. But I am not sure right now. It depend on who Kony want and what commander he call."

The Arrow Boys stood silently and waited for Charlie to continue.

"The army has been gathering during the last month, but I am not sure if they have set off in smaller group since I escaped. And gun? Plenty. There are plenty plenty gun. Some in use, some stored."

"Stored?" Jonasan asked.

"Yes, in the cache, hidden for raid and for time when more children are trained to be soldier and more weapon are needed."

Jonasan moved closer to Charlie. "Do you know where any of these cache are?"

"I do."

"Where?"

Charlie took a stick and drew a line on the ground. "If you head north and walk for perhaps one day and a little more, you will find a creek where it meet a little lake. There you must turn into the bush and travel toward a cane field. At the end of the field is a large tree; the flower look like the flame of a mighty mighty fire. At the base of that tree are some AK-47 with about thirty magazine."

He drew another line, extending from the line that represented the creek. "And here there is another, past the field just that grow the pineapple and has three row of orange tree standing taller than you and Naboth put together."

"And is there one here?" Fire said, pointing to a spot north and west of the cache Charlie had just pointed out.

Charlie thought for a moment. "Yes, there is."

"And one here?" Fire asked again.

"Yes." He looked at the diamonds that surrounded her dark eyes. "How do you know?"

She drew in a quick breath as she pointed to the bones and horns, shaking her head as if in disbelief. Their positions corresponded identically with the caches Charlie had drawn on the ground.

Chapter 7

Patience attracts happiness;
it brings near that which is far.
~ Swahili proverb

The stars were beginning to fade into the morning sky when the Arrow Boys returned to Fire's hut.

Jonasan yawned and wiped the sleep from his eyes. "Where is Naboth? I told everyone last night we had to make an early start if we were to find the cache." He crossed his arms over his chest and leaned against a tree.

"You did not sleep well through the night in the comfort of your hut, Jonasan?" Peter asked.

"No. When we have all the gun from the cache, then I will sleep." He glanced into the bush. "And if Naboth do not arrive soon soon, we will go without him."

Fire finished her breakfast and threw some dirt onto the dying coals. She grabbed a small sack and tossed in some *simsim* patties, cassava chips, and a few pieces of dried fruit. Tightening the lid on a bottle of water, she tossed it into the bag and tied the bag with a piece of rope.

She hoisted her bag of pots, plates, and rice onto her hip and carried it to the grain bin that stood between the two huts. "I do not know if the bag will be safe here from the rat and the monkey, but it is the only place I have to keep my kitchen," she told Charlie as she tucked her sack into the beehive-shaped structure.

"You do not have to come," Charlie said. "It is perhaps best that you stay. It is a long long walk."

"Yes, it is long. But you may need me. You do not have eye in the back of your head."

He nodded in understanding. "Will you be wanting to place this in there too?" He took Fire's black bag from the hut and carried it over. He felt its weight. "What is in here?" he asked as he ran his hand over the top.

She grabbed the bag and clutched it to her chest. Her words were quick and angry. "It is nothing, and it is of no concern to you." Charlie backed away as she set the bag into the bin and gently stroked its side. She secured the door.

A girl approached her. She held the hand of a

young boy who was sucking on a piece of sugarcane. Wrapped tightly to her back in a yellow printed shawl was a small child, asleep and content.

"*Itye nining*, Fire?"

"I am well. And how are you and your family?"

"We are good also. The child still does not sleep through the night, but I am still rested."

"Eeh. This is good, Salume."

Fire removed the cloth that tied Maisha to her back and placed her baby in the young girl's arms. She reached into the folds of a scarf tied around her waist and brought out a small bag of leaves. "Here, take this. You told me your son has a cough. Boil it in the water and let it sit for the morning, then make him drink. It will help." She bent down and kissed her son on his forehead. "He is a good boy. He should not fuss," she said as she caressed his cheek. "Be safe, my ka-man. *Maa* will come home soon." She placed her bag on her head and stepped onto the path leading away from the hut.

Naboth rushed out of the bush and limped to the group. He had a rifle slung over his shoulder.

"Look what I have," he said, panting and holding the gun out to show everyone. "I found it last night, near to the creek, on my way home. It was where we found the ka-boy and the girl last week when we scared away the two LRA soldier." He pulled the action open and pointed inside the chamber. "And look. It still have the bullet inside."

"But you are sure you know how to use it?" Jonasan asked.

"Yes. Yes. It does not take any brain to point and shoot." He slung the gun strap back over his shoulder and looked at Fire. "And what are you doing? Why are you coming with us?"

"I am coming because we cannot trust it all to Charlie memory. If we cannot find the cache, then I will summon the spirit and ask for the help. That is why I am coming."

Naboth glowered and shook his head. He went to the back of the line.

Charlie glanced at each of the boys as they stood in line behind Fire. The one they called Peter, the one who had tied his wrists, was first. With such long arms, the boy couldn't help but remind Charlie of a gorilla. Peter was talking to another teen, the one Charlie recognized as Michael Jackson. They both carried a bow and a quiver of arrows slung over one shoulder and a hoe over the other. For a moment, he remembered a person he had met who had two names: John Paul, a soldier they were told to call J.P. He didn't have many good things to remember about him. He wondered, *Why would a mother and father give their child two name? Was one not enough?*

Next in line was Jonasan, carrying his bow and

a quiver of arrows, and Naboth, standing tall as he brought up the rear. Naboth glared at Charlie, who dropped his gaze and stared at his feet. He couldn't blame the boy. And he wouldn't. This was how it was going to be, and there would be no changing it. The hatred was there and it always would be.

Fire interrupted Charlie's thoughts. "Let us go. We have mile and mile ahead of us." She readjusted the bag on her head and stepped aside so Charlie could take the lead.

Charlie stepped onto the pathway and took a deep breath. He straightened his shoulders and stared ahead.

Fire rested her hand on his shoulder. "Are you ready?" she asked.

"No. But we will go just." He followed the path.

The Arrow Boys kept up with the quick pace Charlie set. They continued on in silence, passing abandoned huts, treading over pathways once clear and smooth from years of use, now showing signs of overgrowth. In the forests of Uganda, it didn't take long for any seed or tendril to make its claim on an unused piece of soil.

When they came upon the edge of a forested area, Charlie turned to the shelter of the trees. He led the group into its thick foliage and pushed his way through the branches, barely making a sound.

They traveled for several more kilometers, the boys walking carefully, leaving as little sign of their trail as possible. Finally, when the sun was at its highest point in the sky, Charlie stopped and stood in a small clearing among the trees. He wiped the sweat from his forehead and took a drink from his bottle of water. "We will rest here for a bit, until the sun move away from the top of the sky," he said, sitting at the base of a tree. "We will stay in the cover of the tree until we make it to the river. From there we can travel under the safety of the dark and reach the cache before late late night."

The boys sat on the ground and took long sips from their bottles. Fire walked to a spot near the group and leaned against a tree.

Jonasan gathered the arrows from Peter and Michael Jackson's quivers and set them on the ground beside him. "I will check them for straightness," he said as he held one up to his face and gazed down the long shaft.

Peter cocked his ear and listened. "I hear water," he said. "I hear it faint faint, but there is a creek near here. It is not flowing fast, but I hear it." He turned to Michael Jackson. "Come. We can fill the bottle." The boys gathered the half-full bottles of water and crept into the bush.

Charlie rested his head against an immense tree trunk. A shadow loomed over him, blocking the rays of light that reached the forest floor. He looked up and saw Naboth glaring down at him.

"You are stupid," Naboth said to Jonasan. "You close your eye while this ka-boy think only of slitting our throat while we sleep."

Jonasan shook his head. "Eeh, the pot has boiled and the tea is made, Naboth. Can you see he is not a threat? The boy was captured by the LRA, he escaped, and now he is helping us. Can you not see the courage it take for him to do this?"

"You think it is courage? The hyna has courage when it face the lion. This is not courage. It is stupid stupid. It could be a trap. He could be leading us right to the LRA. And what could we do against them? Our one rifle against their many? Our arrow and machet against their bullet? It is foolishness."

Fire took a step forward. "Even the hyna know what is a threat and what is not. And I do not see him as a threat."

"Eeh? We do not listen to you. You are a whore. Sit down, ka-girl, and shut your mouth."

Fire glared. "No. I will not shut my mouth." She took a couple of more steps and stood in front of him. "I have had enough of this stupidness. You stand there like a peacock, all full of pride and thinking you know so much, but really you are an *opego*. A dumb dumb *opego*!"

"I will not take this from you!" Naboth's

nostrils flared. "I said, shut your mouth, whore! You do not call me a pig!"

Fire spun around and kicked him in the back of the legs. His knees buckled and he fell to the ground. She yanked her scarf from her waist and wrapped it around his neck and pulled tight. Naboth's face turned red. While twisting the scarf with one hand, she snatched up his gun and pressed the barrel to his head. Jonasan grabbed his bow and reached for an arrow.

"Stop now, Jonasan. Or I will shoot," she said calmly. You will be dead dead with the bullet in your heart faster than it take you to reach the arrow. Throw the bow away."

Jonasan obeyed.

"Now let us see what it is like. Take it." She placed the gun in Naboth's hands and twisted the scarf tighter. "Take it, I said!"

Jonasan and Charlie stared at Fire, confused.

She stood behind Naboth, using him as a shield between her and Jonasan. "Now aim. Aim it at Jonasan." She pulled the scarf even tighter. Her words came out slowly. "And shoot him."

Naboth struggled. He dropped the gun and tried to grab at Fire. She tightened the scarf again. His face turned red and his eyes bulged.

"Pick it up! Now!"

Naboth obeyed. His arms shook.

"Now whose life will it be, Naboth? Yours or your leader? Decide!" She yanked the scarf.

Naboth gasped. He placed his finger on the trigger and pulled back. It clicked.

Nothing happened.

Fire leaned forward and spoke into his ear. "You need some brain if you are to point and shoot. You left the safety on."

Peter and Michael Jackson stepped out of the bush as Fire released her grip on the scarf and Naboth fell to the ground, fighting for air. Peter rushed to Naboth's side as Michael Jackson grabbed his bow and reached for an arrow.

"No," Jonasan said. "Leave her. The viper has learned the strength of the mongoose, and the mongoose has learned the strength of the viper."

Michael Jackson let his bow fall to his side.

Fire grabbed the gun and emptied the bullets out of the chamber, wrapped them in her scarf and tied it back around her waist.

"Now stop being stupid." She walked to a tree, sat down, and leaned against the trunk.

Naboth sat up and rubbed his throat. He glanced at Charlie, then dropped his gaze to the ground. Peter offered him some water.

Charlie walked toward Naboth. "I understand this. Trust is earned, not given. Here." He took a small coil of rope from Jonasan's side and handed it to Peter. "Tie me. Naboth can hold the rope. When you trust me, Naboth, the rope can come off."

Peter wound the rope around Charlie's wrists, pulling the coils tightly around his scars. He tugged on the final knot, securing it strong and fast.

Charlie looked at the knots and then at Naboth. He nodded. "I should have more than rope around my hand, Naboth. Perhaps a chain as well, because I deserve all your hatred. But there is nothing I can do to change this. Perhaps someday you will understand. But I do not know how this can happen. I do not understand myself. For now, I accept your hatred. Throw it at me again and again."

Charlie sat on the ground. He closed his eyes and leaned his head against the tree. "There," he said. "Let us get some rest. We have a long way to go still."

Chapter 8

A small house will hold a hundred friends.
~African proverb

Charlie rubbed the back of his hand across his face, feeling the tightness of the rope coiled around his wrist. He looked up and noted the position of the sun. A brown African hawk eagle, perched in an upper branch, held his attention for a moment as it spread its wings and lifted itself into the air. Charlie followed its flight until it became a mere speck in the sky. He watched the bird for a moment longer and then turned his attention to the leaves of the tall acacia trees as they lifted with the slight breeze. The leaves changed color as they reflected the variable light: dark green, lime green, and occasionally a bright yellow that speckled the foliage with a fleeting touch of the trees' own sunshine.

He felt the tug of the rope and followed its trail,

glancing at Naboth, curled up against a tree. Even in his sleep he clutched the end of the rope in a tight fist. Peter, Michael Jackson, and Fire were also asleep; only Jonasan was awake, running the edge of his knife up and down the shaft of an arrow. He squinted down the long thin stick and placed it inside his quiver.

Charlie observed. His childhood, until he was taken by the LRA, was spent farming, working in the cassava and bean fields, caring for the fruit trees with his mother and father, tending the goats in his family's herd, and living a nomadic life. Some people traveled out of the village area to hunt an occasional wild animal like a hartebeest or a kob, but it was very rare to see a man or a boy carrying a bow and arrow. When it did happen, Charlie was in awe, wishing he could follow along with the hunters and share in the thrill of the chase. He sighed. The admiration he'd had as a young child for this primitive weapon was long gone.

"Do you really think you stand a chance with your bow and arrow against the LRA and their gun?" Charlie asked.

"We stand a better chance than with nothing and doing nothing," Jonasan said, focusing on his work. "I know you think we are foolish, perhaps even stupid, but we have done some good. Last week just, a boy and his sister went out to gather

their cow and were taken by the LRA. We followed
their trail and found them with two LRA soldier and
three young boy soldier. We killed the two men, but
the three boy ran away. Then we brought the
brother and sister back home and kept a guard on
their place for several day. We want to stay as guard
there, but we cannot. We do not have enough boy to
do the job everywhere."

Jonasan put the arrow aside and picked up
another. "You see, Charlie, we have some
advantage here. The LRA do not expect us to fight
back. No one has before. So we have a surprise
tactic right there. And then there is the bush. We
know it. We know the terrain—all the hill, each of
the river—and if the LRA come into our area we
have a good idea where they will be heading. And
we can meet them and ambush them before they
even know what is happening."

Charlie imagined the looks on the
commanders' faces when a barrage of arrows flew
at them while they were trying to sneak up on a
village. Then he imagined himself, part of the LRA,
trying to escape from the arrows while the LRA
commanders were breathing down his neck. Death
could come to him from a bullet or an arrow. It was
like his mother said: *sufuria au moto*. He could be
in the fire or in the pan. It was all the same.

Jonasan interrupted his thoughts. "And we have

this," he said. He took a small metal box from his pants pocket.

Charlie leaned closer and looked at the shiny red object the boy held in the palm of his hand.

"What is it?"

"A cell phone."

"A cell phone? What is that?"

"Look." Jonasan opened the device to reveal several buttons covered with numbers and letters. He touched a few of the buttons, then passed it to Charlie. Charlie held the phone and rubbed his fingers over the smooth surface. A voice came from the phone.

"Gway!" Charlie yelled. He dropped the phone and jumped back. The voice from the phone grew louder and louder.

"Hello? Hello?"

Jonasan let out a loud guffaw.

"What kind of devilry is this?" Charlie asked as he took a cautious step forward.

Peter woke, looked at the phone on the ground, then at Charlie's horrified expression, and started to laugh. Suddenly, the whole group was awake, watching Charlie. Michael Jackson doubled over and held his sides while tears streamed down his face. Peter slapped Jonasan on the back, and Jonasan fell to the ground. His arms and legs shook in the air as a huge belly laugh erupted from his body. Fire clapped her hands over her mouth as she tried to hide her huge smile. Naboth glared. Charlie stared at Fire and shrugged, then smiled.

Finally, Jonasan calmed himself and picked up the phone. "Hello, Ben. Yes, we are about sixteen mile in now. We have stopped the footin' and are resting for a short time, but we will head off soon soon." He paused, nodded, and talked some more. "Yes, it is going fine. No. No trouble. Yes, he is here. Do you want to speak to him?" Jonasan handed the phone to Charlie. "Here, Ben is needing to talk to you."

Charlie took the phone with his bound hands and held it to his face just as he had seen Jonasan do.

"*Hujambo? Hello?*"

He jerked his head back in surprise. Peter, Michael Jackson, Jonasan, and Fire burst into laughter again. Naboth scowled and turned his back. Finally, Charlie spoke. "I . . . I am fine. And how are you and your family?"

He furrowed his brow and stared into the distance. The group watched him intently as he listened to Ben, shrugged, nodded, and shook his head.

"You have to say yes or no, Charlie. Ben cannot see you, you know," Jonasan said.

"Oh." Charlie spoke into the phone. "Yes, I

will do that. Thank you. He handed the phone back to Jonasan and sat beside Fire.

"What did Ben say to you?" Fire asked.

"He said, '*Apwoyo matek*, brother.'"

Jonasan closed the cell phone, put it back in his pocket, and sat down. "That was Opio Ben. He is the leader of the Arrow Boy and gave us the okay to look for the cache you know about. He say it is brave of you to go back into the bush after you escaped just. He say he want to meet you when we come back with the gun."

Charlie smiled. Ben had called him "brother". Charlie didn't know him. He had never met him, and yet he had called him a name given only to someone loved and well respected. His smile grew and his eyes moistened, so much so that when he looked at his wrists he didn't see the rope that wound around them, binding him like a captured animal.

Chapter 9

The kingdom of heaven is within you; and whosoever shall know himself shall find it.
~ Egyptian proverb

Charlie stopped where the bush met the road and waited. It was still dark. They had made good time. Perhaps they would be able to dig up all four caches and leave before the sun rose. Looking across the dirt road, he took in a beautiful sight. The light from the full moon brought the *opok* tree into view, showing its flaming red flowers. It was a sure sign they were well into the rainy season. He breathed deeply, hoping to catch a whiff of its heavenly scent. He closed his eyes and smiled. It smelled like life, new beginnings and hope. It was beautiful.

Jonasan crept closer to Charlie. "Is this where a cache is?"

Charlie nodded.

"Show me where another one is, and I will get a couple digging while you have the other digging here."

"No," Charlie said. "We all stay here and dig together. It is better that we get one hole dug than two part hole, in case we are spotted. Plus, the less activity the better. Less chance of being heard."

Jonasan nodded. "Yes, you are right."

The boys jogged across the road, following Charlie in single file back into the cover of the surrounding bush. Naboth kept a tight hold of the rope that bound Charlie's arms.

"It is right here," he said, using both hands to point at the base of a tree.

"Take the rope off him, Naboth," Jonasan said. "He cannot do the work if his hand are tied."

Naboth glared at Jonasan out of the corner of his eye, then looked at the rest of the group. Peter nodded while Micheal Jackson shrugged in a "Why not?" sort of way. Naboth stared at Fire for a second, then looked away. He yanked Charlie toward him and untied the knots. Charlie winced as the rough rope jerked across his skin.

"And give it to me," Jonasan said. Naboth handed him the rope. "We will not be needing it again."

Naboth scowled. "I am watching you," he said. He shoved Charlie toward the tree.

Charlie drew a quick square on the ground. Immediately, Michael Jackson and Peter put their hoes to work, coaxing the red clay from the ground. Jonasan pulled the chunks of dirt away from the hole, clearing the way for more.

Charlie grabbed a rock and began to help.

"Now I do not want no piss hole. You dig it deep."

Charlie threw the blade into the ground as his breath came out in noisy huffs. Over and over he gouged the earth; again and again he pulled the clay from the ground. Soon, beads of sweat formed on his forehead and the palms of his hands perspired, causing him to lose his grip on the hoe.

He glanced at the young boy beside him and tried to remember if he had seen the face before. No, *he thought,* he must be new. *He wiped his palms on his pants and repositioned his hands on the hoe. The large shadow of the commander loomed over the hole, unintentionally offering some relief from the sun.*

The commander moved and a small pod from a flame tree fell into the hole. It must be nearing the beginning of the dry season, *Charlie thought. Soon the ground would be covered with the boat-shaped seed coverings. He remembered the piles of brown pods littering the ground when he was taken from his village and forced to walk to the camp.*

It had been a year since the soldiers came and took him from his village.

He grabbed the pod and put it into his pocket. He offered the young boy a quick smile. The boy's hands were shaking and his breath was quick and shallow. Charlie threw the blade of the hoe into the ground with greater intensity, trying to cover for the boy's feeble attempts.

"Slow down," Charlie whispered as he got down on his hands and knees. He brushed aside some dirt and revealed the corner of a soiled burlap bag. Naboth helped him remove the rest of the dirt and lift the bag. Charlie untied the rope and opened the sack to reveal its treasure: ten AK-47s and a heap of ammo. He reached down to take a gun.

"No." Naboth grabbed Charlie's hand and held it tight.

Fire scoffed. "Let it be, Naboth. We are close close to the LRA camp, and we need the gun. Unless you know how to use them, you should stand back and let Charlie show us."

Naboth scowled.

"Let him be, Naboth," Jonasan said. "We trust him. You must learn to do the same."

Naboth released his grip on Charlie and stepped

back. Charlie reached into the bag, pulled out a gun, and inserted a magazine. Naboth watched intently, grabbed a gun, and followed his lead. Within seconds both guns were assembled and ready. Charlie placed the gun strap over his shoulder and adjusted it until the gun lay perfectly parallel with the ground. He inserted his finger near the trigger, swung the gun back and forth, then lifted a small lever on the side and clicked it into place. "The safety," he said. "Keep it on at all time. Until you need it." Then he pushed the tip of the gun down and readjusted the strap, leaving the gun resting against his side.

Every move Charlie made was watched with intense scrutiny. Naboth passed a gun to each one of the boys, and they repeated Charlie's steps. Charlie stepped back and watched.

They filled the hole and covered the disturbed soil with dead leaves and branches. Fire took the rest of the magazines, put them into her sack, and placed it on her head.

"Come," Charlie whispered, leading everyone farther into the bush.

He walked until the faint sounds of flowing water could be heard. A slow-moving stream, meandering through the bush, gurgled past them.

Charlie dropped to his knees and plunged his face into the river. The frigid water instantly cooled him, sending a rush of prickling pins and needles over his body. He cupped the water in his hands and brought it to his lips, gulping the liquid down, feeling his stomach tighten and cramp with each mouthful. He glanced to his side and watched the young boy do the same. The boy's spindly arms shook. His breaths were short, raspy, grating.

"Here," Charlie said. He reached into his pocket and pulled out the seed pod. He placed the brown shell into the river and watched the boat-shaped vessel drift away. "I used to do that when I was a ka-boy. I would pretend I was on the water, floating off somewhere far, far away."

The little boy watched the pod until it went around a bend in the river and was lost from sight.

Charlie turned to his right, took a big step, and began counting his lengthy strides. *"Acel, ariyo, adek . . ."* until he reached twenty and stopped. Directly in front of him was an orange grove, three rows of trees standing on the edge of a sugarcane field. He walked toward the grove and counted again—*"Acel, ariyo, adek, angwen, abic"*—and stopped. He scribbled a square on the ground and stepped back. Again the boys dug with their hoes and pulled the earth away until another bag was exposed. Michael Jackson pulled it from the hole and began to undo the rope.

"No," Charlie said, "leave it in the sack. We

have enough gun on us to protect us."

Michael Jackson tucked the bag under his arm. The rest of the boys threw the dirt back into the hole and used the decaying leaves and twigs to cover up the freshly disturbed dirt.

Charlie walked farther into the bush and led the group to the third cache. It was ten paces from a termite hill. The mound that covered the cache looked like a smaller termite hill, a small village next to a larger city. The group began to dig.

"What is your name?" Charlie said under his breath.

"William."

William's arms trembled as they pulled the dirt from the hole.

"It is going to be okay, William. One more hole after this one just. You can do it." Charlie pulled the dirt from the ground and threw the chunk far from the hole. He tossed the large chunks of clay to the side, leaving William only the smallest pieces to carry.

The boy tripped and stumbled.

Charlie caught him and lifted him up. It was too late; the man placing the guns in the bag saw everything. "Hurry!" he yelled.

William struggled to quicken his pace. Charlie pulled up a huge chunk of clay and threw it out of the hole, only to see it hit the ledge and fall back in.

William reached for the piece, staggered, and fell onto Charlie's hoe.

"Stop." Jonasan spied a fragment of cloth. "There it is."

The boys brushed the dirt away from the sack, pulled it out of the hole, and hoisted onto Peter's shoulders.

"Quick, fill this hole back in and we will find the last cache," Jonasan said, turning to follow Charlie's lead.

Peter peered into the hole. "Wait, I see something else in there."

"No," Charlie said. "It is nothing. Leave it. We must go."

Charlie lifted William's limp body and watched the boy struggle to open his eyes. "Come on, William. Get up!" Charlie shook him. "Get up, William!" William's eyes closed. His breath left him in a long sigh. "William!" Charlie yelled. He listened to the boy's heart, then felt his pulse. Nothing and nothing. He cradled William's head in his arms.

A shadow loomed over the hole.

The commander looked down at Charlie. "Leave him. We do not want to attract the hyna. Bury him with the gun."

Peter leaned his load against a tree and jumped back into the hole.

"I said leave it." Charlie tried to hide the anxiety in his voice. "We have been here long long already."

"Here," the commander said, throwing the sack of guns into the hole. "Cover them up. And I do not want to see any sign of us being here. You understand?"

Charlie nodded, took his hoe, and began to fill in the hole. He stifled the sob that threatened to escape from his lips.

"One second just," Peter said. He brushed aside some dirt and pulled up a small skull.

Charlie covered William's body while he said a short prayer. He pictured William sailing in a little canoe, floating down the stream, going somewhere far, far away. Everything was all right now.

"Put it back," Fire whispered. "We must not disturb the child spirit. It is angry as it is. Quick quick, cover it again."

The boys filled in the hole while Charlie took two sticks and fashioned them together into a small cross. He pushed the cross into the ground and finally allowed his tears to fall.

He had wanted to do that for a long time.

Chapter 10

*Speak softly and carry a big stick;
you will go far. ~ West African proverb*

Charlie woke with a start and listened.

The *koo-WEEU, koo-WIRIRIRI* of the nightjar
and the soft *hoot-hoots* of the eagle owl were gone.
Fire tapped Charlie's knee and held her finger to her
lips, then pointed. Naboth, taking his turn as
watchman, was leaning against a tree, fast asleep,
his gun draped over his shoulder, his finger resting
lightly on the trigger.

"It is too quiet," she whispered.

Charlie nodded. "Wait here." He slung his gun
over his shoulder, dropped to his hands and knees,
and crawled through the bush to the edge of the
road, then glanced in both directions. It was clear.

He turned, then stopped. A twig snapped and a man laughed.

"It is only the snake and the bug that crawl. Get up, ka-boy."

Charlie felt the end of a rifle at the back of his head. He stood.

"Give me the gun."

He passed the gun back.

"Walk," the voice commanded.

When they entered the small clearing, the Arrow Boys and Fire were on their knees with their hands laced behind their heads. Two soldiers, one sporting dreadlocks, the other a red beret, pointed their guns at Fire and the Arrow Boys, their feet spread, arms taut, and fingers resting lightly on the triggers. Two little boys—Charlie guessed they were around eight and nine years old—stood to the side, cowering, their wrists tied, shirts tattered, and dirtied faces streaked with tears.

The commander took a quick look at the sacks and the guns lying on the ground and laughed. "Eeh! What do we have here? Oh! Yes! The Arrow Boy! Come to steal our weapon, have you?" He pushed Charlie toward the group. "Kneel!" Charlie obeyed.

The man swaggered toward Charlie and stared. Looks of recognition crossed both their faces. Charlie froze.

"Charlie? What are you doing? You have left the LRA and joined the enemy, have you? That did not take you long long. Eeh, we will have much amusement with you when we bring you back to the camp." He stuck the end of the rifle into Charlie's chest. "Or perhaps we should start our fun here and let the Arrow Boy see what we do to our traitor?" He took a rope that hung from his side and tossed it to one of the boys. "Tie them," he ordered.

The boy in the dreadlocks stood guard while the one in the red beret unraveled the rope. He tied Peter's, then Naboth's hands, pulling the rope tightly around their wrists. It cut deep. Peter squeezed his eyes shut as he gritted his teeth. Naboth scowled at the commander, his nostrils flaring in anger.

"Eeh! Look here," the commander said, turning his attention to Fire. "We got ourself a girl." He stood in front of her and stared, looking first at her face, her breasts, and then her hips. "Hmm . . ." He paused as he licked his lips. He ran his finger over Fire's cheek, down the nape of her neck, and then onto her breast. "A beautiful girl. And what is your name, my dear?"

Charlie glared. "Take your hand off her!" he yelled. He rushed at the commander, grabbed his gun, spun around, and shot. The bullet found its mark. The commander fell and lay dead on the jungle floor, his eyes open, staring, but not seeing, the star-filled sky.

The soldier in the dreadlocks swung around and aimed his gun at Charlie, his finger at the trigger.

"No!" Jonasan yelled. He grabbed the gun from the commander's side and aimed it at one soldier and then the other. "Put your gun on the ground and step back."

The soldiers raised their arms. With deliberate slowness they placed their guns on the ground and backed away. Charlie stepped between them and their guns. He aimed his rifle, pointing it at their chests. His arms didn't shake. His breath was even.

"You can go," he said to the soldiers. "Turn and walk away. But if you try to follow us, I will kill you. I will."

The soldiers walked into the bush. Charlie released his breath and relaxed his hold on his gun. The soldier in the dreadlocks turned and rushed at him and grabbed for his gun.

"No!" Fire yelled. She yanked the gun from Jonasan and shot. Her expert aim hit the soldier in the head. He fell to the ground.

Jonasan stared at Fire, and then at the still body and the blood that began to pool at his feet. He couldn't move. The soldier in the red beret ran into the bush; the sound of breaking branches carried into the trees until it faded into the night air.

Finally, Jonasan looked up. He glared at Naboth. "Whose watch was it? Was it yours?"

Naboth lowered his head and stared at the ground.

"No, it was mine," Charlie said. "I took the next watch. I heard something and I went to see what it was."

"You left us? Without a watch? Why didn't you wake someone?"

"I did not think of it. I did not think I would be long. I am sorry."

"Sorry?" Jonasan shook his head. "We could be Kony kid by now. I thought you knew better, Charlie."

Charlie hung his head. Fire looked at Naboth as he glared back at her.

"Let us go," Jonasan said. "Let the hyna feast tonight. We have no time to bury the body." He took the rope off Peter's and Naboth's wrists and threw it to the ground.

The two young boys stood perfectly still. They raised their hands. Their arms shook. Fire spoke softly to one. "What is your name, ka-boy?"

The first young boy stared at the ground. The only sounds that came from him were muffled sobs.

"And you?" she asked the second boy.

She was met with the same silence.

"That is fine. I understand. You do not have to

tell me. When we get back to our village, we will remove the rope then. For now, we do not trust you, and I am sure you do not trust us." She checked the tightness of the ropes and loosened them a little. "And do not worry," she said, "We will not torture you or poison your food. I know the soldier tell you that and it is not true. But we will look after you." She took a few steps, stopped, and turned to face the boys. "Kony does not know where you are or where you are going. He only say that to the children to scare them. The spirit do not tell him where this child is or what that child is thinking." She turned to Jonasan. "Let us go. It is going to be light soon, and we have all the gun we are able to carry." She gave a gentle pull on the rope and stepped in behind Charlie.

*   *   *   *

The sun had reached its highest position in the sky when everyone stopped near a creek to refill their bottles with water and find some shade.

"We eat and then we rest for a short while," Jonasan said as he gulped down his water. "Michael Jackson, you take first watch, then wake Peter. You know the order." Fire passed the rope that tied the boys' hands to Michael Jackson. "And hold the rope. Do not be tying it to some tree and then falling asleep. The last thing we want is for the boy to take off and get lost. Are we together?"

The Arrow Boys nodded.

Within minutes, after Fire passed out the *simsim* patties and everyone licked their sticky fingers, the group was asleep. Some leaned their backs against a tree, while others lay exhausted, flat on the ground.

The two young boys sat wide-awake and stared into the surrounding bush. Their *simsim* lay untouched on the ground. The smaller of the two boys laid his head on the other's chest and squeezed in closer. The older boy whispered something in his ear and rested his cheek against the boy's head.

Michael Jackson squatted on his knees and smiled at the boys. "What village are you from?" he asked.

The boys glanced at him, then quickly lowered their gaze. They reached out and held each other's hands. *Brothers*, Michael Jackson thought.

"You do not like the *simsim*?" he said, pointing to the sweet cake lying on the ground. "Or perhaps you are not hungry. I can eat it for you, then. I am always hungry." He brushed the dirt off and took a nibble.

The boys looked up.

"Eeh? You are hungry now?"

Michael Jackson broke the *simsim* patty in half

and placed a piece onto each of their outstretched hands. He stepped back and pouted. "Whatever you have left you can give to me. That is not a lion you hear making the growl. It is my own belly." He grinned as he watched the boys devour the sweet cake, then nestle back into each other's arms. Their eyelids closed and soon they were fast asleep.

Michael Jackson sat at the base of a tree and leaned against the smooth trunk. He stifled a yawn and forced his eyes to stay open. Then he began to sing, quietly, mouthing the words in a bare whisper. First he sang an upbeat song about a girl dancing in the moonlight, and then another song about a baboon stealing a crown from the king of a village. The song grew quieter and quieter until his head dropped to his chest and the only sound that came from him was a deep-throated snore.

* * * *

Fire woke and saw Michael Jackson sound asleep on the ground, curled up in a ball, resting his head on one of the young boy's shoulders. She cleared her throat. He was totally oblivious. She cleared her throat again, this time louder. Michael Jackson rolled onto his back and smacked his lips. The expression on his face was one of complete euphoria, as if he didn't have a care in the world.

"Get up, *kapere*!" She glared, kicking him in the leg. "If Kony was here we would be well on our way to his camp. How dare you fall asleep, you worthless nobody!"

Michael Jackson jumped to his feet. He glanced at the boys around him, still fast asleep. He sighed with relief. "I am sorry. I am sorry," he whispered. "Please do not tell Jonasan. He would be mad mad. And I would never be an Arrow Boy again."

"We trust you with our life. And you cannot stay awake to keep guard?"

"I told you I am sorry. What else can I do?"

"Do not do it ever ever ever again." Fire jabbed her finger into his chest, then turned. "Wake everyone up. It is time for us to get going. We have slept long enough."

Michael Jackson shook each of the boys awake. When he came to the young boys, he knelt and gently touched their cheeks. "Come on, ka-boy. It is time to go. I am sorry sorry we cannot eat now. Perhaps later. But when we get to my village, I will bring you to my hut and my *maa* will make you the best sorghum you have ever tasted. It is so good the bee hover around my mother as she stir the pot and ask her for the recipe. It is sweet sweet."

The boys gave a slight smile.

While the group stayed hidden in the bush, they each took turns crossing the road and filling their

bottles from a creek. Michael Jackson filled his,
brought it over for the boys, and watched them gulp
it down in seconds. He ran across the road and
refilled it again.

"That is all you should have, ka-boy. If I give
you more, your belly will cramp and you will have
many many trouble footin' it. Come, we must go."

Without another word, they gathered the bags
and set off.

*   *   *   *

Charlie slowed his pace as he led the way
through the bush. He knew the heavy loads they
were carrying were growing heavier and heavier
with each mile they left behind them. They couldn't
keep up the brisk pace he had set on the way in.
They walked toward the sun as it began its descent.
Everyone knew it was imperative they keep
walking, even if it was daylight. The farther they
got away from the caches and the dead bodies, the
better. The group walked in total silence, taking
turns carrying the bags of guns, shifting the weight
from one person to the other whenever a boy tired
of carrying the load, or when someone thought the
bearer needed a rest.

They walked and walked, watching the sunset
and the moonrise. Using the light of the moon, they

continued on their way until they stopped and sat for a short break. After eating a handful of peanuts, Charlie took a drink from his bottle and stood. The rest of the boys stayed in their spots, some already leaning against the trees and closing their eyes.

"No, we cannot stop here. It is best to make it home while we have the dark and the moon," Charlie said.

The boys rose, got in behind him, and followed. Soon the forest filled with the sounds of the night birds, the flittering of bats' wings, and the occasional screeching howl of a jackal. It was all the company they were given as they traveled into the night and watched the moon follow its path across the sky.

When the blackness of the sky turned to purple and the faint lightness of the sun began to creep above the treetops, Charlie stopped to listen to the twitters and trills of the morning birds. The first rays of sunlight had just warmed his cheeks when he finally stepped into Fire's yard. He stopped at the fire pit and waited until the rest of the group arrived. Michael Jackson followed, holding the rope that bound the two children. The rest of the boys walked into the clearing, while Fire brought up the rear.

Jonasan cleared his throat. "We will bring all the gun with us and put them in the latrine at the school. Then we must meet there after the noonday sun passes. I will call Opio Ben and tell him to bring as many of the Arrow Boy as he can find. Now get some rest."

Charlie nodded half-heartedly, passed his gun to Jonasan, and turned toward the hut. He could only focus on the mattress lying on the ground. He stumbled into the hut and fell onto the mat and closed his eyes.

Fire opened the door to the grain bin and checked to see if the bags were inside and unharmed. They were. She ran her hand over the black bag and sighed. "I will be back with Maisha right away," she said.

Charlie mumbled goodbye and fell asleep.

Chapter 11

To get lost is to learn the way.
~ African proverb

Charlie opened one eyelid and attempted to focus on the broken beams of sunlight that came through the roof. Two round beady eyes stared back at him. He rubbed his hand over his face, yawned, and looked again. This time the two eyes were joined with a yellow beak and a tuft of brown feathers.

"I see you have made yourself comfortable and now think I am a nest."

He stroked the soft feathers of the bird, then rubbed his fingers over its beak. The hen responded by pushing its head under his hand and rubbing its comb under his palm.

"Do not get too comfortable there. Because we are friend does not mean you will not find your way into the supper pot soon soon."

As if in reply, the chicken sat up and squawked, then jumped onto the ground.

Charlie looked where it had sat and lifted up a brown egg. "*Apwoyo,* ka-girl."

He glanced out the door and watched Fire cooking something in a small pot set on a few hot coals. Maisha was wrapped tightly to her back, sound asleep. Charlie made his way to the fire and sat.

"Here. Your chicken has provided you with breakfast." He placed the egg into Fire's hand.

"My chicken? No, she is not mine. She was here when I came. She must have belonged to the family that escaped when the LRA attacked this area." Fire placed the egg into a pot, poured some water over it, and placed it on the coals. "But she certainly has a liking for you, so I would say she is yours now."

She spooned a large clump of rice into a bowl and passed it to Charlie. "We need to get going soon. Jonasan and the group will be waiting for us at the school. The rest of the Arrow Boy will be there, and Opio Ben. He will be wanting to talk to you." She readjusted her baby on her back, then sat down to eat.

Charlie scooped the rice with his fingers and shoved it into his mouth. He swallowed it without pausing to chew. Twice more he grabbed a big handful and gulped it down. He passed the empty bowl to Fire. *"Apwoyo matek,"* he said, wiping his mouth with the back of his hand.

Fire refilled the bowl but paused before she handed it to him. "The LRA stole many thing from us. Even the pleasure the mouth had to enjoy the food. You are free now. There is no hurry to put the rice into your stomach." She placed the bowl into Charlie's hands.

He took a nibble and chewed slowly.

"See. It is not all that hard. And your stomach will not cramp up."

Charlie closed his eyes and swallowed. The tenseness of his body began to subside. He opened his eyes and looked into the trees and watched a mother vervet monkey walk along a tree branch with her baby clinging to her belly. He took another bite, chewed, and swallowed. Then he took another. He paused, drew in a long, deep breath, and smelled the freshness of the jungle. He smiled.

When the egg was boiled, Fire cracked it down the middle and offered half to Charlie.

"No. I had the last one. You eat it. You are feeding your child too."

"But you are growing."

Charlie took the half of the egg and popped it into his mouth. Two quick bites and it was gone. Fire frowned.

"Oops," he said.

She took a small bite of her egg and chewed. Smacking her lips, she rolled her eyes and smiled. "See. The fine taste of that egg was a big waste on you. Next time I will eat the whole thing." She winked.

After the dishes were washed, they set off at a quick pace, taking a path that led east, away from the school and farther into the bush. When they neared another set of huts, Fire stopped and spoke to Salume. A few children were playing in the yard, kicking around a soccer ball made of leaves and twine.

Two big rocks at either end of the yard designated the goalposts, but with so few players, there were no goaltenders. The children yelled and screamed, running and kicking the ball whenever it came close to them. While each of the kids showed great skill, Charlie couldn't help but pay closer attention to one boy. The ball flew across the yard whenever his bare foot connected with it, and his skill in snatching it from the other boys and girls was uncanny.

The boy paused at the end of the yard while he held the ball with his foot. He glanced at Charlie, then kicked the ball. It landed right at Charlie's feet. The boy gave him a quick smile.

"Gweye! Gweye!" the children yelled. They

jumped up and down with their arms flying in the air.

Charlie stared at the ball.

"You have the speed and the cunning of the jackal, Charlie."

"Eeh? You think so? But I must be like the jackal. We cannot let Christopher team win again. It go to his head, and it is already puffed up with so much pride. One more goal and then we can go."

"Gweye! Here! Pass it to me!" The boy clapped his hands against his thighs. "You will be happy you kick it to me. I will make the goal. Watch." He stared at Charlie and waited.

Charlie tossed the ball into the field and ran. He jumped in front of a boy dribbling the ball down the center and lunged. He took control of the ball and passed it between his legs, then ran in the opposite direction, dribbling the ball and keeping his eye on the goalie and the small space between him and the posts.

The men yelled, their deep voices rumbling like a war drum. "Go, Charlie! That is it! Go!" The women waved their scarves in the air as Charlie ran closer to the goal. He shifted his weight to one side and aimed his foot. The goalie moved to the right. Charlie hopped to the left and kicked the ball. It took the goalie by surprise. He rushed to the left, but it was too late. The ball sailed through the air, past the post, and into the surrounding bush. The field erupted in a loud celebration of clapping and shouting. The women called out, their voices rising like a chorus of songbirds. Charlie's teammates ran to him and lifted him into the air and shouted. "The Jackal! The Jackal! The cunning Jackal!"

Charlie ran to his mother and wrapped his arms around her waist. "It was a good game, eeh, Maa?"

His mother laughed. "Yes, it was a good game, Charlie. But you should be gone by now. It is getting dark already. Here, take this." She pressed a blanket, and a small loaf of bread wrapped in brown paper, into his hands. "I will see you in the morning. Go."

"We will play again tomorrow, and you will wave your scarf again and again. Yes, Maa?"

"Yes, now go. You know it is not safe for you to be here at night. Kony could be watching us right now."

A flash of fire flew over their heads and landed on the grass roof of their hut. The roof burst into flames. Instantly, the air filled with screams of panic and confusion. Then came the sound of the guns. A shower of bullets riddled the ground near their feet, sending clouds of dust into the air. Charlie's maa grabbed his hand and ran toward the bush. A soldier stepped out of the trees and aimed his gun at them. He shook his head and smirked. Charlie's maa stopped and turned. They ran toward the field.

Charlie's dad ran toward him, his arms outstretched, ready to lift him up.

"Charlie! Margaret! Come!"

Then his father stopped. His eyes widened and emptied of all life. He fell to the ground. The back of his shirt, ripped with bullet holes, turned crimson. Charlie stared down at his dad. He could not move. His body, his mind, were numb. Charlie's maa grabbed his hand and ran.

"Please." The boy's enthusiasm was replaced with a hesitant smile. "Please."

Charlie stared at the ball, his eyes vacant and unseeing. He walked away.

"I have to go," Fire said quickly. She kissed Maisha on his forehead and ran toward Charlie as he headed down the pathway. She rushed past him and stopped him in his tracks. He stared into the trees.

"Charlie? Charlie, are you okay?"

He brushed past her and continued on his way.

Fire stepped in front of him again. "Stop. You must tell me. What happened?"

He turned and looked at her; the images momentarily swept away. "And what must I tell you? Why would I want to say in word what I see in my head? Is it not enough that the picture are there, in my head, to see again and again? One time to see it is enough. To tell you would only make it real. No, I do not want to tell you."

"Yes. Once is enough." She placed her hand on Charlie's shoulder, then let it fall. Turning, she led the way. "Let us go," she said, quickening her pace. "We are late late."

They walked along the pathway until they came to the open field near the school. It was completely deserted.

They crossed the field, passed the school, and drew into the bush that lined the edge of the building, keeping themselves covered in the dense foliage. Fire stopped and listened. The faint sound of people talking in a classroom could be heard. She crept up to an open window and looked inside. She motioned to Charlie as she climbed onto the window ledge and hopped into the classroom. He followed.

Thirty teenage boys and men, ranging in age from about twelve to twenty, crouched in a circle, while a teenager sat in the middle and drew on the floor using a piece of chalk. Michael Jackson, Peter, Naboth, and Jonasan glanced at Charlie and Fire, then returned their attention to the center. Charlie and Fire walked to the edge and glanced down. Crude lines and *X*s marked out an attack plan.

"You are here, Charlie." The teen rose, wiped the chalk onto his pants leg, and extended his hand.

Charlie caught his breath. He glanced at the teen and dropped his head, squeezing his eyes shut. But the boy's face brought back a horrid memory. It hit Charlie full force: mismatched flesh, brown and pink scars where there should have been a nose, jagged flaps of skin where there should have been lips.

"Hello, Charlie. I am Opio Ben." His voice was nasal and distorted. "I want to ask you how you and your family are, as is our tradition, but as of late I am afraid to do this. It only remind me of our loss. So I will ask you, Charlie. How are you?"

Charlie raised his head and looked at Ben once again. His breath caught in his throat, squeezing his lungs. He gasped for air. He shook.

"Come here, boy. Come and show the lady how sharp the machet is. Show her the damage it can do."

Charlie covered his ears. "No!"

He pushed his way through the group and rushed to the door. He ran across the field and into the bush, hearing Fire's footfalls close behind him. He stopped and collapsed on the jungle floor. His breaths were short and quick. His eyes opened wider and wider until he stared unblinking into the forest, glancing from tree to tree and from sky to ground.

He hugged his knees to his chest and rocked back and forth.

"I am here, Charlie. I am right here," Fire said, kneeling down beside him.

Acama took the machete from Charlie and walked toward the woman.

"Do not cry or scream, woman. Or you will be killed right away."

The woman knelt on the ground and turned to see a commander standing behind her swinging a machete from side to side. Her body shook.

Fire wrapped her arms around Charlie and held him close to her. They rocked back and forth in a slow, steady rhythm.

"Noooo," he moaned.

The boy swung the machete down and sliced the woman's lips from her mouth. Blood poured down her chin and throat, darkening her dress. Tears filled her eyes and overflowed, falling down her cheeks. Her mouth quivered as she stifled the screams that threatened to escape from her throat. The boy stepped back and surveyed his work. He studied the woman's ears; with one fluid motion, he sliced off one ear and then the other. He wiped the machete clean on his pants and returned it to Charlie. He stood beside the commander, who nodded his approval.

"Go," the commander said to the woman. "Go and show the other. Tell them if they do not speak the truth or hear the truth, then we will cut their lip and ear off, too."

The woman stood and held her hands to her lips; blood dripped from her fingers and fell to the ground. She turned and stumbled, then slowly walked away.

Charlie blinked, then stared into the bush.

"I do not want to see that again," he said.

Fire shifted her position and faced him. She rested one hand on his shoulder and lifted his chin with the other. She looked at his face and held his hands in hers.

"No. You should not have seen it. It should not have happened." Fire held him in a firm embrace.

The sound of footfalls came closer. A hand pushed aside the bush, and Jonasan and Ben stepped forward.

"How is he?" Ben whispered, bending down on his knees.

"I do not know. He is young. They have done terrible horror to him. And there is nothing my magic can do. It is the *ajiji*. The vision have entered his spirit and have a strong hold on him."

Charlie looked past Ben and Jonasan, lost again in the images in his mind.

"We need your help, Charlie," said Ben. "You

105

know how to use the gun. We are farm people. We have held the plow, not the gun. If we are going to fight back, we need you to help. *Ojone*. Please."

"He himself is in need of help, Ben. He cannot do what you ask."

Ben nodded and stood. His shoulders dropped as he sighed. He walked into the bush. Jonasan followed.

Charlie rested his head on Fire's chest as she hummed. A lone bird perched at the top of a thorn tree and called out into the jungle. Its mate flew down with a twig in its beak and wove it around the edges of a tree branch. It stretched its neck and ruffled its feathers, sending a chorus of notes into the canopy. The pair flew off, over the treetops and out of sight, then returned moments later with twigs and long blades of grass. They wove the branches into the beginnings of their nest and flew away to collect some more.

Fire continued to hum until the tune took on words and became a song.

"Take the stone from the heart,
take them from the mind.
Lift them from the hand that saw mercy denied,
then fill the heart and fill the mind with
forgiveness overflowing.
Let the hand feel the earth once more,
and see the seed of sowing."

The song ended and they sat in silence.

Charlie took in a shuddering breath and let out a long sigh.

"I need to go back to the school," he said, standing. "I can show everyone how to hold the gun and change the magazine. I am good at that."

Chapter 12

*An army of sheep led by a lion
can defeat an army of lions led by a sheep.*
~ Ghanaian proverb

They stared at Charlie when he reentered the classroom.

"Let us get back to the task at hand, Arrow Boy," Ben said, finding his spot on the floor again. Charlie took his place on the outside of the circle. Fire inched in closely beside him, while Jonasan stood on his other side.

"Our scout have told me that Kony has sent many of his soldier into different direction. Some of the group have headed northeast into the Kitgum district, some south to Apac, and there are even report that a group of thirty is entering the Congo right now. One scout sent word that a group of twenty has made it way south toward our area, but we have not heard any more.

"I think it is wise to assume that the LRA could be coming closer to us and could attack any day now. But since Charlie has led us to their cache and we have the gun, our strategy can change. We will still rely on surprising the LRA, but now we can use their own weapon against them.

"If this information is true, the LRA will follow the tip of the Ka-Achwa River until it end near to all the Gu-rock." Ben used a piece of chalk to draw a line on the ground to represent the river. He drew a round shape at the base of the line to show where the rocks were positioned. "This is the best place to attack," he said, pointing to the rock. "They will be weary from traveling through the bush and will still be far enough away from our village that they will not expect anything, and of course the rock will provide good cover. We will set up the post here, here, and here," he said, marking the spots on the floor with an *X*. "Connor, I want you and all your boy here," he said, pointing to the first *X*. "It is the place where Mr. Erebu field backs onto the river. If my memory serves me correct, there is a large treed area near the back of the property that will be perfect for you to hide. And your group can go here, Emora." He indicated the second *X*. "Right near to the place Mr. Olela used to keep his bull. You have more experience with the arrow and the club. And here," he said pointing to the last *X*, "is where I want your group to go, Jonasan. Near to the old orange grove."

Jonasan rubbed his chin and nodded.

"This way we have them surrounded on all three side. As for me, I think this is good. Yes?" Ben stood and wiped the chalk on his pant legs.

The group nodded.

Charlie stared at the markings on the floor and imagined the plan coming to life. If he had still been in the LRA and was part of this battle, he would have had no hope. And neither would any other kid who had been forced to hold an AK-47 and shoot or be killed.

He cleared his throat. His words came out slow and shaky. "But what about all of the kid?" he asked. "The kid in the LRA. They do not want to kill. They only do it because they have no choice. You must know that."

The group was silent.

"We will try not to shoot at the kid, Charlie," Ben said. "We know that some of our own kid from here may be in the group. But that is all we can do. We have tried to bring the kid out of the bush, driving down the road, calling out to them from a megaphone, telling them we will protect them. We have even gone on the radio, hoping they will hear our message that their parent are missing them and want them back."

"I know you have. I have heard those message. But they do no good when you know if you try to escape you will be tortured and killed."

"Then tell us, Charlie. Tell us what we need to do."

Charlie paused. "We need to be smart. Smart like Waswa when he tricked Sesota. The trouble is you are attacking the snake from the front and side. That is where the youngest of the children are. The one that are most afraid, because if they do not stay standing and shooting when the bullet are flying, they will be shot from behind by their own commander. If you want to kill the snake, you have to go for it tail. That is where the commander are. Kill all the commander in the rear, then the children will not fear for their life and will lay down their gun."

Each member of the group nodded. Jonasan smiled.

"It might work. It is worth a try." Ben passed the piece of chalk to Charlie. "Show us where we should attack, then."

"It is the same as what you have here, but change this," he said, erasing the X from the top of the drawing, "to this." He made another X near the end of the river.

"But we will have to sneak up from behind."

"Yes. But that is the only way."

"Then that is what we will do. I want each leader from the subgroup to meet me here tonight, and every night when the moon crest above the tree just. We will set out when I get more word on where the LRA is heading." Ben placed his hand on Charlie's shoulder. "*Apwoyo matek*, Charlie," he said. He walked to the window and jumped out.

"We are going to need more instruction with the use of the gun, Charlie," Jonasan said. About fifteen boys stood behind Jonasan—Michael Jackson, Peter, and Naboth among them.

"Yes, let us get started," Charlie said.

The boys jumped out of the window and headed into the bush. By the time Charlie and Fire reached the group, everyone was standing and waiting beside the pile of guns.

Michael Jackson hurried over to Charlie and Fire. "The boy we found have told their name. My *maa* know their tribe and think they are from Kitgum. She is taking them to the refugee camp so she can find someone to bring them home. That is good good, yes?"

Charlie smiled.

"Yes, that is good good," Fire said. "I am happy to hear this news."

"I am glad we found them," Michael Jackson said. "They are only ka-boy. What would Kony want with small small children? He is stupid, this Kony. Stupid stupid."

Jonasan walked up to the group and placed a rifle into Charlie's hands. "Let us get started. It will be turning dark soon, and I want to be ready. I want to chop off the snake tail."

Charlie stared at the gun, looking from one end to the other. He felt its weight, then hoisted the gun strap over his shoulder, holding it straight from his waist. It felt heavy and cold.

"In the army, we were told that our gun was our best friend, and when you are out in the bush it is true true." Charlie swept the end of the gun back and forth. "When you have a gun, you have power. But you must have total respect for your gun. If you do not look after it, it will not look after you. Do not drop it, do not dirtin' it, and keep it with you at all time. No matter what.

"When we were in the front attacking the UPDF, we walked like this just." He swept his gun back and forth while pretending to hold the trigger. "The gun is fast and many bullet come out."

Each boy stared intently at Charlie and the gun.

"Sometime there would be twenty of us in a line, bearing down on the UPDF, coming up to their defense, and we would keep on coming just while they sent their bullet at us. Sometime kid would get hit—some would die, some would live. That is how it work in the bush.

"But that will not work here. If you want to shoot at the commander, you must be more accurate and not waste the bullet. We do not have many. First, you must switch the gun from the automatic fire to the single shot." He flicked a small lever on the side of the gun. "Now you will be able to shoot the one bullet. But to have the good aim, you must hold the gun like this." Charlie hoisted the strap around his neck and held the gun with his right hand.

Each of the boys picked up a gun and did the same.

"You ram the butt of the gun into this part here, beside your shoulder. That keep it steady steady."

The boys followed his lead.

"Then you hold it here," he said, indicating the black grip handle, "and point this finger forward. Then you hold the front with your left hand, like this." Charlie glanced at everyone's grip on their guns.

"Then there is only to press the trigger and fire. It will kick back some, but if you hold your feet firm and spread like this"—he stood with his legs apart—"it will keep you strong. You must keep this leg like this, and the other leg like this. Not so much turned as the other. See. See?"

The boys watched and nodded.

"And you must bend your knee. But only little little. If you bend too much, you will lose the balance."

They bent their knees, imitating Charlie as best as they could.

"That is good good. Now lean forward. But only a little. Yes, that is it. Now grab a magazine and do this." Charlie took a metal cartridge and knocked the first magazine from the gun. Before it fell to the ground, he had the second cartridge inserted and ready to fire.

Everyone, including Fire, looked on in amazement.

Charlie shrugged. "It take practice just. Now you try."

Everyone did as Charlie said. Magazines fell to the ground, attempts were made to insert the cartridges as quickly as possible, but no one came close to matching his speed.

"Keep on trying. Do not try for speed. Work on getting the clip in properly; practice again and again, then the speed will come."

Charlie watched Peter fumble with the clip, awkwardly forcing it into the gun until it finally clicked into place.

"My mom still call me her *latin gunya*," Peter

said, putting the butt of the rifle into the ground and trying to yank the magazine out. "It is these long arm, eeh. Sometime I think my real dad came from the forest in Bwindi."

Charlie laughed.

"I think that explain why I have this urge to climb tree all the time."

"As long as you do not want to start building your bed up there and grow fond of leave and termite."

Peter tilted his head and looked at Charlie through narrowed eyes. "Eeh. I do not know if I am far far off. Sometime when the food was low at the refugee camp, I would look at those termite hill and wonder."

"Oh, termite? They are not bad bad. They taste like carrot."

"Really?"

"Yes. But not as crunchy."

Peter shuddered and Charlie laughed.

Charlie turned his attention to Naboth and watched him knock the magazine out of the gun and reinsert the other cartridge with ease. Naboth then took a step to the side, spread his legs, threw the butt of the gun into his shoulder, and aimed it at an imaginary target. "Those commander, they think big is big. But we will show the gu-men that they are nothing but ka-boy." He turned his back to Charlie and aimed at a bird perched on a branch.

Charlie walked away from the group and leaned his head against a tree.

"Yes, sir. I will do that, sir," the young soldier said as the commander turned on his heel and walked away.

"You are a latunge ki remo. *You know that, eeh?" Charlie laughed. "You put your nose up that commander butt any farther and you will smell nothing but* cet *for the rest of your life."*

"You call me a brownnoser? You laugh now, but you wait. Soon I will be a commander and you will be listening to me, ka-boy."

Charlie went quiet. "You are serious here, Acama? Tell me you are not."

"You are stupid, Charlie. Look at what the commander have: more food, less work. They are feared. No one touches them. They give the order on who will live and who die. I am going to be a commander."

Charlie shook his head. "But what are you a commander of? This place reek of evil."

Acama stepped back. "Reek of evil? What evil? You heard it yourself. The LRA is here to protect us from Museveni. Our own president. He is the one who has sent his army to kill the Acholi. He is from the south. He hate us in the north. You heard what Otti said. Museveni sent in the soldier to steal our cattle. Our cattle. That which show us we are rich. Museveni is the one who force us into the crowded camp and take our land from us."

Charlie resisted clamping his hands over his ears. He had never heard his friend talk like this.

"We should be proud to be soldier in the LRA. At least we are fighting for our people. Those people who do not provide us with food and supply, the parent who do not give of their children willingly to be soldier—they are the enemy."

Charlie shook his head in disbelief; he looked away.

"Come, we need to teach these people a lesson. They say our gun are rusty. We will show them."

Charlie followed Acama as the group made their way quickly through the bush, but with stealth, careful not to make any noise, until they came to a clearing. Charlie glimpsed a school building, and heard the chatter of the students and teachers as they reviewed their lessons. The pair crept to the rear of the building and edged to the first door. Acama stepped into the room, raised his gun, and pointed it at the teacher. The teacher calmly placed the piece of chalk on the ledge.

"Take your gun and your evil out of here!" he demanded as Charlie peered around Acama.

"Our evil? And what evil could that be?" Acama replied. "You are the one who is evil. We

*come to free our country, and you," he said,
shoving the gun into the man's chest, "you dare to
seek the protection of the UPDF? You dare to take
the side of your enemy! Only a coward would do
that!"*

*   *   *   *

"Charlie?"

Fire touched him gently on his cheek. He
looked in her direction, but he stared into nothing,
seeing nothing. She grasped Charlie's hands and
held them tight. She pulled him closer to her and
held his gaze, then waited until he blinked and a
glimmer of recognition came to his face.

"Charlie," she said firmly.

He looked at her, startled. "It was more *ajiji*."
His voice dropped to a whisper. "It took me away. It
took my spirit and it made me see it. Again."

"And once is enough," Fire said, still holding
onto Charlie's hands.

"Yes, once is enough."

The group stared at Fire and Charlie in silence.

"I think we should all head to our home and
eat," Fire said calmly. "We have learned lots
today." She passed her gun to Jonasan and took
Charlie by the arm. "Let us go, Charlie. I am
craving an egg."

Chapter 13

*If you observe attentively you will even find
wisdom in shadows. ~ African proverb*

Fire waited for the small flames to turn the
wood into hot coals, then poured some water into a
pot and threw in a couple of handfuls of rice. She
placed the pot on the embers and covered it with a
flat stone then set another pan on the fire and
poured a tiny amount of oil into the middle. With
experienced hands she took a small ball of dough
from a bowl and quickly turned it into a perfect flat
circle. The oil sputtered as she put the dough onto
the pan. She closed her eyes and breathed in the
tantalizing smell.

Charlie sat on the ground beside her and
grabbed a little piece of dough from the bowl and
flattened it between his hands.

"Here," she said, taking the dough from

Charlie. "Turn it around and around as you flatten it, and push at the side. Then it will come out like this." She held up a near-perfect circle. "Then it will brown evenly and you will not have the burnt spot."

He took another handful of dough and bit his lower lip as he tried to form a patty as she had shown him. He held out an oval piece, thick on one side and thin on the other, and passed it to Fire.

She glanced at it and smiled. "Much better," she said as she evened it out and placed it on the pan. She gave Charlie another piece and took one for herself.

Within minutes the pan was filled with the small brown patties. The oil bubbled around their edges. The smell was heavenly. Charlie swallowed and grabbed a stick to spear a piece.

"No. You will have to wait. They will be hot and need to cool."

He stuck out his bottom lip and looked at Fire with his big brown eyes. She laughed.

"They will be cool in a couple of minute," she said, taking the pan off the fire and setting it on the ground. "But while we wait I want to show you something."

She placed a basket on the ground beside her and crouched on her knees, facing Charlie. Reaching into the basket, she set out a pile of stones and a handful of flowers. She ran her fingers over the stones' rough surfaces, then brought a flower to her nose, breathing in its perfume.

"I have been filling my mind with many thought this evening," she said. "And I would like to put word to these thought, if you can sit with me and hear them."

Charlie nodded. She began.

"When you were born, there was a great celebration and much happiness." She placed a flower in front of Charlie. "And there were many many good day that followed." She picked up another flower. "You were given a name," she said, setting it next to the one lying on the ground. "And you learned to walk and talk, and to give love, and to be the one to receive this love." She placed more flowers in a row. "And you drew water from the well, and you tended the goat, and you studied your lesson, drawing all your letter in the dirt under the acacia tree." She added more flowers.

"But in this life of yours, you also learned about hatred." She placed a stone between two flowers. "And pain," she said, adding another stone, "and anger." She drew another stone from the pile and disrupted the long line of flowers.

"There was the first time you learned that no one could live forever, and not even your love could bring them alive again. And then there was the first time you realized not all could be fair. There would be those who have plenty and those whose belly would grow swollen with the hunger.

"But despite all this, your life was good because there were more flower than stone."

Charlie looked at the line of flowers and stones and nodded.

"But then Kony came." Fire grabbed a handful of stones from the basket and dropped them at the end of the line. "And there were no more flower. Only fear and pain and suffering and death. And even as you try now, after you have escaped, there are no more flower, for the stone keep falling and falling."

Charlie's eyes moistened.

Fire scooped the rest of the flowers from the basket and laid them on top of the pile of stones. "I am thinking that you are in need of many many flower to do away with the stone that keep falling."

She lifted Charlie's chin and gazed into his eyes, watching a tear course down his cheek.

"My *maa* told me this: we all have two shadow. When you turn your back to the sun, the shadow of your past will always be in front of you. But if you face the sun, your shadow will fall behind you and you will only see the future. You must learn to face the sun, Charlie, and leave the past. But I do not know how you can do this." She paused and picked up a flower. "I can search, but it will not help you.

123

You need to find your own flower. But remember this: the flower does not grow well if it is in the shadow. Turn your back, and if it is possible you will see your own flower grow. And then, perhaps, you will be able to feel your freedom." She dropped the flower into Charlie's hand. He squeezed it and held it tight in his fist.

Fire stood and brushed the dirt from her dress. She grabbed a couple of plates from her bag and set them on the ground and divided the patties between the two of them.

"There," she said. "That is all I have to say. I have told you my thought, and perhaps it will help you, perhaps it will not. But it is something you can think on."

She took the stone off the pot and spooned the rice onto the plates.

"We will eat, and then I will see Maisha for a moment before we head back to the school."

Fire passed a plate to Charlie and sat on the ground holding a plate to her chin. She scooped a handful of rice into her fingers, brought it to her mouth, and paused. She dropped the rice onto her plate, turned her head toward the bush, and listened. The only sound she could hear was the screeching of the monkeys and the squawking of the birds in the high canopy. She placed her plate on the ground, reached into her bag, and pulled out a handful of stones and bones. "Maybe the spirit will speak to me again, like they did when they showed me the cache. Perhaps they are on my side now." She knelt and shook the stones and dropped them onto the ground.

Charlie leaned over and stared. "What is it?"

"There is something out there. But the spirit are not speaking to me. I am confused. They are very silent."

She leaned forward, staring at the stones, cupping her chin in her hand.

"No. It is useless. Kony magic is strong. And I think it is getting stronger." Fire leaned back on her knees and closed her eyes.

She began to hum and chant, but the words did not come from her mouth; they came from her throat, guttural and strong. *"Ik i . . . Ik i . . . shay me no . . . shay me no . . . shay me no . . ."*

Fire stopped and silence filled the yard. She opened her eyes and looked at the stones and bones again. "No. I see something, but it is too faint for my eye. The color are blurred and the line are not keeping all the image in their place."

She placed the charms back in the bag and returned to her seat. Then she put her plate on her lap and scooped up a handful of rice. "No. I will try again later." She chewed on the rice, slowly and methodically.

Charlie lifted his plate to his lips and brushed the last of the rice into his mouth. *"Apwoyo matek."*

Fire nodded as she continued to stare into the bush.

Charlie grabbed a handful of long grass from behind the hut and sat beside her. He took off his shoes and removed a pile of dried grass from the toes and threw it onto the coals. Then he crumpled the new grass into a ball and shoved it into the toe of one shoe, packing it in tightly.

"What is with the shoe, Charlie?"

"My angel has big feet."

"Your angel?"

"Yes, Bruce, my angel. He is big big. He look like he is a man but he is a boy just. He footed it with me on the road to Lira." Charlie laughed. "I did not know he was an angel. I thought he was only a stupid white boy."

"White?"

"Yes, he was as white as the cloud before they take on the rain, and he was as stupid as a *romo*, but without the woolly coat. He did not know a thing. Nothing about the war or why we were footin' it to Lira. And he did not think. He stole food, and when it was found out he was a thief we were put in the *jela*."

"Jail? They put a young boy like you in the jail? Now why would they do that?"

"I did not know. But I was scared scared. I told the chief I had been taken by Kony, and when the officer heard this he made plan to kill me. I was terrified and mad at my angel. How could he do such a stupid thing and put my life in danger?" Charlie's brow furrowed. "I could not think. In my mind all I could see was my body hanging from the great branch of an acacia tree and my feet dangling in the wind."

Fire shook her head. She didn't like the image either.

"But my angel Bruce is very strong. And now that I think, he was not so dumb after all." He laughed again. "He did this thing with his head"— Charlie brought his head down quickly, imitating a head butt—"and the officer, he fell to the floor just, like a dead dead stone, and he did not get up."

Fire narrowed her eyes at Charlie. "You are sure of this?"

"Yes. And then he spread his wing and he flew away, carrying me to a tree where he fed me manna and washed my feet and gave me his shoe."

"This angel, Bruce, he had wing?"

"Oh, yes. They were large wing, for he was very large too."

"And he gave you his shoe?"

"Yes. And then he put me into a deep sleep, and when I woke he was gone. He had done his

127

work and had to go to help someone else."

"I see."

"That is what angel do. They help someone, and then they must leave so they can help another."

"Yes, that is the way of the angel. I think they are busy busy." Fire nodded.

"And then another angel came to me. And this one, his name was Scott. I think God must have many many angel. But he was also stupid. Scott thought he knew so much, but he was like Bruce just. I do not know if all angel are stupid like this, but Scott talked to me when I was in the deepest of sadness and told me I was a good person. He made my heart stronger and made me want to escape again."

A smile flickered across his face. "He gave me a stone. And he told me to give it to Kony. He said the stone had the power to change people, and if I was to give it to Kony it would make him change and the war would end."

He let out a long sigh. "But I do not think the magic is working because Kony is still taking children, and he is still evil. He has not changed."

Fire placed her hand on his shoulder and stood. "No, you are right. He has not changed."

Charlie reached into the bag and pulled out a small basin and poured some water into it. "I miss my angel. Even though Scott and Bruce were not all that smart, they were good good angel. I do not know if I will see them again."

"Eeh, I am sure if they want to they will fly down and see you again."

Charlie shook his head. "No, that is not how they are able to come to me. It is the stone that bring them to me. The stone have power."

"Stone? Like the stone you gave Kony?"

"Yes, a beautiful green stone. With a thread of silver that move over it as you turn it in your hand."

Fire added the plates to the water and began to wash them. She shook her head in disbelief. "Stone that have power, angel with wing, and manna. I can believe it, and yet I do not."

"But why? Why do you not believe?"

"There is much evil. Sometime I think this will all end, but it has gone on for a long long time. I do not remember a day in my life when we did not have this war. And it make me wonder—and I hate myself for thinking this—but perhaps God has left Uganda, Charlie."

"Left Uganda?"

"Yes. I think he has let the devil take the throne and he has forgotten us."

"But what about my angel?"

"I do not know about your angel. All I know is sometime I am on this side of the line where I am happy and I know that good will win over the evil, but other time I am on the other side and I cannot see the end in sight." Fire sighed and stood, stretching her back. She looked into the trees and the deep blue of the sky. "But you know this, Charlie?"

"What is that?"

"It is a thin thin line."

Charlie watched the embers from the fire slowly turn from red to black. He sighed.

Fire put the dishes into the bag and went into the hut. "We must go soon soon," she said as she brought the water jug out and felt its lightness. "We need more water. While I go to see Maisha, you go and fill the jug. The well is down that way." She pointed to the path that had brought them to the hut from the school. "Head down it for a bit just, until you see the termite mound that stand above your head. Then turn left. The path will take you to the well."

Charlie grabbed the jug. "I will be back soon."

"And I will meet you here. We will leave then." She placed the sack into the hut. Before she stepped out the door, she ran her hand over the black bag tucked safely inside.

*　　*　　*　　*

Charlie hurried down the pathway and turned at

the termite hill. A small space between a pair of trees marked the beginnings of a trail. He followed the traces of a path made long ago until he stood in front of a broad cement circle in the middle of some tall grass.

He positioned the jug under the spout and lifted the long arm of the pump. He swung it down, then raised it again and again until a trickle of water flowed. Another pump of the arm and the water gushed out, filling the yellow container in seconds. He moved the jug to the side and stuck his head under the tap. The water soaked his hair, back, and legs until goose bumps covered his skin. He sat under the tap and splashed the water up onto his head, rubbing his hands over his hair, face, and arms. He closed his eyes and turned his face toward the sun. The coolness of the water and the heat from the sun sent a shiver through his body that passed from his head to his toes and back up again.

Then he began to sing. A song from long past. A child's song about a hippo and a crocodile and a battle to see who ruled the Nile. "He thrashed his tail, he chomped his teeth, to show he was the king of beast!"

He pushed the lever down, and the last drops of water fell to the cement and flowed to the outlying grass. He stretched his arms out and threw back his head. The sun's rays dried the droplets from his body, chasing the goose bumps away. He smiled. He screwed the top on the jug, hoisted it onto his head, and held it in place with both hands as he walked back to the hut.

"I filled the jug," he called out as he placed it in the hut. He looked around the yard and peered into the other hut. Fire was not there. He sat by the fire pit and watched the last of the coals give off their heat and turn to gray ash. The white-browed robin-chat sent his call into the dusk: *ko kweer, ko kweer, ko kweer ki, ko kweer ki,* filling the evening air with its loud, raucous song, while the sun began to hide behind the trees. Charlie stood and walked toward the path Fire had taken before to get to Salume's hut. He paused and faced the hut, then turned toward the path again.

"Where is she?" he muttered.

He followed the path for several minutes until he heard the sound of children's laughter. He entered the clearing and looked around. Salume was busy at her water basin, washing the dishes. Fire was not to be seen.

Charlie called out. "*Itye nining,* Salume! I am looking for Fire. Do you know where she is?"

"Eeh?" Salume stood up and wiped her hands on her dress. "She left long ago."

"Where?"

Salume pointed at the path behind him. "There,

the same path you came by just. She should be at her hut by now. Did you not see her there?"

Charlie stared at Salume, turned, and ran down the path as fast as he could.

Part II

Chapter 14

*The wise create proverbs for fools to learn,
not to repeat. ~ African proverb*

Sam grabbed the lever of the Juicy Fruity machine and jerked it up, cursing under her breath. A thick pile of bright yellow froth slid down her forehead and landed on the counter with a splat. She gritted her teeth as she pushed a lid on the top of the plastic cup and rammed a straw through the hole in the center. She forced a smile as she passed the cup across the counter to a young girl.

"Here. One tasty lemon Juicy Fruity. Enjoy." She tried to say it pleasantly, just as her boss had instructed her, but failed miserably.

The girl took the cup and stared at Sam. The goo oozed down Sam's forehead and slid slowly down her nose.

"Next," Sam called. She wiped her nose and

sent the goo splattering onto the floor.

Two boys approached the counter.

"Hey, Sam. When did ya start working here?" The boy leaned over the counter and started playing with the straw dispenser.

"Obviously not too long ago," the other boy replied, looking at the stain on Sam's head. "But I kind of like the neon-yellow highlights. What about you, Brendan?"

"Yeah, but I think it needs a bit more. Say, something in pink, perhaps. I'll have a cherry Juicy Fruity," Brendan said, smirking.

"And I'll have the super neon kiwi, double flavor burst," the second boy added.

"I think the pink and green will look pretty cool with the yellow. What do you think, Dylan?"

Imitating the long, drawn-out nasal voice of a fashion designer, Dylan replied, "Wonderful. Absolutely wonderful."

Sam drew in her breath and glared. She turned her back to the boys and filled each cup with the bright fruity syrups, then threw a huge scoop of ice into each. After she placed the cup under the beater, she turned the machine on, then carefully lifted and lowered the cup, watching the syrup blend with the ice until it became a neon pink. She held the cup in one hand while she reached across and hit the off switch with the other. The machine came to an immediate stop. Carefully, she began to pull the cup away and reached for a lid.

The machine gave a quick jerk and sent the still rotating beater into the juice. Gobs of neon-pink foam flew into the air and landed with perfectly aimed precision on Sam's head. With great restraint, she wiped the goop away before it had time to slide down her nose again.

As she placed the cup on the counter, she glimpsed her boss. The woman was shaking her head and looking none too pleased. Sam forced another smile. "Two dollars and fifteen cents, please." Her voice oozed with syrup while her eyes shot daggers at Brendan.

Sam took another deep breath and repeated the steps: place cup under beater, turn beater on, lift and lower cup, turn off switch, remove cup from holder.

"Shit!" she yelled as the beater fell into the cup and the neon-green ice flew in all directions. She stepped back as the ice landed on the counter, the walls, and the ceiling. A massive gob that had hit the ceiling lost its battle with gravity and landed on the front of her shirt and slid down, leaving a long streak of green from top to bottom.

Sam forced smile number three and passed the cup across the counter to Dylan.

"I don't know if it's what I was looking for, Dylan, but I think it'll work," Brendan said.

"Yes, yes," Dylan replied, using his nasal fashion designer voice again. "Sporting the Juicy Fruity ice freeze look, this model is proving that yes, food can accessorize the latest look."

Sam stepped out from behind the counter and stood in front of him as he reached for the door.

"Just a sec," she said, reaching for the cup. "I didn't give you enough." She yanked the lid off and grabbed the front of his jeans. With one single jerk, she dumped the juice down his pants, dropped the cup on the floor, and walked out the door.

"Now, that's plenty," she said, slamming the door behind her.

She pulled her bike from the rack and took off. "Stupid assholes. Stupid friggin' assholes," she muttered under her breath.

She sped down the street until she was forced to slow at a red light. She glanced to her left and turned at the corner. A car flew past her, the driver honking the horn and yelling. Sam's bike jerked and twisted into the curb. She jumped onto the boulevard and pulled her bike off the road. She stared at the flat front tire.

"Stupid piece of junk! I fixed you last week!" She kicked the tire and her foot caught in the spokes. She yanked it free, bending several spokes out of place at the same time. A passing vehicle slowed as a woman looked out the passenger window.

"I'm okay! I'm okay!" Sam yelled as she lifted her bike to her shoulder and walked down the sidewalk. "Just made a stupid fool of myself, lost my job, and I look like a friggin' freak from a circus sideshow, but other than that I'm perfectly fine. I mean, what else could possibly go wrong?"

Sam repositioned the bike on her shoulder as a huge raindrop landed on her head. She felt another one and then another, until the sky burst open and the entire contents of one cloud poured on her, her hair, her bright orange uniform, and all of the neon pink and yellow and green syrups she wore as accessories.

"Yep. Just when I thought things couldn't get worse . . ." Sam shook her fist at the cloud. She walked on.

When she reached the front steps of the Museum London, Sam locked her bike to a rack and walked up the front steps. A Canadian flag flapped in the wind. An elderly man, huddled under a small overhang, put his hat out toward Sam. His worn jacket, pants, and shoes had seen better days. He flashed a quick smile, his white teeth contrasting with his black skin. Sam looked at him from the corner of her eye, stepped to the side, and pushed the heavy wooden doors open. She leaned over the counter at the reception desk. A middle-aged

139

woman sat in an overstuffed office chair, focusing on a computer screen while her fingers flew across the keyboard.

"Crazy Bill's out there, again."

"Uh-huh." The woman looked briefly at a paper on the table and continued typing.

"Then send someone out there to get rid of him. He scares people."

"No he doesn't. Just leave him alone. He's harmless." The woman paused to look up at Sam. "Well, aren't you a lovely sight today. You going for the Goth look, mixed with a little neon disco?"

Sam gave her a dirty look. "Where's my dad?"

"He's finishing up with a kids' group right now. If you wait he should be here soon."

"No," Sam said, turning on her heel. "I just want to know where he is so I can avoid him. Don't tell him I'm here." She ducked into the door marked EMPLOYEES ONLY, walked down the hallway, and turned into the staff room.

She poured herself a cup of coffee and added five sugar cubes, then stirred in a couple of spoonfuls of coffee whitener.

"Hey, Sam, I thought you were working today." A boy dressed in khaki pants and a green shirt sporting the museum's logo walked into the room and threw his lunch bag on the table.

"Nope. Quit."

"Oh. Your dad's gonna be likin' that. What is this now? Job number ten?"

"No. Job number three, asshole. And mind your own business, Jake."

Jake sat down and took a sandwich from his bag. "So, what happened this time?" he said, taking a huge bite out of his sandwich. "Do tell me. No, let me guess. You suggested that a customer go to the tent store to purchase a dress in her size. No, that can't be it. You did that at Pier 21 a few weeks ago. Or maybe you told an old lady to—"

"Shut up, Jake."

"No, I don't think it was exactly those words. Wasn't it something more like, 'Stick your Big Mac where the sun don't shine'?"

"I said shut up. And don't you dare tell my dad anything." Sam slammed her cup of coffee on the table and stormed out the door.

She stopped and stood in the hallway. She drew in a deep breath. *One . . . two . . . three . . .* She let the air out and inhaled again. *One . . . two . . . three . . .*

"Oh, screw it," she blurted out. "What do psychiatrists know, anyway?"

She walked to the end of the hallway and pushed her way through a set of metal doors marked STORAGE. The spacious room was filled with shelves, crates, and boxes of various sizes. A pile of canvases, rugs, and other packing material lay in the corner.

She pulled out her cell phone and set her alarm to 5:15. "That should work," she mumbled, lying on the rugs and pulling a canvas over her head. "Sweet dreams, Sam." She closed her eyes, but it was only for a few seconds. The metal doors slammed shut, followed by the sound of footfalls on the cement floor. She was wide-awake. The footfalls drew nearer and nearer.

Sam lay perfectly still, holding her breath.

The canvas was pulled off her and thrown to the ground.

"I've had it, Sam. I've lost it. I can't take it anymore."

Sam sat up. Her dad glared.

"Aren't you gonna ask me what happened, at least?"

"Why should I? It's always the same thing. You don't try. You don't think. You lose your temper." He crossed his arms over his chest and sighed. "I'm right, aren't I?"

"No. Well, yeah. But I did try. The stupid juice machine kept on screwing up. And these two boys came in and—"

"And you took the liberty of emptying the entire contents of a Juicy Fruity cup down someone's jeans. I know. Sheila called me. You know, the only reason she hired you was because we're friends and I asked her to do me a favor. She had enough staff already. She was not impressed, Sam."

"Yeah, but you should have heard what they were saying to me. That I looked—"

"I don't care what they said. You shouldn't have done it. You know that. End of story." He shook his head. "You know, it's like you just don't care anymore."

"I don't."

Sam's dad sat on the pile of canvas and studied her face. "Don't say that. Please, don't say that. It's hard right now. It's hard for both of us. But you have to get rid of this anger, Sam. It's not good. You have so much going for you."

Sam rolled her eyes. "Not this talk again, Dad. Spare me."

"No, because you do. You're smart. You have a way of figuring things out that I've never seen in anyone else. Like your bike. The other day you had a flat, and when we didn't have any more of that rubber glue or a patch, you went and got that rubber molding from Mom's craft room and heated it up and used it with a piece of window screen. And it worked. You rode your bike to work today, didn't you?"

"Yeah, but the stupid thing didn't last. I had to

carry it here 'cause the glue didn't hold."

"Oh," Sam's dad said, biting his lip. "But that doesn't matter. The point is, you gave it some thought, you tried it—and it worked—for a while, anyway."

"Big deal."

"Yeah, it is a big deal."

They sat in silence.

"Listen. Tomorrow's going to be a busy day. Remember that exhibit I was telling you about? The one that's been traveling around Canada? The one from Egypt? Well, it's coming tomorrow, and we could use some help unloading it. We could have supper and then come back in the evening when the truck arrives. What do you say?"

Sam got up and walked toward the doors. "Yeah, whatever."

Her dad followed and pushed the door open, holding it while she walked into the hall.

"Oh, by the way. One of the custodians called in sick today. How about you help Jake wash the floors on the main level? After all that rain, lots of mud's been tracked in. And you know how much Jake would appreciate it."

Sam stopped and drew in another deep breath. *One . . . two . . . three . . .*

Chapter 15

*You do not teach the paths of the forest to
an old gorilla. ~ Congolese proverb*

Sam sat on the edge of her bed and rubbed her
hand over her face. She looked out her window and
blinked as the late morning sun glared into her
bedroom. "Morning to you too, Mr. Golden Sun,"
she said as she snapped the window curtains shut.

She walked to her dresser and turned on her
clock radio and set the volume to max. The tinny
sound of bass and drums filled the room, pushing
the stillness and quiet out the door.

Wrapping her housecoat around her small
frame, she walked into the bathroom and stared at
her reflection. She ran her fingers through her
hair—jet black, brown roots. "You'd think by now

you'd have lost the freckles, Sam," she said and stuck her tongue out.

She stepped into the shower and stood in a daze as the water fell. Leaning her head against the shower wall, she covered the drain with her foot. The water rose above her feet and ankles until she moved her foot and the water drained away. Finally, she washed her hair, rinsed, and shut the water off.

Standing in her bedroom doorway, she sighed. A wooden trunk lay at the end of her bed. She opened the lid and ran her fingers over the cover of a well-worn children's book that lay on top. *"Sammy the Super Snail,"* she whispered as she held the book to her chest. Tears rolled down her cheeks, dropping onto her housecoat.

"Yeah, right." She tossed the book back in the trunk, slammed the lid shut, and brushed the tears from her face. "How many times did you say, 'There's always tomorrow,' Mom? Too bad you didn't listen to your own words." Her words were hateful, stinging. "Such a hypocrite. Such a friggin' hypocrite."

She walked into the kitchen, poured herself a bowl of cereal, and sat in front of the TV. "Come on, Shaggy and Scooby-Doo. Make my day," she said as she turned it on and shoved a spoonful of Froot Loops into her mouth. She laughed as Shaggy and Scooby-Doo scrambled over each other, trying to run from a ghost sporting a long white gown and an eerie smile.

Sam's dad walked into the kitchen. "I see you're at it again. Froot Loops and Scooby-Doo. The breakfast of champions." As she continued to watch the TV, he added, "You know, I'm having my lunch right now. Along with the rest of the population of London."

"Uh-huh. And I'm sure you have a point to all this, old man."

"I did, but my Alzheimer's is kicking in again and I can't for the life of me remember what it was."

Sam gave a little laugh.

"I got you a present." Her dad pulled a cardboard box from behind his back and placed it on the coffee table.

She put her bowl down, picked up the box, and examined the return label. "No way. You didn't. Really?"

She tore open the box and revealed hundreds of shiny, rubbery bright pink paintballs. "Oh, you are going to be so dead and so pink when we go out, Dad."

"Listen, lady, I bought the pink paintballs because I know it's your favorite color and you look so good in it. Don't you be threatening me."

"So when's the match? Or are you too scared

147

your little girl is going to kick your butt again?"

"How about right now, little girl? You versus me. Me versus you. The Terminator Field. Fourteen hundred hours."

"But what about work?"

"I quit." He smiled.

"Yeah, right."

"Nah, someone has to pay the bills here. I just thought I would take the afternoon off since I have to work tonight. You up to a game or two? I think we could both use a break, huh? Get our minds off things for a bit?"

"Yeah." Sam gulped the last of her cereal down and ran to her bedroom.

"Loser makes supper, and I want KD, extra ketchup!" she yelled, grabbing her camouflage pants and a T-shirt.

*   *   *   *

In the prep shack Sam filled her hopper with the small pink balls and secured the lid. She checked her air tank and hoisted the gun, feeling its weight. As her dad pulled his camouflage shirt over his head and adjusted his neck guard, she grinned. "You are so going to need that, Dad. You're dead meat already."

"Oh, don't be so sure about that, princess.

Experience is more valuable than speed and agility. At least that's what I keep telling myself." He grabbed a couple of handfuls of paintballs, filled his hopper, and pushed down the lid. "Here," he said taking an extra handful. "Take these for your spares. You're going to need them."

Sam placed the balls in the extra-large pants pocket on her thigh. "You are going to be so covered today," she said, laughing. "Just wait."

Her dad laughed as he put his helmet on and tightened the strap. "Shall we get this over with, sweetness? Oh, by the way—I want steak, done on the barbeque, medium rare, baked potato, and Caesar salad on the side. Plenty of sour cream. On the potato, of course."

"Best not to think of something that's not going to happen, Dad."

Sam ran out of the shack, across the field, and took her position behind a pile of tires. She crawled through the tall grass and came to a wooden barrier, then peeked through a tiny hole at the bottom. A blur of camouflage flew across.

"Gee, Dad," she muttered quietly, "the whole idea of wearing camo is not to be seen. I can see fast-moving targets."

She stuck the barrel of the gun through a hole and squeezed the trigger, sending a paintball splattering on the opposite wall.

"You're wasting your ammo, princess!" her father yelled.

Sam grinned.

She jerked her gun out of the hole and crawled toward a pile of logs. Her dad raced across the field again and dived behind a bush. She fired her gun again, this time hitting a tree. A bright pink spot confirmed her poor aim.

"Nyah nyah nyah nyah nyah!" her dad yelled out.

Sam crouched and studied the arrangements of tires, logs, and bunkers. She crept to a thick stand of evergreen trees and watched her dad make his way to the pile of tires she had hid behind just moments earlier.

"So the ol' man can move, eh?" she mumbled. "Not for long . . ."

Sam fired another shot. The paintball hit the tires, adding a bright pink circle to the myriad of green, blue, and yellow spots left from other games.

"Ha ha ha ha haaaa!" her dad yelled. "You're losing your touch, princess!"

She crouched and inched her way toward a tall tower. She took an oblong green grenade out of her pocket, pulled the pin, and threw it over the tires. Without a moment's hesitation, she scrambled up the wooden slats nailed to the side of a tree. The grenade landed with a huge splat.

"You're going to have to practice that toss, Sammy. You throw like a Yankees pitcher!"

Sam sat and leaned against the wall of the tree fort. "That's what you're supposed to think, Dad." She smirked.

She looked down onto the field through a small hole in a board. Her dad was still crouched behind the tires, looking toward the stand of trees she had been hiding behind. He crept toward the bush, then jumped in front and stopped. He looked from side to side and shrugged. Sam held her hand over her mouth to keep from laughing.

He edged toward a pile of logs and slunk around its base, holding his gun in position. Sam watched as he jumped around the edge, expecting to see her, and then shook his head again.

"I better put the guy out of his misery," she whispered, sticking her gun through the hole in the board.

A barrage of bullets plastered her dad, covering his camouflage outfit in neon pink. "Ow! Ow! Ow!" he screamed, pulling his arms over his head and running for the nearest bunker.

She held her finger to the trigger and hit him in the legs, his helmet, and his back. With one final shot she aimed for his butt. The paintball made its mark.

"Mercy! Mercy! Mercy!" he yelled.

She climbed down the ladder, hoisted her gun to her shoulder, and walked up to her dad.

"You scream like a banshee, Dad," she teased.

*   *   *   *

The streetlights came on as Sam closed the door to the house and her dad locked it. She pulled her jacket on as she felt the chill of the evening air. "Great meal, Dad. You make a pretty mean bowl of KD. Not too hard, not too soggy. I think you finally got it this time."

"Good to know. I was worried we might have to start eating steak and potatoes for a change."

"Can I drive?" she asked as her dad unlocked the car.

"No. You don't even have your beginner's."

"But I've been practicing with Uncle Darren out in his field."

"Uncle Darren's been letting you drive?"

"Yeah. What's wrong with that?"

"Well, like I said—"

"But why does it matter if I don't have my beginner's? I know how to stay on the right side of the road."

"No."

Sam slid into the passenger side of the car. "You're no fun, Dad. No fun at all."

Her dad started up the car. "I don't know about that. Seems you had a lot of fun pelting me with those paintballs this afternoon."

"Oh, yeah. That reminds me." She reached into the glove compartment and pulled out a CD. "I've got your theme song here." She pushed it in the stereo and the music pulsed from the speakers:

"He bit the dust. He bit the dust.

Hey, it's a shame. It's a crying shame."

"Ah! Very funny!" her dad said, starting to sing along. "'Hey, it's a shame. Hey, it's a crying shame. He bit the dust. He bit the dust.'" He smiled. "For your information, I did not bite the dust."

"Oh, yes you did. You bit it and swallowed it, and you're still choking on it."

"That's not dust I'm choking on. Next time, request something other than Kraft Dinner for your victory meal. Please."

He pulled the car into the museum parking lot and they got out. A large truck pulled up and started backing toward a wide garage door.

"You ready?" he asked.

"Uh-huh. You?"

"Oh, yes," Sam's dad rubbed his hands together like a little boy in a candy shop. "It's the first time this museum has ever had anything like this. Imagine mummies and shabtis and amulets and all those ancient treasures taken from the tombs of pharaohs and delivered right to our doorstep."

He stopped and looked at Sam. "You don't seem to be that excited about this. Are you?"

"Yeah, yeah. I was just remembering how Mom and I would come here every time a new exhibit arrived. And we'd watch you open the boxes and ooh and aah over everything."

Sam's dad put his arm around her shoulder and gave her a squeeze.

"Hey, Jim!" Jake stuck his head out the museum door. "We're ready whenever you are."

Jake held the door open while they walked into the dimly lit museum. "What's with the army fatigues, Sam?"

"Dad and I went out for a little game of paintball before supper."

"And how come you're not in your outfit, Jim?"

"'Cause he wouldn't be caught dead wearing neon pink."

Jake gave Sam a puzzled look.

They all walked through the museum, past the displays and into the hall.

Two stuffed wolf statues sat at the edge of a First Nations exhibit, their glass eyes reflecting the light from the red EXIT sign. "Kind of creepy in here when the lights are low, huh?" Sam said.

"Yeah," Jake said. "Makes you think of *Night*

at the Museum, doesn't it?"

"Yeah," Sam said.

The first of the crates to be unloaded were on the smaller side. After they were placed in the corner of the loading dock, Jake removed the screws from one of the wooden lids with a drill, lifted the lid, and looked inside.

Sam peered over his shoulder. "Dad told me to help over here. He wants me to unload everything, put it on the tables, and check the inventory." She held a clipboard and a pencil in her hand.

"Be my guest," Jake said, stepping back. "I'll get to those other crates over there."

Carefully, Sam reached into the crate and pulled out an item covered with layers and layers of bubble wrap. She removed the tape and took the plastic off, placing the wrapping into a cardboard box. She turned the object over to see its inventory numbers and found the same numbers on the paper. "Item number AF/EGY-2309, Ram's Head Amulet." She placed it on the table beside her and pulled the next item out.

Time passed quickly, and within two hours Sam had most of the objects placed on the table and was working on the last crate. She had thoroughly enjoyed checking out the canopic jars, rings, necklaces, Saqqara-type birds, sistrums, and all the other items taken from the ancient tombs in Egypt.

"You ready for a break yet?" Sam's dad stood by one of the tables and began looking at the set of canopic jars. "Let's see if I remember this right. The baboon-headed jar contains the lungs, the jackal holds the stomach, the human-headed one has the liver, and the falcon holds the intestines. Kind of disgusting, don't you think? The Egyptians brought us many wonderful inventions and fine art, but I have to admit that some of their beliefs were a tad off."

"Well, I don't know. Seems to me there are all kinds of religions with beliefs in things you can't see. Angels, spirits, gods, demons . . . heaven, hell."

"Yeah, I suppose you're right, Sam. That idea of heaven kind of keeps us going, eh?"

"Yeah, I guess so." Sam checked off another item on the list. "You go ahead. I want to finish this first. I'll be there in a couple of minutes."

"Okay. I'll put the coffee on." He turned to Jake and the truck driver. "You ready for a break?" he asked.

"Sure. I was ready hours ago," Jake said as he placed an empty crate in the corner of the room.

"Sounds like a great plan," the driver replied. They walked out the door.

Sam reached into each corner of the crate and felt around in the mound of Styrofoam chips for anything she may have missed. "Hey, almost missed this one," she mumbled. She pulled out a small package and removed the wrapping to reveal a wooden box. Carvings of birds, lions, elephants, and snakes adorned the top and sides. She turned the box over to record the artifact number and paused. "Strange," she muttered. "No number."

She unrolled the wrapping and looked for the label, in case it had fallen off in the packaging, then looked into the crate. Nothing.

"Hmm." She scanned the list of the items for that crate on her clipboard and scratched her head. "All of the items are accounted for. There's no 'wooden box' listed here."

She turned it over and over again. "Filthy thing," she said, wiping the black dirt on her pants. "Let's clean you up."

She grabbed a small paintbrush hanging from a hook on the wall and carefully brushed the soot and grime away from the wood. The images became clearer and clearer.

She took a closer look and noticed a series of wavy lines traveling in different directions around the box. Short lines traveled upward while longer lines moved lengthwise.

With a few more quick strokes of the brush, she blew the dirt and grime away until each line became distinct.

"This isn't a solid piece of wood," she

whispered. "It's like a . . . a puzzle. A set of blocks put together, each holding the other like a log house, but . . ." She turned the box over and over in her hands. "But it's more complicated than that."

She paused and held the box to her ear. "Anything inside?"

She shook the box. Something rattled.

"Dad's going to kill me for doing this, but, oh well."

With one hand Sam held the box and with the other she tried to pry a wooden piece from its place. Nothing budged. She tried another piece, and then another. Still nothing moved. She traced her finger over the lines.

"Wait. It's like one of those Rubik's cubes from the old days. You have to think ahead. The pieces have an order to them and . . ." Sam sighed. "This is going to take some work."

She placed her finger on one of the bottom corners and followed the length of the piece and stopped. Using one finger as a marker, she traced the next line as it moved upward to the top of the box.

"Now if I move this piece and then this one at the same time, then . . ." Wedging her nails into the grooves, she pulled at the pieces, then turned the box over to get a better grip and pulled again. Nothing happened.

"Now this is pathetic. Come on, Sam. You can figure this out."

She traced her fingers over another set of lines, stuck her nails into another groove, and pulled. Nothing budged.

"Now I'm getting upset," she said.

Sam's dad, Jake, and the truck driver returned to the room.

"No more time for coffee, dear. Glen just told me he's got to get going. Can you help us with the last crate?" her dad asked.

"Is it the coffin?"

"Well, sort of. A replica, actually, but I've heard you can hardly tell the difference."

Sam placed the box on top of a file folder on a side table and went over to help.

All eyes were on the crate as the driver used the forklift to carefully place it on the floor. In a way, Sam wished she didn't know the coffin was a fake. It took away the thrill of seeing something people had created thousands of years ago. But when the wooden lid of the crate was lifted up and the canvas pulled away, everyone stood in awe.

"Look, they even etched in the cracked age lines to make it look authentic," Sam's dad said, running a gloved finger over the coffin. "And look at this paint job. Even the colors are faded in some spots, and the paint is chipped. If I didn't know better, I'd swear it was the real thing."

The driver closed the doors to the truck, thanked Sam's dad for the coffee, and drove off.

"You want to open the lid, Sam? Jake?"

Both nodded eagerly. They lifted the coffin's lid, placed it on a table, and looked inside. The second coffin inside it was even more colorful and more elaborate than the first.

"See, this part here is the cartouche," Sam's dad said, pointing to a series of symbols at the chest area of the coffin. "It's kind of like the pharaoh's signature. And these hieroglyphs tell us he was a pharaoh and a high priest."

Sam examined the coffin, taking in the brightly colored human eyes, trees, animals, gods and mythical creatures.

"I've got some more info here." Her dad pulled out his briefcase and opened a hefty folder. "They're handouts for the tours."

They each took a paper and studied the hieroglyphs. Sam looked from the coffin to the paper and back again. She took a pen and circled the symbols as she found them on the coffin and wrote notes along the borders of the paper.

Her dad yawned and looked at his watch. "Oh my, it's getting late. Come on, Sam, Jake. We still have to move these things into the display room. He tossed his pile of papers and folders onto the side table and grabbed a trolley. Sam and Jake carefully placed the items inside.

"I'll take it to the display room if you want to fill another cart while I'm gone," Jake said as he pushed the cart through the doors.

Sam went to the supply room to get another trolley while her dad gathered his file folders and papers and threw them into his briefcase.

When the second trolley was filled, Sam pushed it through the doors, down the hallway, and toward the new display room. Her dad followed, locking the storage room doors behind him.

Jake came up from behind. "Mind if I get the keys from you now? I have to open up early, and I really want to head home now."

"Sure. I'll see you around ten," Sam's dad said as he passed him the keys.

"Thanks." Jake pocketed them and walked out of the room.

"Is Madge going to be setting up the display tomorrow, Dad?" Sam asked, wheeling the trolley into the room.

"Yes, she's got some help coming from the museum in Toronto. Why do you ask?"

"Oh, just wondering if she'll need any help." She paused. "I'd rather do that than the Juicy Fruity job any day."

"She probably will. So nice of you to ask, Sam.

Now let's get going home. I'm exhausted." He turned toward the front entrance. "We have to leave out the main doors. I locked the back ones already."

"Sure, but one thing. Can I have the keys to the storage room? I want to show you a box I found in the last crate. I left it on the side table. It's really cool. And strange thing, there's no artifact number on it, and it's not on the list either."

He yawned. "Sorry. I just gave Jake the keys. It's going to have to wait until tomorrow. I'm sure it'll be safe there for now."

"Crap. Well, I guess it'll have to. But you're going to like it. Kind of a mystery thing."

"Hmm. Now you've got me intrigued." He placed his hand on Sam's shoulder. "Let's go home and have some hot chocolate. I'm pooped."

Chapter 16

*Advice is a stranger; if he's welcome he stays
for the night; if not, he leaves the same day.*
~ *Malagasy proverb*

Sam took a long sip from her cup and made herself comfortable in a pile of cushions on the couch. "Thanks for the hot chocolate, Dad."

"No problem. You earned it." He paused for a moment. "It was a good day, huh?"

Sam nodded and took another sip.

"Better than yesterday," he added.

Sam put her cup on the coffee table and sighed. "I really don't want to talk about yesterday, if that's what this is all about. Let's just enjoy this time right now. I don't want to ruin a good day." She grabbed the remote and turned on the TV.

"And when do you think it would be a good time to talk about it, Sam?"

"Never." She flicked through the channels. "We don't need to discuss everything." The tone in her voice revealed her impatience.

He turned the TV off. "I disagree. We need to talk." He sat on the couch beside her. "Sam, you have a temper, and it's getting you into trouble. And I'm afraid if you don't learn how to control it, it's going to get the better of you and you'll end up in a lot more trouble than just losing a job."

She leaned back on the couch, stared at the ceiling, and didn't respond.

"Well? I'm open. Talk to me. Tell me what's going on."

"Tell you what's going on? Are you totally stupid?"

"No, Sam. It's tough. I know it is. I'm going through it, too. But—"

"But what?"

"You seem to think you're in this all on your own. Talk to me. Tell me what you're thinking."

Sam drew in a long breath. "Okay, you want to know. Here goes: I met up with Mrs. Peacosh yesterday. She'd been in Arizona for the winter. Said she was catching up on the news, looking through the newspapers, and she came across Mom's obituary. Said she was sorry and all that crap. And then she had to ask how Mom died." Sam felt her face tense. "No. She couldn't leave it alone.

She had to know. And you know what I did, Dad?"

He placed his hand on hers.

"I walked away. Yep, just turned 'round and walked away."

"I'm sorry, Sam. I'm sorry."

"Sorry ain't worth shit, Dad." She turned to go to her bedroom and paused. "And you know what makes it worse? You. If for once you treated me like some spoiled teenage brat who's not getting her way, you'd be wringing me out. Yelling at me, grounding me for losing my job. But no, you're not. You're all nice and sweet and patient 'cause . . . 'cause . . ." She stopped. "Forget it, Dad. It ain't worth shit." She ran into her bedroom and slammed the door behind her.

She leaned against the wall and listened to her dad climb the stairs, walk down the hall to his bedroom, and close the door. Moving to her bed, she leaned against the headboard. She took a stuffed green lion from her night table and held it on her lap. The hand-sewn eyes, with their frayed eyelashes, stared back at her. She wiped her tears with her sleeve and held the lion close to her and squeezed.

A jumbled mass of feelings and thoughts tore into her mind, destroying any self-control she possessed. She screamed and threw the lion across the room. It hit a lamp, causing it to crash to the floor. The bulb broke into a thousand pieces, leaving the room in darkness.

"You bitch!" Sam yelled. "You bitch!" She punched her mattress. The anger refused to be quelled. She slammed the wall with her fists. It became a punching bag as she hit it over and over. Her knuckles bled as tears filled her eyes and flowed down her cheeks. The wall became a blur as her breath came to her in shallow, short pants. Her knees buckled and she collapsed to the floor. She held her fists to her chest and leaned against the wall and sobbed.

"Sam! Sam! Let me in!" Her dad pounded on her bedroom door.

She stared at the blood on her fists. "Go away, Dad. Go away and leave me alone." Her voice shook, but the tone was firm and full of hate. She drew in a long, deep breath and then another.

"Sam? Please, let me in."

She didn't respond.

"Please."

Another long pause. "Go away!" she yelled. "I don't want to talk!" Sam inhaled sharply. Finally, she spoke, her words measured, controlled. "I'm okay, Dad. Just leave me. I'm fine."

"Are you sure? You don't sound fine."

"I am. Just leave me to think. Okay?"

There was silence on the other side of the door

until he said, "All right. All right. But if you need me, you know where I am."

She listened to the silence that followed and her dad's footfalls as he turned and walked away.

She went to the opposite wall, turned on another light, picked up her lion, and stroked its woolen coat. She grabbed a fistful of tissues and dabbed at the blood on her hands, then sat on the floor next to her trunk. Its lid was closed, beckoning her, inviting her to open it and revisit the treasures inside.

More emotions stirred in Sam's heart. Treasures revisited only brought more pain, and yet they offered the only comfort she could find: things from the past that shared traces of good days filled with bitter sweetness. It was like a dull toothache after gorging on a candied apple. She opened the lid.

Next to her book lay a small stone. She picked it up and felt its cool touch. It was an ordinary piece of gravel: gray, nothing pretty. But yet it held something special.

"Here. I've got something for your treasure trunk."

Sam's mom pulled a rock out from her pocket. "I don't think you'll remember it, but you gave it to me when you were just a little girl. We were walking through the park one day and you picked it up from the pathway and gave it to me. You told me to keep it forever because it was a very special rock. It's been in my pocket ever since. Never took it out."

"Why are you taking it out now, then?"

"'Cause I thought you'd take better care of it now."

She turned and walked out of the room. Sam placed the stone in the trunk.

Under the stone lay a faded baby blanket. Sam held it to her nose and sniffed it. It still held the smell of the soap her mom had used when she was a young girl. A corsage stuck in the corner of the trunk caught her attention next. She ran her fingers over the silver ribbon that was tied around the pink rose, now faded and dried.

"What's this all about, Mom?"

"Your dad gave it to me on our first date. A dance at the school. I thought you might like it. It's a treasure too."

Sam put the corsage back and pulled out a gold-colored medal. A large paintball gun was embossed in the center over top of a splattered blue paintball. The words "Most Valuable Player" were written on the bottom.

Sam's mom took one look at the medal hanging around Sam's neck. "Hmph. So did everyone get one of these?"

"No, just one member from each team, Mom."

"How many people in each team, then?"

"Five."

"Well, there's not much competition then, is there?"

"No. I guess not." Sam took the medal off her neck and stuck it into her pocket.

She ran her fingers over the lettering and dropped the medal into the trunk. The tip of a brown envelope caught her attention. She pulled it out and opened it. A sketch she had drawn back in elementary school fell out. She looked at a picture of a dog leaping up into the air to catch a ball and smiled. As she placed the sketch back into the envelope, she noticed a scrap of paper stuck inside. She pulled it out. "My artist extraordinaire" was scribbled in her mother's handwriting.

Sam stared at the medal and then at the picture. If she could describe her life using two objects, these would do just fine. Life with her mother was like being on a bumpy roller coaster ride full of highs and lows. She could never tell what each day would bring. Compliments, hugs, "I love you," or stares into space and hurtful words: "Get out of here. Leave me alone."

Sam placed the medal and the picture back into the trunk and closed the lid. She stood and sighed as she placed her green lion on the end of her bed. As she opened her door to walk to the washroom, she spied her cup of hot chocolate on the coffee table in the living room. *A hot cup would do quite nicely right now*, she thought. She carried her cup to the kitchen and set it in the microwave to warm up. Her dad's snoring came from the other end of the hallway. It comforted her as she took a sip of the creamy liquid and let it settle in her stomach. She stared at the clock on the kitchen wall: 2:35 a.m. Late. But there wasn't a tired bone in her body. Sam carried her hot chocolate downstairs and stopped in the foyer. Her dad's briefcase leaned against the wall beside the door.

She opened the case and sifted through the papers until she found what she was looking for: the paper she had written on while looking at the coffin. As she pulled it out, something dropped to the bottom of the briefcase—not a file folder, but heavier. She reached in and her hand brushed against something hard and solid. She pulled out the wooden box she had left on the table at the museum.

"How the hell did this get here?" she asked.

She tucked the box under her arm as she walked into her bedroom. Then she closed the door behind her and sat on her bed. "Now let's see what we can do here."

Again, she traced her fingers over the short

wavy lines and turned the box over and over. "This has got to be the most complicated piece of woodwork I've ever seen. There must be some way to figure it out."

She took a piece of paper from her desk, held it over the box, and lightly rubbed a pencil over each side and the top and bottom until she had a complete template of the box. The paper looked like a Grade 5 geometry assignment, with instructions to cut, fold, and tape together to make a 3D prism.

Sam stared at the paper. She followed the paths of the pieces, glancing from one part of the rubbing to the other.

"If I was to push this piece, then this piece would push this one . . ." Sam's brow furrowed and she rubbed her hand across her forehead. "But then this piece would hold it here and then . . . No, that won't work." She turned the paper around and looked at it from a different angle. "But . . . if I push this one here, it will move this one, and then . . ."

Sam picked up the box and pushed a small piece of wood in the corner and pulled at a piece on the opposite side. The box fell apart and lay in pieces on the floor. A little leather sack sat in the middle of the pile.

"What the hell is this?" she asked, picking up the sack and pulling the leather tie that wrapped it closed. She opened it and looked inside. A pile of green stones lay nestled in the bottom.

She dumped the stones onto her bed and picked one up. A faint thread of silver passed over its polished green surface as she turned it over and over.

"Pretty, but . . . not what I was hoping for." She ran her finger over the stone and felt its coolness. "Diamonds, rubies, even a few gold nuggets or a ring would have been nice."

She yawned and looked at the clock on her nightstand. It read 3:17. "Maybe I am tired," she said, laying her head on her pillow and pulling her blanket over her body. "I'll change my clothes tomorrow." She took one last look at the stone as she held it tightly in her hand. "Tomorrow will be another day, Sam. Tomorrow will be another day."

A girl's quiet voice came from the darkness: "If there is a tomorrow."

Chapter 17

Where a woman rules, streams run uphill.
~ Ethiopian proverb

Sam caught her breath. She glanced back and forth as she twisted her head from side to side. The surrounding air, the stench, and the heat were stifling. Her eyes adjusted to make out a clay wall, about shoulder height, almost surrounding her in a large circle. Atop the wall, huge logs rose above her head, meeting at the center. Long leaves and stems of grass covered the roof. Small gaps between the roof and the wall allowed the sunlight to pour in, bringing into focus a young girl standing near the center post.

The girl, her eyes closed and head hanging down, lifted her hand to her face and wiped away the beads of sweat that covered her brow. Sam's eyes widened as she took in the whole picture: the girl's long white dress, which contrasted with her dark skin, was ripped and soiled, clinging to her body. Her arms were wrapped around the post, almost hugging it, while her wrists were tied securely with a rope. Her feet were bound to the bottom of the post, making any movement impossible.

The girl opened one eyelid and looked at Sam. Faded white diamonds painted around her eyes gave an ominous glow. She gasped when she noticed Sam's camouflage shirt and pants. "You have to get out of here," she whispered. "They will be coming back soon soon."

Sam shook her head in confusion. "Who? What are you talking about? Where am I?"

"You are in Kony camp, girl. Now get out of here. Otti is coming back."

"What?" Sam stepped back. She didn't understand what this girl was talking about. She didn't know where she was. She didn't understand anything but the cold fear that sent the hairs on the back of her neck standing on end.

The girl turned her ear toward the door, a space in the wall where a thin piece of cloth hung from a stick resting on the top.

"They are here. Hide. Get behind those sack and throw the blanket over you. Do something, girl.

They do not like soldier coming here uninvited."

"Soldier?" Sam looked at the girl and then at the camouflage shirt and pants she was still wearing after her paintball game with her dad. "I'm not a—"

"Hide!" the girl commanded.

Sam dived behind the sacks and pulled the blanket over her head, attempting to cover every inch of her shaking body. Tightening herself into a ball, she held her breath and stayed absolutely still. Footfalls drew nearer until she heard a sheet being pushed aside as someone stepped into the hut.

"Lovely Eseza. You have been waiting for me. My heart is so happy to find you here." A man's voice came from behind the center post. Sam's heart pounded against her chest. She closed her eyes as tightly as possible, wishing she could make herself disappear.

"Take your hand off me. When Kony come back he is not going to be happy with you. You wait. I will ask him to tie you to this very post and leave your body to rot."

Despite the confidence the girl tried to muster, Sam detected a tremble in her voice.

"Eeh, what is this you say? Now I think you are mistaken here, dear Eseza. Joseph does not take too kindly to one of his wife taking off. It has been four month since he held his child. Where have you been, precious Eseza? Sharing a hut with the soldier of the UPDF? With all the enemy in the government army? I think this is what I will tell Kony. He will not be happy. No, beautiful Eseza, it is you who should be afraid."

Sam listened. She could have sworn she heard the girl spit.

"Ha ha ha! You are a strong woman, Eseza!"

Sam heard a loud slap and then a gasp.

"Come with me, whore. I will give you a taste of what Joseph will do to you when he return."

Sam listened to the faint sound of ropes being untied and the dragging of feet across the dirt floor and out the door.

"Untie me now, Two-Victor." The girl's voice sounded more confident. "Untie me, or Joseph will learn how you are part of Otti group. And have been trying to gain the support of all the soldier and replace him as their leader."

"Hmf! You speak all lie, whore!" Another vicious slap followed.

"You know exactly what I am talking about. Do not take me for a fool. I have seen you giving special favor to the soldier. Extra ration, letting them help themself to more of the spoil from all the village we attack. Joseph has been suspecting it for some time. I only need to say what is the truth and he will place you in front of a firing squad."

The man laughed. "You may be a strong

woman, but you are stupid. Who do you think stand before you now? All of these men here are under *my* command. All of them are faithful to *me*. Me, and only me. No one here will listen to you because you are a wife to Kony."

There was silence. Sam shifted her weight as her legs began to cramp. Voices came from a different direction.

"Hey di da!" a new voice called out. "Look at what I see."

Sam tried to figure out how many more people had arrived. By the sound of the footfalls, three, perhaps four. It was hard to tell.

"*Itye nining*, Eseza. You have come back to us." The voice was very deep and had the same effect on Sam's ears as the pounding of a bass drum.

The voice continued. "Now why do you have her tied, Two-Victor? This is not the way you treat a wife of Kony."

"You know as well as I do, Kokas, that the girl escaped. And she did not take too kindly to our finding her and bringing her back."

"Of course she did not. She still had much work to do. Do you not know that Kony sent her out as a spy to the lower area? He has suspicion of UPDF sympathizer banding together and planning to attack our camp. A young girl and her child is perfect cover for this. No one would suspect a thing. You did not."

"And why was I not told this? I am second-in-command."

"But not always the second to know. Kony does not tell you everything. I suggested the plan to Kony. That is why I know. Now untie her."

In a moment of silence, Sam imagined the ropes being removed.

"And where is the child, Eseza?" the deep voice asked. "Where is Kony son?"

After a short pause she answered. "He is dead. The malaria got him. I buried him two month ago, shortly after I arrived at the village."

"That is bad bad."

"Yes, but it is the way of the bush. I do not worry. I will soon have another."

"Yes, it is better to think this way. There is no use in the tear, for it will not bring the child back. Some of the girl cry and cry over the loss of their child, but no matter how many tear fall the god will not breathe new life into the child."

Sam listened to the slap-slap sound of bare feet walking across the packed ground. Kokas continued. "Linda, we are hungry. Prepare the meal. And do it quick quick."

Sam heard footfalls approaching the door. She froze.

Eseza spoke. "No. Let me prepare the meal for you, Kokas. It is my honor to."

"Eeh? Do not talk the foolishness, girl. Sit. And you will tell me what you learn. Linda, go. Prepare the meal."

"But I can prepare your favorite."

"No. Sit," Kokas commanded. "Linda. Prepare the meal. Now."

The footfalls came closer and closer as Linda entered the hut and walked to where Sam was hidden among the bags under the blanket. Linda threw the blanket to the side.

Sam stared wide-eyed at her. "Please. No," she whispered.

The girl screamed.

Two-Victor rushed into the hut. He stopped and looked confused, then lowered his gun and pointed it. He smirked.

Sam lifted her arms above her head. The fear that had never left her since she arrived in the hut was now magnified a hundred times.

"Get up!" Two-Victor shouted.

Sam rose.

"Out."

She kept her hands above her head and walked out the door. The bright light from the sun blinded her, and she squeezed her eyes shut. She opened them and took in her surroundings: men, black men, wearing army uniforms, all pointed their guns at her. Trees, tall leafy trees and bush. The chatter of monkeys and the unfamiliar cry of a bird as it flew high above her head. Voices in the near distance, calling to one another in a language she had never heard before. A hut made of mud and a roof of grass. And a hot, hot sun.

Africa?

She glanced at the soldiers' shirts, searching for any identification, any sign of what country they were from, but she was confused. They seemed to be from different countries. One man wore the blue, white, and red striped flag of France on his arm sleeve, while another had the white, blue, and red horizontal stripes of a Russian flag. *Strange,* Sam thought, *they don't look French or Russian.* Others wore fatigues, much like the ones she was wearing, with no flags or embroidery above the chest pocket signifying what army they were from. The only thing they had in common was the blackness of their skin and the tight dreadlocks that clung to their sweat-covered heads.

Two-Victor kicked the back of Sam's knees. Her legs buckled and she fell to the ground. Her arms were wrenched behind her and a rope was wrapped tight around her wrists, then pulled until it cut into her skin.

She winced. "How dare you! Get this off me,

you assholes!"

Two-Victor pushed his rifle barrel to her head.

"No," Kokas said. "Leave her. We make her talk first. Then we kill her."

Sam's breath caught in her throat.

Two-Victor yanked the rope and dragged her toward the edge of the bush. She had no choice but to stand as he wrenched the rope up and slammed her against a tree. He rammed the back of her head against the rough bark.

She gasped. Bright stars flashed across her eyes. Two-Victor tied a rope around her shoulders and waist, and finally her knees. She couldn't move. Kokas stood in front of her and smiled.

Sam glared, clenching her teeth, balling her hands into tight fists.

"A white woman," he began. "Why would a white woman, a white soldier woman, be in our camp, boy?"

The emphasis on the word "soldier" was not lost on Sam.

Kokas turned his back and walked a couple of steps away. He spun on his heel and faced her again. "And a soldier who does not know the respect that is owed a commander."

He rammed the butt of his rifle into Sam's stomach. She gasped.

"You will address me as Commander Kokas or

sir. I will accept either of those, but I will not accept 'asshole.'"

He swung the end of his rifle and hit Sam on the knees. She screamed.

"Do you understand?"

Sam gritted her teeth. "Yes, sir," she said. Tears welled up in her eyes and fell down her cheeks.

"Now, tell me, dear, what is your name and what army send you here?"

Sam returned the commander's glare. "My name is Samantha Wallace, but I'm not in any army. This isn't a soldier's uniform if that's what you're thinking . . . sir."

The commander studied her briefly. "Samantha. A pretty name for a pretty girl. It would cause me great sadness to change any part of you, Samantha, because you do not wish to tell me these little detail just. Tell me where you are from and I will not take the machet to your lip."

Kokas placed his hand on the long knife that hung from his belt.

Sam thought quickly. *London? London, Ontario? Would he know of such a place? If this is Africa, I doubt it.*

"Canada, sir. I'm from Canada."

The man rubbed his hand over the stubble on his chin. "The Peace Corps? Did you lose your little blue beret? I can find you one. We took several off all the Kaibil peacekeeper we strung up last month." The commander smirked as he looked around at the rest of the soldiers. They laughed in response. "And how did you get here? In the middle of the LRA camp?"

Her mind raced. *LRA camp? What the hell is an LRA camp?* Whatever it was, she was sure it wasn't any Boy Scout camp.

She replayed the last few moments in her mind: looking through her trunk, finding the box in her dad's briefcase, and figuring out how to open it . . . the pouch of stones, then finding herself here. In Africa? In the middle of some war?

Sam quickly decided that telling the truth wasn't the best option. She doubted her explanation of suddenly appearing here would go over well. "I don't know, sir. I must have gotten lost."

"Lost?" Kokas turned toward the bush. A group of men and boys were heading into the clearing. Sam stared, not at the men and the rifles, but at the boys that followed along with them. Young boys. Young boys carrying guns and looking quite comfortable with them hanging over their shoulders.

"Eeh. You have returned soon soon," Kokas said.

A tall man, wearing a green bandanna wrapped

around his head, pushed his way through the group while pulling a teenage boy by a rope that bound the boy's wrists. The man pushed the teen to the ground. He lay still, his eyes closed and the rise and fall of his chest barely visible.

"We found one of the Arrow Boy. He will not talk, but that will change. Now."

The teen's legs were covered in dried blood, and what clothes he wore were ripped and clinging to his sweat-drenched body. His face was swollen, and the blood from a fresh gash on his forehead oozed down his face. A fly landed on his lip and another on his eyelid. He didn't lift a hand to brush them away.

Each of the soldiers smiled, then turned their gaze on their commander. Eseza circled the boy and bent down to examine his face. She stifled a gasp.

"His name is Emau Naboth," the soldier in the green bandanna said. "We found him near the same village we found the girl. Some of my boy took the liberty of interrogating him in the back of the jeep while we drove here. Hope that was okay with you, Commander."

Kokas nodded as he walked closer to the boy.

"We could not get anything out of him. No other name, no plan, nothing. The only reason we know his name is that one of the boy recognize him as Samson brother. I sent a boy to get Samson.

Maybe he can get him to talk."

Eseza grabbed the teen's hair and pulled his head up to study his face. She released her grip, allowing his head to fall to the ground. "No. You are wrong. He is not an Arrow Boy. I know this one. He is a simple beggar boy. I have seen him on the street with both his hand out. He cannot work because his leg are filled with bullet. You will see when he walk. No, you are wrong. He is only a beggar boy."

Eseza stood and wiped her hands over her dress. "But," she said, pausing, "he will be good in the kitchen. He can cook. If not, he will learn quickly. Bring him into the hut and tie him," she ordered a boy standing guard near the door.

The man who carried the rope stepped in front of Eseza. "I say he is an Arrow Boy, and he stay with me."

She smiled. "Until Kony come, he is with me. He is not an Arrow Boy. I know the people of that village, and I know this boy. Look." Eseza wiped the blood from the back of the boy's legs. "See the bullet mark. There are many. He is no threat to us. He cannot run. He cannot be a fighter. He cannot even work. He is a beggar boy. Take him into the hut now."

The boy obeyed and dragged the limp body inside.

Eseza glanced at the soldier as he adjusted the bandanna on his head. "Next time you go out, find something of more use than a beggar boy."

She walked into the hut, allowing the cloth door to fall down behind her.

Chapter 18

Rain does not fall on one roof alone.
~ African proverb

Sam stared into the darkness and shivered as a cool breeze passed over her bare arms. She swallowed, attempting to relieve her parched mouth, then raised her shoulders, trying to lessen the stiffness that had crept over her and made any movement painful or impossible. She drew in a deep breath, then another, trying to focus, trying to calm herself, but failing miserably in the attempt. Another wave of panic flooded over her. Her breaths came in short gasps and she shuddered as each one left. A creeping coldness settled in, and the tears came again. They fell freely down her face, onto her chin and along her neck.

A fluttering of wings caught her attention, and she turned her head to follow the sound. A bat swooped down into the clearing and abruptly changed direction, then swooped again, repeating its haphazard flight. Soon more flew down until the area was filled with bats, swooping, arcing, going one way, then the other, all in a manic yet orchestrated dance.

Then the bats ascended in unison and flew high into the sky. They covered the moon with their dark wings and soared into the jungle. It became eerily quiet. Too quiet. And Sam returned to trying to make sense of something that was beyond anything she could understand.

She closed her eyes and opened them. The blackness, the ropes, the tree, the hut: they were still there, visible under the moonlight and very, very real. Try as she might, she couldn't figure out how she ended up in this nightmare. The fear that had taken hold of her was intensified by the confusion that filled her mind. The simple questions, "Where am I?" and "How did I get here?" repeated themselves over and over again, but the question that terrified her the most was: *Am I going to die?*

A young boy sat on the ground, leaning against the hut. Everything about the kid disturbed Sam. He watched her too intently, never taking his eyes off her. His fingers continually ran back and forth over his gun as if he needed constant reassurance of its presence. And after he drifted off to sleep, he startled awake and stared at her with an even greater intensity.

Exhaustion took hold of her, and Sam fell into a fitful state of sleep that had one foot in reality and the other in a dream-like trance.

A gentle touch on her cheek startled her, and she woke to see two brown eyes, surrounded by faded small white diamonds, staring at her. Sam glanced at the boy holding the gun. He was fast asleep.

Eseza whispered into her ear. "Here. I can help you." She unwrapped the rope from Sam's shoulders, waist, and knees. "Sit," she said.

Sam's body resisted. Pain shot through her legs, up her back, and into her head. She forced her legs to bend, then slid down the rough bark of the tree until her legs spread out in front of her, resting on the ground. Eseza retied the rope.

She held a tin cup to Sam's mouth. "Drink," she said.

Sam gulped the water down. Its lukewarm temperature did little to quench her thirst. "Thank you," she whispered.

Eseza crouched down and put her head near Sam's. "I can help you," she whispered. "But you need to tell me when your unit is planning to attack. Did the commander send you ahead to scout the area? Are there other with you?"

Sam shook her head. "No. I'm not part of any army. I told you . . . I don't even know how I got here. I don't even know where 'here' is."

"You are in Kony camp, girl. North of Gulu, close to the border just."

Sam's voice rose slightly above a whisper. "Where the hell is Gulu? And who the heck is Kony?"

Eseza looked confused. "Gulu. Northern Uganda. Kony. The leader of the LRA. The Lord Resistance Army."

"What?"

"You really do not know what I am talking about, do you?"

"No."

"But how did you get here?"

"I don't know. It's crazy. I was in my bedroom at home. Home in Canada. I've tried to think of the last thing I can remember before I got here, but it's always the same. I was figuring out how to open this box, and when I finally did, a pouch of stones fell out. I picked up one of them and was just looking at it, and suddenly I'm . . . here . . . I don't remember leaving my house or getting on a plane or anything that would tell me how I got here. All I remember is looking at this box and . . ." Sam thought for a moment. "Eseza, this is a dream, right? A very real dream, and I'm going to wake up in the morning and find myself safe in my bed, right?"

Eseza scoffed. "A dream! No Samantha, this is not a dream. It is a nightmare. It is a nightmare because it is all real: Kony, the LRA, the evil . . ." She stopped. Shouting and yelling came from the bush.

Eseza thrust her hand into her pocket and pulled out a handful of cooked rice. "Eat," she said as she cupped her hand to Sam's mouth. Sam chewed the rice and spat out a pebble and a couple of dried rice husks. "Eat. Quickly." Eseza looked over her shoulder. "There is no time for pickiness. It is getting light and they will be here soon soon."

Sam took another bite and swallowed the food in one gulp, then quickly finished what little was left in Eseza's palm.

Eseza wiped her hand on her dress and ducked into the hut. The darkness in the night sky began to fade as the rising sun sent golden tendrils of light over a steel-blue horizon. Sam pulled her legs to her chest, placed her head on her knees, and closed her eyes. But she rested only for a moment.

She heard footfalls, and Kokas walked into the clearing, wearing a red beret, slightly tilted to the side. A soldier followed him; his hair was in dreadlocks and he wore tall rubber boots.

The young boy on guard jumped to attention as

Kokas walked into the hut and dragged Naboth into the yard. Eseza followed. He kicked the boy in the ribs. Sam gasped.

"Get up." Kokas commanded.

Naboth struggled to rise, but his bound hands made it very difficult. He stood for a moment, wavered, and collapsed on the ground. The gash on his forehead split open and fresh blood dripped into his eyes.

"Get up!" Kokas kicked him again.

The teenager stood, his legs apart, trying to steady himself. He stared at the ground.

"I have a surprise for you, Emau Naboth. Your brother."

An older boy who Sam guessed to be in his early twenties, walked into the clearing and stood in front of Naboth.

Naboth lifted his head and looked at the soldier for a second. His eyes widened for a moment until he blinked and dropped his head to his chest, returning his gaze to the ground.

"Is this your brother, Samson?" Kokas asked.

The soldier stood straighter and taller. "I have no brother except those who are loyal to the LRA, sir!"

"Then get the boy to speak. I do not believe he is a simple beggar boy. He know of many thing and refuse to tell us."

Kokas threw the rope to Samson and stepped back. Samson yanked the rope and shoved Naboth against a tree, then tied his legs and chest tightly. With deliberate slowness, he lifted Naboth's arms until they reached out directly in front of him. "Do not move," he commanded. His voice was cold.

He pulled a machete from his belt and lifted it high in the air.

Naboth squeezed his eyes shut. He stifled a sob. "No."

The word came from his mouth in a tightened whisper. "No."

The word was louder. "No!"

Naboth stared at Samson. He stared back, indifferent, unfeeling.

"I will speak."

Kokas spat on the ground. "Such a ka-boy. A small, little ka-boy," he said, laughing. "But you have wasted time." He circled Naboth then untied the ropes and let them fall to the ground. He rammed the butt of his rifle into Naboth's stomach and the boy doubled over, grasping his middle. He clouted Naboth on the shoulders, then kicked the back of his knees, forcing him to fall to the ground. The commander grabbed a stick from the bush and threw it to the boy who stood guard. "Teach the boy he should speak when he is spoken to." He stepped back and crossed his arms over his chest.

Sam squeezed her eyes shut.

Whack! Whack! Whack!

She brought her legs up to her chest and buried her head between her knees, pressing her ears against them, trying to shut out the sound. It was no use. The blows penetrated through her skin and shook her inner core.

Whack! Whack! Whack!

Again and again the young boy whipped Naboth. Again and again the noise carried through the forest until it stopped. Sam cautiously peered over her knees. The young boy dropped the stick and returned to his post. Naboth lay perfectly still. His shirt was soaked in blood.

Sam stared and wondered at the courage of this teen. Not once did he yell or scream or cry.

Kokas stepped in closer. "Get up."

Naboth slowly lifted his head.

"Get up!" Kokas kicked him in the ribs.

He pushed himself up and staggered as he tried to stand. His head fell to his chest, and short, raspy breaths came from his mouth.

"Now, tell me, ka-boy. We have sent out spy into your village, and we know you are planning to attack. And we know you have found some of our gun we have hidden. But I want to know the name of those who dare to go against us. Who are they?"

Naboth lifted his head and stared at the

commander. He spoke, but the words were mumbled and disjointed.

"Speak up, ka-boy!" Kokas leaned in closer.

Naboth spat on the commander's face.

Kokas glared as he wiped his cheek. He grabbed the stick from the ground and hit Naboth across the face. Naboth's head twisted and fell to his shoulder. He lifted his head and stared at the commander.

"Tell me!" Kokas yelled. "Tell me who dares to fight the LRA!"

Naboth smiled. He spat into Kokas's eyes.

Kokas grabbed him by the neck and dragged him to a wooden bench that stood beside a fire pit. He flung Naboth's arms over the bench and stomped on them with his steel-toed boot. He pulled his machete from his belt and held it above Naboth's wrists.

Eseza walked over to Kokas and stood by his side. "Do you think this is wise, Commander? To use the machet? A dead boy cannot speak." She stared down at Naboth. "If you leave him, perhaps his stomach and his thirst will make him talk."

The commander paused for a moment and nodded. "Yes, that is what we will do."

"Tie him against the tree," Eseza ordered the young boy. "The sun will do what we cannot."

Samson dragged him to the tree, and the young

boy wrapped a rope around Naboth's chest, tying it securely to the trunk.

Kokas stared down at Naboth and spat on his head. "You will suffer, ka-boy. You will suffer."

Chapter 19

Kindness is a language that the blind can see and the deaf can hear. ~ African proverb

Eseza placed a cup in Kokas's hands and hurried back to the fire. She filled another cup with a thick brown liquid and brought it to Samson, then backed away, keeping her gaze to the ground.

Sam swallowed as she watched the two drink from their cups. The smell from the pot left cooking on the fire teased her stomach which grumbled in protest. She turned her head and looked at Naboth tied to the tree beside her. His breathing was barely visible as the flies gathered around the blood and cuts on his body and face.

A new boy Sam guessed to be around ten or eleven years old had replaced the other guard on duty. She decided she didn't like this one any better. He seemed a little too much on the strange side, holding his gun a little too tightly, turning at the slightest noise. Nothing on his body seemed to rest; he continually looked from Sam to Naboth and to the surrounding bush, and he had a nasty habit of twitching whenever he turned his head from side to side.

"Squirrel," Sam whispered.

Eseza pulled a knife from a bag and swiped its blade back and forth over a flat rock. She grabbed a piece of meat and cut it into several pieces. The meat sizzled as she placed it into a pot that sat on the fire. Sam caught a whiff of the tantalizing smell. Her mouth moistened.

"Great," she murmured. "Just friggin' great."

The boy holding the gun turned his attention from Sam and stared at the pot on the fire. He breathed in the aroma.

"The boy there," Samson said, tilting his head toward Naboth, "would make a good soldier."

Kokas snorted.

"He has the gut. After all, he spat on you not just once but twice, sir."

"He will not be making it past the week, so do not start thinking of adding him to your group. As soon as we get all the name from him, we will be feeding him to the vulture."

"Shame. I do not think it would take long to break him."

"He is too old. I tell this to Kony all the time. Get the boy and girl when they are young. They learn to obey quick quick." Kokas emptied the rest of his cup and put it on the ground. Eseza took the cup and filled it again, then placed it in his hands. "Yes, that is what I tell him," Kokas continued. "This one would only try to slit your throat in the middle of the night. He is too filled with the idea of his village."

Samson walked to the fire and filled his cup and stared at Naboth. "But if we trained him, he could slit the throat of those in his village. It can be done."

Kokas looked at Naboth and grunted. "No. We get what we want, and then we kill him."

"What about the white girl? What are you going to do with a *muzungu* in Africa?"

Kokas stared at Sam and rubbed his hand over his face. She raised her head and looked in his direction.

His eyes met hers briefly and he smiled. "General Chadet has come through with our request for more gun. I think he should get more than his request for a hundred boy and girl. She would make a nice gift, do you think? No?"

Sam's breath stopped in her throat.

"So you are sending her to Sudan?" asked Samson.

"Yes, but not with the children. I will send her with Otti when he goes to secure the deal. I do not want to spoil the white meat."

Sam froze. The words "white meat" stung.

Eseza took the cups from Kokas and Samson and brought them to a basin holding a little water. She washed them and placed them to dry on a wooden rack set near the hut.

Kokas stood and looked into the pot on the fire. "That is smelling good good. But do not be putting any of the yam in with the meat. It spoil the flavor." He sauntered over to Sam and crouched down. "Otti will be here soon. You will tell us everything then." He walked toward a pathway leading away from the hut. "Come, Samson. Let us round up all the kid."

The pair followed the path until the surrounding bush hid them from view. Eseza sliced a yam into pieces and placed it into a pot filled with water. She stirred the goat meat, pausing to breathe in its enticing smell.

She knelt beside Sam and pulled a banana from the scarf tied around her waist, peeled the bruised fruit, and brought it to Sam's lips.

Sam turned her head away from the fruit. Her eyes welled with tears. "They're going to use me as a gift for some general. To thank him for the guns he's supplying them with." Her voice caught as she took in a breath. She shook.

"Shh. Eat." Eseza brought the banana to Sam's lips again.

Sam bit off a piece and forced it down. "He called me 'white meat.'"

"Yes, I heard. Eat."

Sam swallowed the last piece of the banana and leaned back into the tree trunk. "You have to let me go. Now. Please. Just untie me."

"And where will you go?"

"I'll run into the bush. I'll find someone, somewhere. Just let me go."

"There is no one to run to here, my sister. And you would not last in the bush."

"I'd rather die in the bush than be used as a sex slave for some general. I've seen the movies—I know what happens to girls who are abducted and sent off to some foreign country. And that ain't happening to me. Let me go. I'll take my chances."

"If I let you go, they will kill me and the young boy you see over there. And not until we have endured hour and hour of torture on the *goyo* tree. No, I will not let you go."

Eseza poured some water into a cup and brought it to Sam's lips. "Drink."

"But there's got to be a way."

"No, there is not. If it was that simple, I would have escaped long ago. I did not choose to be a soldier. I did not choose to be a wife. No, Samantha, there is not." She tipped the cup to Sam's lips and the water spilled down her neck and onto her shirt. "Drink. You will need your strength no matter what is decided."

Sam took a long sip and swallowed.

"Good, good." She paused and whispered into Sam's ear. "I am sorry for this, my dear Samantha."

Eseza set the cup beside the water jug and returned to the fire to stir the meat. "That is done," she said, removing the pot from the fire. "Now I think I will go and shuck the peanut." She arched her back and looked up into the sky. "It is going to be another hot day. Look at that sun, how it burn, and it is only morning." She glanced at the boy. "I think I will shuck all the peanut inside the hut and stay out of the heat." She pushed the sheet aside and walked in.

Before the sheet had fallen back into place, the young boy rushed to the fire, grabbed a piece of meat, and threw it into his mouth. He took another piece and swallowed it whole. He did the same with a piece of yam, but this time he stopped to chew it once or twice before swallowing. Then, just as quickly, he returned to his post, sat under the shade of the roof, and held his gun.

The boy licked his lips and rubbed his sleeve across his mouth. Sam smiled. Squirrel was a survivor.

Seconds later Eseza returned from the hut and filled two cups with water. She passed one to the boy and then crouched down at Naboth's side, lifting his head. She placed the cup to his lips and whispered, "Drink."

Naboth opened his eyes to half slits, then closed them.

"Drink." Eseza lifted the cup. The water dribbled down the sides of his mouth. The young boy with the gun walked to the pathway and stood with his legs spread, his gun held firmly in his hands.

"Good boy, Squirrel," Sam whispered. "You keep watch."

Eseza lifted the cup to Naboth's lips again. "Come now, Naboth," she said. Again the water trickled down his chin, landing on his shirt.

Eseza sat back on her heels and sighed. "You have to drink, Naboth."

Naboth opened his eyes. He lifted his head and looked at Eseza. He gasped.

"No. You do not know me," she whispered sharply. "If you do, they will kill us for sure. Now drink."

She raised the cup to his mouth. This time the water did not spill.

"Halt!" Squirrel yelled.

Eseza placed the cup behind Naboth's back and

hurried to the fire.

A young teen walked into the clearing. He wore the same camouflage fatigues and sported the same dreadlocks as many of the other soldiers. Like Samson, he wore a pair of rubber boots. "You do not tell me to halt, ka-boy!" he commanded. He smacked Squirrel on the side of his head and sent him flying to the ground.

Eseza grabbed a cup from the rack, quickly filled it, and brought it to the bench. The teenager sat and swallowed the liquid in one long gulp, then passed the cup to Eseza. Again she filled the cup, and again he downed it within seconds.

"So you are back," he said.

"Yes, Dominic. There is not much to report. The people are weak and very afraid. They do not even dare to mention Kony name."

"Eeh? That is what I thought. They think like the warthog and run like the kob."

Eseza stabbed a piece of meat with a fork and passed it to him. He held the fork under his nose and took a deep sniff. "Goat, eeh? I have not had meat for a long long time."

"Sudan is giving us more weapon, I hear," Eseza said. She sat on a rock and faced Dominic.

"Yes, and I am to lead the group again." He put down his fork and sighed. "Do you know this is the third time I have taken the trip to get the arm? The first time I was a kid just. I know it like it was yesterday. Such a long trip. We left many on the path, dead. And I know that is what is going to happen on the trip again." He reached into the pot and took another piece of meat. "I have told Omick I will be needing one hundred fifty children, at the least. That way, when we arrive there, I will have maybe one hundred to carry the gun. And even then, this is not good. You know many more will die on the way back, and that only make it worse because the children will have to carry a bigger load. Less will have to carry more." He paused and shook his head. "No, no. It is not good."

Dominic stood and looked down into the pot. "Goat again for the commander belly, eeh?" he said, turning on his heel. "We must raid another village soon and take what belong to us. The food from the last raid is growing thin, and I am growing weary of spoiled rice and cassava." He walked down the pathway, slapping Squirrel across the head as he passed. "Do not tell me to halt again."

Eseza watched the soldier disappear into the bush and then went to Naboth's side, taking the cup from behind his back. She filled it with more water and gulped it down. She sighed. "I am sure this is going to end someday. God is not pleased when he look down on Uganda. No. I think he shake his head just and regret that he create us."

She walked into the hut and returned with another banana in her hand. She shook Naboth by the shoulder. "Eat," she said, taking a morsel and pushing it into his mouth. The piece fell and landed on his shirt. She tried to force it between his lips. "Do not be stupid, Naboth. Eat or you will not live."

Naboth's head fell to his chest. Eseza lifted his chin and pushed another piece of the overripe fruit into his mouth. "Eat and swallow. You need to live." She crouched closer and spoke into his ear. "You would like to spit in the commander face again, yes?"

He smiled for a second as he swallowed the food. Eseza brought another piece to his mouth. "Here, eat more."

Naboth's head dropped and his eyes shut. His chest rose and fell in a gentle rhythm. Eseza popped the rest of the banana into her mouth, brushed the dirt from her dress, and sighed. She filled another pot with water and set it on the fire. "The general will be wanting tea with their lunch." She placed a lid on the pot and sat beside the fire.

Sam closed her eyes. It was time to think. As much as she wanted to believe it was a horrible dream, she couldn't. It was all too real. Too real. *But how did I get here? How come I don't know anything? Amnesia? Did I come here on some trip? With who? Why?* She shook her head, trying to clear her mind. *It doesn't matter how you got here, Sam. The point is, how do you get out?* Waves of panic washed over her, squeezing her chest, leaving her breathless. *Get a hold of yourself, Sam. Get a hold of yourself. One . . . two . . . three . . .* She tried to clear her mind. *Think, Sam, think. Look at the options. Weigh each one. You'll end up dead if you let fear take control of you. Used, beaten, and dead. Think.*

She decided the option she had proposed wasn't going to work: Eseza refused to let her go free. As much as she could tell that Eseza was on her side, Sam knew she was right. If she escaped, Eseza and Squirrel would be killed. She knew she couldn't live with that. But . . . what if they were to escape with her? Now how could they do that?

Sam looked into the surrounding trees. They would have to go into the bush; that went without saying. Would Eseza and Squirrel know enough to help her survive in there? And how far would they have to travel before they found a place or someone they could trust who would help them?

Then there was the question of when they could escape. Nighttime should work best. She needed to talk to Eseza and convince her to escape with her. And then, when everything was quiet under the cover of darkness, they could run away. Simple, right?

Sam drew in a long, unsteady breath.

The plan was simple, and the simpler a plan was, the less chance there was of any foul-ups. *But, she thought, if the plan is so simple, why hasn't anyone ever tried it before?* And then it became all too clear. *'Cause they'll torture you, Sam. Beat you and beat you until you're dead. Just like Eseza said.* Sam took in another breath, this time steady, assured. *No, I'll find a way to escape. And if they catch me, they catch me. And if they beat me, they beat me until I'm dead. And I'd rather be dead than be used as a whore for some general.* She closed her eyes. It was time to think.

Chapter 20

Only a fool tests the depth of a river
with both feet. ~ African proverb

Sam looked up when she heard the sound of parting branches and heavy boots on the hard ground. A young teen, carrying his gun over his shoulder, walked into the clearing. Eseza filled a cup with water and brought it to him.

"Pffttt!" The teen spat the water out and glared at Eseza. "This water is as warm as piss!" He grabbed a large yellow water jug and marched over to Squirrel. "Give me your gun!" Squirrel obeyed. The teen leaned the gun against the wall of the hut. "Now get fresh water or I will make you drink your own piss!" Squirrel grabbed the jug and ran down the pathway.

The teen ambled over to Sam, looked down at her, and smiled. "So this is the *muzungu* girl. I have seen the *muzungu* pastor who lived near to our village. And one time I saw a *muzungu* woman. But never a girl." He shifted his gun and ran his fingers over Sam's hair. She flinched. "Hmm. It is soft."

He turned to Eseza. "The commander want you now. Otti is wanting the girl too." He walked to the fire and looked into the pots. "And they are wanting the food."

Sam stiffened. Otti was here. He would be asking her questions she didn't know the answers to. Then he would be taking her. She couldn't wait for the cover of darkness to escape—she had to think fast.

"Then you must wait for the water to boil for the commander tea," Eseza replied. "He does not like it cold. And you must help me carry. I cannot do it all myself." She placed the lids on the pots and passed the one containing the goat meat to the soldier.

She untied the rope that held Sam to the tree. "Up!" she commanded, giving the rope a jerk. Sam jumped.

"Now how am I expecting to do all this when you have sent the boy away? I cannot carry the yam and the tea," Eseza said.

"Give a pot to the *muzungu*. She can carry and make herself useful."

Eseza untied the ropes that held Sam's wrists

behind her back and pulled her arms in front. She retied it, leaving it looser so Sam could hold the pot.

"I think the commander would be honored if he was served tea from a *muzungu*, eeh?" Eseza wrapped a cloth around the handles and placed the hot pot in Sam's hands. The heat from the fire radiated through the cloth onto Sam's bare skin.

Eseza took the pot of yams and placed it on her head, then lifted the pot of rice to her hip. She pulled on the rope and walked down the path.

"Hmmph! Imagine that. A *muzungu* serving tea to the commander!" Eseza laughed. "I wonder what he will think of that. A white serving a black for a change!" The teen led the way, joining in Eseza's laughter. Eseza followed, pulling Sam behind.

They followed a well-worn path from which several smaller paths branched off. Sam glanced down a trail and noted another hut and a couple of teenage girls preparing a meal around a fire. An older man sat on a wooden chair while a third girl filled his cup with water from a yellow jerrican. *So that's where all the voices are coming from,* she thought. *It's just like a little town.*

When they came into the clearing, Sam almost stopped in her tracks. Well over one hundred children were sitting on the ground. They had been subdivided into groups of ten to fifteen, with their hands tied together and one long rope joining each child to the next. It was absolutely quiet. No one spoke a word. They stared at the ground, motionless in the hot sun.

Each group was guarded by two or three soldiers holding guns. All the soldiers wore the same uniform: army fatigues, rubber boots, and dreadlocks. A few wore red or blue berets. Sam gasped. Red berets were worn by plenty of different militia groups, including NATO forces. And blue by the UN peacekeepers. *How the hell did they get those?* And then she knew. The UN came to countries to bring peace. And anyone who went against the UN could only be terrorists or warmongers.

Sam followed Eseza until she stopped before a long table made of split logs. Kokas sat behind the table on a bench between two men. Sam studied their faces. They were old. Not old like her grandparents, but old like her dad. The man sitting to the right of the commander wore a khaki outfit, neatly pressed—not a wrinkle or a speck of dirt in sight. The other man's uniform was just as immaculate, but his sported bright orange tabs on the tips of his shirt collar surrounded by a yellow embroidered design that looked like feathers.

The soldier who led the way approached the table and placed the pot of meat in front of Kokas. A young girl set a plate in front of each of the men, then quickly followed with a fork and knife at each place setting.

Eseza walked forward, looking downward, seeing only the table. She placed the two pots next to the meat and stepped back.

A white truck pulled up beside the table, and a man jumped out and walked toward them. Sam couldn't help but stare. This man *was* old. The white that speckled his hair and the wrinkles on his face confirmed it. He carried an air of great authority as he stood at the table and faced the men.

"Come, Vincent. Sit down. We have goat and yam today. There is no need to rush. Turn off the truck and sit down. The girl is here. She is going nowhere. Eat." Kokas lifted the lid off a pot to show the man the goat meat covered in thick gravy. Vincent glanced in the pot.

"No. It is a long trip and I am late late. Put the girl inside and I will go. Kony want to talk to her personally."

"At least stay for tea, Vincent." Then turning to Eseza, Kokas demanded, "Bring the tea here and pour Mr. Otti a cup."

Sam inched her way closer and looked from the pot to the table and then to the men. She placed the pot, full of water, down and removed the lid. The steam rose into the air. "I'm sorry," she said. She grabbed the pot with her bound hands and flung the boiled water at the men. It splashed onto their faces, hitting their eyes and scalding them. They threw their hands up and screamed.

"Go!" Sam yelled. She grabbed Eseza's hand and pulled her toward the truck. She yanked the door open and shoved Eseza inside.

Sam jumped into the truck and shifted it into gear. Letting out the clutch, she stomped on the gas and drove straight at the table and the men behind it. They jumped aside. Legs, arms, and goat meat flew everywhere. She pressed the accelerator to the floorboard and sent the truck roaring into the bush.

The truck's nose tipped and lunged forward, plunging down a bank, sending leaves, branches, and the occasional tree flying across the windshield.

"Hang on!" Sam yelled.

Eseza grabbed the side of the door, pushed her feet against the floorboard, and looked down. The bank was now becoming a hill, and the hill a very steep mountain. Sam screamed as the truck bounced and jostled and drove through every tree, rock, and bush in its path.

"Oh, no!" Eseza screamed as the bush opened up and a vast river came into view.

Sam stepped on the brake. "Jump!" she yelled.

They threw their doors open and flew through the air, plummeting into the water. The truck soared over the bank and plunged in headfirst. They surfaced, sputtering and coughing. Sam kicked and thrust her bound hands above the water, trying to keep herself afloat. Eseza swam to her side and within seconds untied the knots and flung the rope into the water. They looked at each other, then at the mile-long strip of bush cleared from the mountain. They laughed.

"You have gut, my dear Samantha. Big strong *muzungu* gut."

Sam smiled. "Yeah, but no brains. What the hell are we gonna do now?"

Eseza lay back in the water and lifted her feet, pointing her toes in the direction of the current. "Follow me," she said.

Sam lay back and did the same.

"Keep your feet ahead of you just. That way, when the current get strong, you can push yourself off any rock that may come your way. But do not stand up. The river will push you under if you do."

"Rocks that come my way. Right. Got it."

They bobbed in and out of the water as the river carried them farther and farther away. Everywhere Sam looked was green, from the short reeds that lined the shore to the tall thin trees with spindly trunks reaching into the sky, and all of the flowering bushes in between. Even the water had a green tinge. Sort of green, sort of gray, dark and murky. And everywhere there were birds. Tall birds with long legs holding fast onto the thin branches overlooking the shore, small birds flitting in and out of holes in the hard clay walls that towered over the river, and birds of every size flying through the trees, soaring through the air, diving into the water. A white heron walked among a lush carpet of neon-green leaves while a huge black bird with a long thick beak stood on a rock, looking into the water, searching for any passing fish.

Sam turned her attention to the river ahead of her. It was hard going. Her feet constantly wanted to go under her body as the current pushed her along. And the water, refreshing at first, became bitter, bitter cold. Her teeth chattered and her skin turned a light gray. They passed several fields and some old huts with their doors facing the water. A few cows grazed near a couple of orange trees, the orange fruit peeking through the dark green leaves.

A large stick floated by Eseza. She grabbed it and tossed it to Sam. "Here!" she yelled as she snatched another stick, holding firmly on to the end. "Just in case!"

"In case of what?"

"Croc or hippo," she answered. "I do not know what is worse. The croc, it take you down and roll you under the water, but the hippo will snap you in half like a twig." She clapped her hands to imitate a hippo's massive mouth. Sam shuddered and glanced from one side of the riverbank to the other.

"Do not bother looking for them. The croc hide under the water with only their eye and nostril peeking out. You cannot see them until it is late late. And the hippo, they come from under you and divide you in half—one half for this side of the river and one half for the other." Seeing the stunned expression on Sam's face, Eseza laughed.

Sam looked toward the riverbank with a start. She could have sworn she saw something in the distance crawl into the water.

"Oh, no," she said. "Oh, big, fat, huge, honking no."

She watched the water, looking for any movement, any signs of life.

Just your nerves, Sam. Just your nerves, she thought. *Relax and enjoy the ride.*

Something slammed into Sam's back, pushing her under the water. The current took a hold of her and rolled her around and around until her mind went black and a million stars flashed before her eyes. Then it stopped. She kicked and thrashed her arms and pulled herself above the surface. She gasped for air and turned in a circle, searching the waves and ripples flowing around her.

"Was that . . . ?" she asked.

"Do not move!" Eseza shouted.

Sam obeyed, every part of her body on high

alert. She glanced from side to side, hardly daring to breathe. Eseza watched the water surrounding her.

Two brown eyes surfaced and stared. Sam screamed.

"Hit the eye!" Eseza shouted. "Hit the eye as hard as you can!"

The words had barely registered before the crocodile was at her side, its mouth opening, revealing long rows of fearsome teeth. Before Sam could realize what she was doing, she pointed the stick skywards and thrust it between its massive jaws. The crocodile thrashed its head from side to side, trying to break the stick that stopped its mouth from closing upon its prey.

"No!" Sam screamed as she brought her fist down on the beast's eye with all her might. "No!"

The crocodile spun around and knocked Sam under the water. She resurfaced just in time to see its tail disappear under the murky surface. Eseza rushed to her side.

Sam's voice shook. "Where did it go?" she asked.

Two eyes surfaced behind her. Eseza screamed and thrust her stick into the beast's eye. The crocodile lunged and they threw themselves backward, narrowly escaping its reach. Eseza rushed at it again, ramming her stick into its other eye. The crocodile plunged under the water.

They placed themselves back to back and watched the rippling surface. A long stick floated by and Sam grabbed it. "Come on, you bastard," she said. "Come on. I'm ready."

As if in response to her challenge, the crocodile rose to the surface and lunged at Eseza. Eseza brought her stick down on its snout, breaking the stick in two.

Sam grasped the end of her stick as two thoughts came to her: *Stick! Throat!* As the crocodile came at her, she thrust the stick into its mouth and rammed it down its throat. The water rushed in and a gurgling sound came from its mouth. Sam pushed the stick in farther, and the crocodile slowly sank under the water until only its eyes were showing. It gave one final lunge and disappeared beneath the surface.

They stared into the muddied depths.

"Is it gone?" Sam whispered.

Eseza continued to stare into the water, watching the waves and the ripples swirl into each other until the water became a smooth surface again. "I think you killed it, Samantha," she whispered, shaking her head in disbelief. "We have to get out of here. Follow me, but do not make any quick movement. Slow. Like this."

Eseza pointed her feet toward the shore and allowed the current to carry her. Sam did the same.

Eseza grasped on to a tree root hanging from the riverbank and pulled herself up, then wiggled her way to the shore. She grabbed Sam's arm and pulled. Sam dug her toes into the bank, pushing herself until she crawled onto the top and lay on the grass. Her arms and legs sprawled out like a starfish thrown to the shore.

"Come, we cannot rest here. We need to go into the bush more." Eseza grabbed Sam by the hand and pulled. "Anyone passing in a boat could see us. Come!"

Sam tried to lift herself.

"Come on!" Eseza demanded. "We have come too far to have someone find us now! And the croc love to hide out in place like this just, close to the shore."

Sam needed no more words of encouragement. She groaned as she pushed herself up and half crawled, half walked, into the bush. A couple of hundred yards into the dense coverage, they stopped and lay on the ground.

"Are you hurt? Did the croc get you anywhere?" Eseza crawled to Sam and looked at her arms and legs.

"No, I don't think so." Sam ran her hands over her body. "Just right here," she said, pointing to the small of her back. "Feels like I've been hit by a truck."

Eseza lifted the back of Sam's shirt. "There is a large red mark left by the crocodile nose when it rammed into you. You will have quite the bruise there soon. And you will be sore"—she paused and pulled Sam's shirt back down—"but I can heal that."

Sam laid her head on a soft pile of leaves and sighed. "Just let me rest here for a bit," she said, closing her eyes. "I've had a really tough day."

Eseza sat at the base of a tree and leaned against the dark green bark. She strained to see what lay beyond the bush and trees. "You sleep. I will watch. Okay, big gut *muzungu* woman?"

There was no response.

"Okay," Eseza whispered.

Chapter 21

To be without a friend is to be poor indeed.
~ Tanzanian proverb

Sam opened one eyelid and stared at the dappled sunlight that fell on the leaves and grass just inches from her nose. A large ant maneuvered its way among the growth, dragging a dead fly, while a green and blue spotted butterfly landed on a rock and spread its wings to capture the last rays of warmth from the sun. The *tch tch* sound of a bird came from high above, as its mate answered from somewhere deeper into the forest. Sam lifted her head and stared into the trees.

"Do not get up yet, dear *muzungu* Samantha," Eseza said as she took a stone from a pile of coals and rolled it on the ground. She placed it on Sam's back.

The heat from the rock sent tingling sensations

up her spine, instantly warming every nerve and muscle in her back.

Sam sighed. "Just call me Sam. That's what all my friends call me."

"Sam? But that is a boy name."

"Yeah, I know. But it's okay where I come from. Just call me Sam."

"Then Sam it is." Eseza took another rock, rolled it on the ground, and placed it beside the first stone.

Sam's skin absorbed the heat, welcoming the healing and soothing touch it offered. She closed her eyes. "Why am I here, Eseza?" The words escaped as a heavy sigh.

Eseza placed another stone on Sam's back. "Tell me what you know. Perhaps that will help."

Sam traced her memories back to the events of the night she had arrived in Africa. "The last thing I remember doing was looking at this wooden box. It came from the museum my dad works at. I figured out how to open it, and when I did, this sack fell out. I opened it up and there were five stones inside. Each of them was this really nice shiny green color, and when I held one up to the light it looked like a thread of silver light was running over it."

Eseza's hand stopped in midair as she held the hot stone a few inches above Sam's back. "Say that again?"

"The box, it was like a puzzle and—"

"No, no. Not the part about the box. The stone. What did they look like?"

"Green, a real nice green. Like a fir tree. No, that won't help you understand what I mean because you don't have fir trees around here, do you? Let's see." She glanced around at the trees in the bush and pointed to one in the distance. "See that tree? The one with the long leaves hanging down, in the shade there? They were that color of green. Not a limey green. A darker green. And there was a faint glimmer of silver—"

"Like a thread that ran over it as you turned it round and round?"

Sam sat bolt upright and the stones fell from her back.

Eseza stared at her, shaking her head, and grinned. "The boy. This is what he was telling me!" She held her face in her hands. "I wanted to believe him. I told him I believed him, but . . . I was not sure. Sometime people, they do not know what is the truth. But here you are. An angel! A real live angel!" She looked at Sam's back and placed her hands on her hips. "But where are your wing?"

"Wing?"

"Yes, you are an angel, yes?"

"Me? No, I'm no angel." Sam laughed.

"But you are smart. Not dumb like both the

angel that helped Charlie."

"What are you talking about?"

"You are here because of the stone, Sam. The stone have power. They bring you here, they change you, and you help people. You helped me escape. That make you my angel." Eseza's smile grew broader as she laughed. "Yes, that make you my angel. I am going to have to tell Charlie I am sorry sorry for not believing him."

"What are you talking about?"

"Do you know Bruce and Scott? Because that would really make Charlie glad glad if you could tell him how they are doing."

Sam clutched her head in her hands. "You're not making any sense, Eseza. You need to go back. Start at the beginning. Tell me everything. The stones have what?"

"They have power. They must be ancient stone from the god; that is all I can figure. And you found them in that box. The one you said was made like a puzzle. And when you held the stone, it sent you here, because you are my angel and you came to help me. Which you did." Eseza took Sam's hand and stood. "Come. Let us go back to my hut. Charlie can tell you how Scott and Bruce helped him escape and how the stone work. He will be able to tell you more than I can."

Eseza pulled Sam up.

"But who's Charlie? And who are Bruce and Scott?"

"You will find out soon enough. Let us go."

"But—"

"Do not ask anymore, for I cannot tell you. If you want to find the answer, you must hurry hurry with me."

Eseza took off into the bush, and Sam had no choice but to follow her. They walked for a few minutes until they came to a clearing and stopped. "We have to stay with the bush. It is not safe to be seen in the open," Eseza said.

They returned to the shelter of the trees and continued on their way. The sun was now falling behind the tops of the lower bush, filling the once-blue sky with a crimson glow. Sam wiped the tiny beads of perspiration from her forehead.

A short while later they came upon a second clearing. Eseza crouched behind a tree, pulling Sam down beside her. "I know this spot. There are orange tree here next to the river. I will go get some. You stay here and wait."

Sam peered around a tree as Eseza rushed across the clearing, her dress wrapping around her legs as she ran through the tall grass. Eseza tied her dress around her hips and climbed the trunk until she was hidden within the sprawling branches. Seconds later she jumped down, her skirt acting like a basket, bulging with oranges. She ran back to the bush. "Follow me. We will find a safe place to eat. We are too close to the river and the field."

Sam obeyed. She breathed in the delicious smell of the overripe fruit. Her mouth watered. She had to resist grabbing an orange from Eseza's skirt and eating it, peel and all, right then and there.

When they came to a thick set of trees, Eseza sat down and placed the oranges on the ground beside her. Sam grabbed one and bit into it, ripping the peel away. She sunk her teeth into the fruit. The juice dribbled down her chin and covered her fingers. Within seconds, the orange was gone. She grabbed another while Eseza finished hers. They ate in silence, devouring the fruit, sucking the juice, chewing on the pulpy insides, and licking their fingers.

Sam stared at the pile of peels on the ground. She burped and wiped her hands on her pants. "That was good. Thanks, Eseza."

"You are welcome to it, my *muzungu* woman."

"I keep meaning to ask you. What the hell's a *muzungu*?"

"It is what we call all white people when they come to Uganda."

"Oh." Sam paused. "What does it mean, exactly?"

"It means a person who is lost and does not

know his way. It is a word our ancestor used when they met the first white people. The white people did not know where they were going and they were walking around and around in circle. Like they were dizzy. And *muzungu*, it is the word a tribe in Africa use for 'dizzy.'"

"Well, you got that right. Never felt so dizzy in my life. Don't know how I got here; don't know where I'm going. Don't know anything, that's for sure." Sam closed her eyes. "I'm just picturing my dad right now. He's either livid because he thinks I've taken off, or he's pacing the floor 'cause he thinks I've been abducted. Or both. Yeah, it's probably both. That's my guess."

"Then we must get you to Charlie. Come. Let us go. We can travel in the darkness. I know the way well well." Eseza tossed the orange peels, scattering them in different directions. She walked into the bush. Once again, Sam followed.

As they made their way, the jungle grew thicker and the girth of the trees larger and larger. Sam found herself grabbing long vines and flinging them out of her way as she tried to keep pace with Eseza.

"I would be careful doing that if I were you," Eseza said.

"Why?"

"Because it is not only the *vine* that hang from

the tree."

Sam stopped in her tracks. "Oh."

They continued at a quick pace until they found an old pathway, partially overgrown but still clear enough to make their travel easier. They walked for another mile and came upon a hut, standing alone. Its grass roof was burnt and its mud walls singed with black. A pile of charred logs lay beside it, and next to the logs was a skull. Sam turned her head, not wanting to look. The skull's empty sockets appeared to stare at her, watch her, follow her.

"This is what Kony does," Eseza said as she picked up the skull. "He send his men and boy in. Sometime ten, sometime twenty, sometime a little more, but they are not needing much men to go against us. They have the gun and we have nothing. We cannot fight them."

"But . . . We? I thought you were—"

"Part of the LRA?" Eseza shook her head. "No, Sam. Did you not understand? Did you not see I must be one part but play another?"

She placed the skull back on the ground, grabbed a rock, and began to dig. Sam crouched and pulled the dirt away as Eseza dug.

"It has happened for year now. Many year. Since I can remember. The LRA attack our village. They burn the house, take the food and all the animal from us, and then they take the children.

And they kill those who try to escape and those who try to fight back. Then they leave. And they leave those who are left behind to cry, and to hate, and to feel weak and helpless.

"Then they take us to the camp, and we are made to learn how to use the gun and set the mine and use the stick and rock and machet to torture and punish. And all the girl, we are made to be slave. To be used by the men and then made to be their wife and have their children."

She placed the skull in the hole and covered it.

"And then we are made to murder. And when you have taken the life of your brother and sister from your village, those people you grew up with and who played with and cared for you, you do not want to go back. You are now *konyi pee*, dirt, not human, a stone that give no love and take none in."

Eseza traced a cross in the dirt.

Sam studied her face, trying to comprehend everything she had just heard. "You were made to kill?"

"Yes. Many time."

"And you don't want to go back home?"

"No. Because I am ashamed. I did many horrible thing. Not just killing."

Sam stopped and thought, *What could be worse than killing?* But she didn't say it out loud. She only asked, "What horrible things?"

"Like spy on my own people."

Sam nodded. "But—"

"There were some rumor of a group forming. Something started by the government and the people. They called themself the Arrow Boy, and they received some gun and bow and arrow to fight the LRA when it attacked. I was sent out here to spy and see if the rumor were true and what people dared to go against Kony."

Eseza wiped her hands on her skirt. "I did not want to do this, but I had no choice. I was a good cover. I was a young girl with a young child, and no one would suspect me."

"You have a child?"

"Yes. Many of the taken girl have children in the bush. I am no different." Eseza sighed. "I found an abandoned hut. I painted my face to look like a witch doctor and gathered some bone. It was easy for me to do this. My mother is much respected as a healer in my village. I simply followed her way. But I did not know the way of the voodoo, the *lajok*. I had seen the men and women with their bone and horn and chant, so I did the same just. I said the word I remembered and I shook all the bone. And it was easy. And it was a good cover. People fear the *lajok*.

"Soon the people were coming to me, asking me to cure them and to tell them what the cloud would bring. Sometime they would ask me where their children were, if they were alive. And if I told them they were dead, they would ask me where they could find the bone. It is important to find the bone. They must be buried. It they are not, then the child spirit is angry and they will haunt the parent life."

Sam's mind reeled back to the moment when she was crouching in the hut, hearing the words, "Where is the child, Eseza? Where is Kony son?"

"Your child. Is Kony, the leader of this army, is he the father?"

Eseza dropped her head to her chest and closed her eyes. "Yes, he is. He is the father to many of the children there. He has many wife, like me."

"And your child's dead? I remember in the hut. I heard you say you had buried the child."

"Yes, I said that. But it was only to protect him. If they knew he was alive, they would return to the village and take him and kill anyone who tried to stop them. Kony is very protective of his children. No, my son is well. He is safe with a woman near to my hut. When we get to the hut, I will take him and we will leave. I cannot fight any more battle against Kony. If I were to be caught again, my death would come only after many many hour of torture."

Sam nodded. She understood.

"No, I will take my son and we will leave."

"To find your mother and father?"

"No. I cannot do that."

"Why? Why can't you go home to your parents?" Sam paused and lowered her voice. "Are they dead?"

"No. They are alive, but—"

"But what?"

"I am dead to them."

"Dead? What do you mean?"

"I am a murderer and I am a spy. I cannot be trusted . . . And I am used. I am young and I have a child. I cannot marry now—no man will want me because I am not pure. And I cannot bring happiness to my mother and father life. I will be a burden to them just, and there will be no more grandchildren to put on their lap. The only grandchild they will have is a bastard child. And the father of that bastard is Kony, a murderer of his own people. They will have nothing to do with me or Maisha. No." She paused again. "I am dead to my parent, my family, and my village."

Sam squeezed Eseza's hand. "But you're their daughter and they love you. Parents are supposed to love their children no matter what, right?"

"Not after what has happened. It cannot be undone. They will think I am possessed. That I am capable of great evil. No, they will not trust me."

Sam stared at her runners and then at Eseza's bare feet. In the short time she had been in Uganda,

Sam had already begun to see the differences between them. And it wasn't just the lack of shoes. Eseza's battles were real, fought with real guns against real people. She didn't splatter them with neon-pink paintballs and laugh as they cried for mercy. That was one difference.

And she had a child. How old could she be, anyway? Fifteen, sixteen? Imagine a culture that placed a girl's worth on her virginity and saw her as a burden until she was taken off their hands and married off. That was difference number two.

Eseza's life was a constant struggle. Not only against her enemies, but also against her family, the very people who were supposed to love her. *At least I have my dad and my friends to help me with all the hell I'm going through*, she thought. *Who does Eseza have?*

Me, she thought. She cleared her throat. "I think you're wrong, Eseza. I've seen what you did back at the camp. You let the boy sneak some food. You fed that other boy, Naboth, and gave him water. And you did the same for me. All at the risk of your own life. Wouldn't your parents see that in you? 'Cause I did."

"No. You do not understand the way of our people, Sam."

"But think about what you were up against. An army! And how smart you are! You saved that boy's life more than once. I saw what you did. Telling them he was a worthless beggar boy, bringing him into the shade of the hut, then convincing that ugly commander guy he shouldn't kill him. Your parents will admire you for that. I know they will. They'd have to be stupid not to."

"Please, Sam, let us go."

"But if you told them all these things, they'd understand. They'd see that you're brave. And kind."

Eseza stood. "No. They would not. That is the way of my people. You cannot change what has been carved into their mind for generation after generation."

"But I could tell them. Maybe if they heard of all the things you did at the camp, they'd realize how great a person you really are. And that would make them love you, despite Kony, despite what you were forced to do."

"No."

"But . . ."

Eseza turned and walked into the bush. Sam sighed and followed, watching Eseza's bare feet step cautiously over the twigs and rocks that covered the unused path.

Chapter 22

If the rhythm of the drum beat changes,
the dance step must adapt. ~ African proverb

Sam stood at the edge of the bush and looked into a clearing. The first morning rays of sunlight cast shafts of pink light into the sky, warming the air and waking the morning songbirds from their slumber. A morning thrush called out: *whe-eat, whe-eat ki ki ki.* The silence and darkness of the night was fading.

"Salume and the children are not here," Eseza whispered, walking out of the hut. She looked around the yard. The goalposts set near the edge of the bush were still there, as were the wooden chairs beside the hut. She looked at the goat pen. It was empty.

"There is nothing to show the LRA attacked here. I think Salume has taken my son and her children and they have gone somewhere. They may have gotten scared after me and Naboth went missing and decided to foot it to the refugee camp far far from here. Many many people stay there. They do not think Kony will attack the camp when the government soldier are guarding." Eseza took one last look around. "Let us go to my hut. It is not far from here. Maybe Charlie is there and he can tell us."

They set off again. Sam struggled to keep her eyes open and stifled a yawn as she tried to keep up with Eseza's quick pace. Within minutes they reached another clearing. This one was devoid of any goat pens or any sign of life, past or present.

Eseza cautiously peered into one hut and then the other. She passed her hand over a black bag tucked against the wall. "There is no one here," she whispered.

Sam looked into the mud enclosure. A small thin mattress lay on the ground. She leaned her head against the hut wall and sighed. "One minute," she said. She walked inside and sat on the mat. "Just one minute," she repeated. "One minute of sleep and I'll be ready to go." She put her head on the mat. "Eseza will understand. Just . . . one . . ." She closed her eyes and instantly fell asleep.

*   *   *   *

"Sam?" Eseza called out. "Sam, let us go." She peeked inside the hut. "Sam?" Sam lay absolutely still. "Oh, my big smart *muzungu* Sam. You are tired. You rest. And I will watch."

She sat in front of the hut, leaned her head against the wall, and stared into the surrounding bush.

A weaver bird called out and was joined by another, and another, until the forest was filled with a chorus of *ko kweer* and *ko kweer ki* sounds. Eseza laughed. "Do not worry, young men," she called out to them. "I am sure you will all find a beautiful girl to lay her egg in your nest."

Eseza sighed. She closed her eyes for a second and then startled herself awake. She slapped her cheeks and shook her head and blinked several times, trying to keep her eyes open. The jungle filled with monkey chatter and the tweets and trills of the morning birds. It soon became a lullaby. It was no use—she couldn't shake the fatigue. Her eyes drooped and closed. She fell asleep.

Eseza woke and looked up as a shea nut dropped to the ground and landed at her feet. Another fell, narrowly missing her head. Two large eyes stared back at her. Charlie slid down the tree and stood before her.

He looked at her dirtied and torn dress and then at the rope burns on her wrists. "You escaped."

"Yes."

"You are hurt?"

"No. I am fine." Eseza closed her eyes for a moment and sighed. "Sit," she said, patting the ground beside her.

"I wanted to . . . I mean, I tried to get the other to come with me, Fire, but—"

"There is no need to explain, Charlie. Come. Sit and listen."

Charlie sat.

Eseza drew in a long, deep breath and prepared herself. "I am afraid, Charlie. I am afraid of what I must tell you. Because I may lose you as a friend. But I have been afraid long long. And I am tired of this fear. Perhaps you will listen. Perhaps you will not. But I must speak the truth now. My name is not Fire. It is Eseza. This is the name my father and mother gave me. It is also the name I was called in the camp. By the general, the children, and Kony. But it is my name, and that is what I should be called."

He nodded.

"I took the name Fire when . . ."

Charlie squeezed her hand. "It is fine. I do not need to hear."

"But you need to hear the truth. You have told

me many thing."

"But I already know. It is fine, Eseza. We were all made to do horrid thing. And we all lived in fear."

She returned Charlie's squeeze and smiled. "You are good, Charlie. I am glad I saved you."

"Saved me? But you said it was the spirit who wanted me saved, not you."

"Well, that may not be entirely true." Eseza laughed.

They stared into the canopy of the trees. A troop of vervet monkeys had begun their morning ritual, yawning and stretching. A young pair scampered through the treetops and chased each other, too preoccupied with the game to concern themselves with grooming. Eseza watched them and smiled.

She gazed at Charlie for a moment. The look on his face had become distant and vacant. "Are you still scared? I mean, does the *ajiji* still come and shake you?"

"Yes, but it is not what scare me."

"What does?"

"Living."

"Living?"

"Yes. Knowing that I am alive and I should not be. That I do not deserve to take any pleasure from life because I have done so much evil and stolen much from many other."

Eseza nodded.

"Anytime I find the pleasure in something, like eating a ripened mango or hearing the hadada bird laugh in the tree when the sun show itself in the morning, I am afraid. I cannot take pleasure in it when I am remembering the people I took life from. They cannot take pleasure from these thing anymore. Why should I?"

"Yes. It is inside me, too." Eseza drew in the dirt with her finger. "And I have seen this almost beat you. When I saw you hanging from the rope and your hand lying limp at your side, I saw a boy who had been defeated and whose fight for life had been lost. It was strange when I saw this. I was not afraid for you, but for me. I was scared this would happen to me, that I would come to accept that my life was no longer worth holding on to. And when the time came for me to fight for my life, I would not have the will to do so."

Eseza held Charlie's hands. "When I saved you, it was because I wanted to see if your fight for life would come back. And it did. I saw it. When you held the skull of the little boy and you cried, I knew you were human again.

"But each time the stone fell on you and your mind became the soldier mind, I cried inside, for I knew you were fighting a battle I was too cowardly

241

to face." She squeezed his hands harder. The tears began to fall.

"You have shown me a courage that I want, Charlie."

Charlie smiled. "But you have that courage. You are here, yes? You escaped. There is your courage there. You have it. How can you say you are wanting what you already have?"

"Yes, I escaped. But not of my own doing." Eseza looked into the hut and watched the slight rise and fall of Sam's chest. "If it was not for her, I would still be in the LRA camp, preparing meal for the general, ordering the children, and preparing for the raid on the next village."

Charlie stood and looked into the hut. "Who is that?" he whispered.

"That is Sam. She is *muzungu*. She threw the hot water on the general and took me away in the truck. We traveled down the river and footed it here the rest of the way."

"She is smart."

"Yes."

"Then I am thinking that not all the *bazungu* are stupid."

"No." Eseza smiled and patted Charlie's foot. "She is wanting you to tell her about the stone. It was a stone that brought her here, but she is scared and does not want to stay in Uganda. She is wondering how to get home."

"A stone brought her here? Like Bruce and Scott?"

"Yes, that is what she say."

"Then I must talk to her," Charlie said as he stepped into the hut.

"Wait." Eseza put her arm across the door, stopping him from going any farther. "She is tired now. Let her rest."

"And you must rest."

"Yes, I will. But tell me this. Where are Salume and Maisha?"

"Salume has footed it to the refugee camp. She was scared scared when you disappeared, so she took Maisha and her children there."

"Eeh? It is as I thought just."

"Naboth has also disappeared. There are no sign of the LRA. But we cannot think of—"

"He was taken. I saw him at the LRA camp. They beat him quite badly."

"They were wanting to hear about the Arrow Boy?"

"Yes."

"And did he speak?"

"No."

"Nothing?"

"He spat on the commander."

"Really?"

"Yes."

Charlie shook his head while a faint smile crept across his face.

"But I do not know if he is still alive. When we escaped he was at the commander hut, tied to a tree. I am thinking he is dead now. If he was not willing to talk, there is no reason for them to keep him." Eseza paused. "He saw his brother, though. He saw Samson, but it was not good. He refused to acknowledge Naboth was his brother, saying his only brother were those who were loyal to the LRA."

"He could have said that to keep him safe just. You have seen time when brother were made to kill brother?"

"Yes," Eseza closed her eyes and inhaled a long, wavering breath. The words stumbled from her lips. "And sister to deny sister."

"So there is still hope he may still be alive. Samson would try to do something, wouldn't he?"

"I do not know. His mind is not his own anymore. He wore the dreadlock and the rubber boot."

"Then we must not waste any time. We must go to the camp and find Naboth."

Eseza shook her head. "You are talking stupid. We will all be caught. And you will be put on the *goyo* tree. You know this. Naboth is dead. I am sure of it. There is no need to rescue a corpse."

"But he could be alive. There is always that hope."

"You cling to nothing, Charlie. There is no hope. When he was at the hut, I tried to put the water to his mouth but he had barely the strength to swallow it. With no one there to help him, he will die."

"And that is why we must go."

"Why the concern, Charlie? Why do you want to save someone who tied the rope around your neck and strung you from the tree?"

Charlie met Eseza's gaze for a moment, then lowered his eyes.

"You do not know because there is no reason," Eseza said.

"But there is," Charlie said, still staring at the ground.

"There is a reason to save a boy who tried to kill you?"

"Yes. It is because he tried to kill me that I want to save him."

Eseza shook her head. "You are foolish, Charlie."

He crossed his arms over his bare chest. "Perhaps I am." He paused. "I am going now. I will be back. And do not worry. You can go to sleep. There are many Arrow Boy guarding the area. You are safe. I will talk to this girl who has the boy name when she wake up." He took a couple of steps, then turned. "I am glad you are back . . . Eseza." He walked toward the path.

"Charlie."

He stopped and turned again.

"I am glad I am back too."

Eseza walked into the hut and lay down beside Sam, placing her head on the hard ground. She watched the slow rhythm of Sam's shoulder rise and fall with her breathing. Eseza's eyes closed, and her breathing took on the same beat. Breathe in, breathe out, breathe in, breathe out, much like a pair of drums beating in the African jungle.

Chapter 23

*A fight between grasshoppers is a joy
to the crow. ~ Lesotho proverb*

"But there is no reason to believe Naboth is alive. I am telling you. He was not of his right mind when I escaped." Eseza shook her head.

Jonasan glared. "Yes, you escaped and left him there to die."

"Do not look at me like that, like I am a beast that leave the weak behind for the tooth of the lion. I am not heartless." Eseza straightened her back and stood taller. She returned Jonasan's glare. "But there was nothing I could do. I have told you that it all happened quick quick. I did not know what the *muzungu* girl was planning. One moment I was bringing the pot to the commander, and the next I was in the truck with the girl and we were flying through the bush like a kob with the lion on it tail.

There was no chance or time to save Naboth."

"Hmph." Jonasan crossed his arms over his chest. "Go and wake the girl, Michael Jackson. I want to find out who she is and what she is doing here."

"No." Eseza grabbed Michael Jackson's arm and held it. "She need her sleep. She has been through much. I will wake her when Charlie come back with the food. Besides, she does not have anything to tell. She did not know until yesterday where she was and who the LRA were."

"Wake her. She will tell us something. There will be time for sleep later."

Michael Jackson entered the hut, knelt beside Sam, and shook her by the shoulder. She woke with a start and sat. She stared at the young boy, the mud wall surrounding her, and then at Eseza, standing in the middle of a group of boys with bows and quivers of arrows slung over their shoulders. She gasped.

"It is okay, Sam. They are my friend," said Eseza.

Sam rubbed her hand over her face and rose to her feet. "Oh God. I'm still here," she said, her breath leaving in an exasperated sigh. She ducked under the low doorframe and half walked, half stumbled toward the group. She stood near Eseza.

"Sam, these are the Arrow Boy. They are part

of a group that protect the children here. This is Edach Michael Jackson, Osipa Peter, and Ebitu Jonasan."

The boys glanced in Sam's direction, then quickly looked back at the ground.

"Michael Jackson? As in the singer Michael Jackson?"

Michael Jackson looked up at Sam and smiled. "Yes, it is a good name, is it not? I do not think I have the dance like him, but I am better looking . . . I think." He took a few steps, did a quick twist, grabbed his crotch in typical Michael Jackson style, and let out a loud "Whoo-ooo!"

Peter choked as he tried to stifle a laugh, but Sam had no such reservations. She laughed until it came out in a loud snort. Jonasan cleared his throat and gave the boys a stern look. They stopped and quickly stood with their arms pressed to their sides.

"I am confused, Sam. You wear the uniform of a soldier, but Fire tell me you are not a soldier," Jonasan said.

"Fire?"

"Yes, Fire. This girl here who you helped to escape."

"But her name is Eseza."

Eseza glanced from Sam to Jonasan, then to the rest of the boys. Her breath caught fast in her throat.

"Eseza?" Jonasan said, stepping forward.

249

"What is it, Eseza or …?"

The sound of branches parting and quiet footfalls stopped Jonasan in mid-sentence. Peter grabbed his bow and reached for an arrow.

Charlie stepped out of the bush, laden with ripe red mangos. "It is fine fine Peter. Drop the bow please and come here." He walked to the group and placed the mangos on the ground. He saw the anger in Jonasan's face and the fear in Eseza's. "It is foolish to discuss anything on an empty stomach. That is what my mother used to say. Come. Please. Sit. Eat," he said, sitting cross-legged on the ground.

"And since when do you give the order here, Charlie?" Jonasan asked.

"I do not give the order. We must eat when the food is near. We can speak when it is not. This is what family does. This is what we as Acholi do. Brother and sister, all of the same tribe." He repeated himself, spacing the words out for emphasis. "All of the same tribe."

Peter and Michael Jackson sat and each grabbed a mango, bit into it, and peeled off the skin with their front teeth.

"Sit. Please." Charlie tugged on Jonasan's pant leg. Jonasan sat between Peter and Michael Jackson, while Eseza sat between Sam and Charlie. Eseza stared at the pile of fruit while the rest of the group ate.

Jonasan cleared his throat. Even sitting, he appeared to glare down at Eseza. "So why is it the *muzungu* girl call you Eseza? The snake and the lion cannot share one name." He glowered at her.

"No talking until we have finished eating, please." Charlie said as he grabbed a mango and tossed it to Jonasan. He placed a mango in Eseza's hands. "You must eat too"—he paused as if for emphasis—"Eseza."

Eseza hesitated and then bit into the fruit. The group ate in silence as Charlie smacked his lips and sucked on a seed. He grabbed a twig from a tree branch and used it to clean his teeth, then placed a small pail of water in the middle of the circle and washed his hands. The rest of the group followed suit. Finally, they sat and waited.

Jonasan spoke first. "So what is your name? Fire or Eseza? Or should we call you traitor or spy? Perhaps these name are more suited for you."

Eseza stared back at Jonasan. His eyes narrowed and the muscles in his face tightened around his clenched teeth.

She lowered her gaze. "*Ojone*. Please. All I ask is that you listen. Then perhaps you will understand."

"Speak, girl," he commanded.

Eseza closed her eyes for a moment as she

found the right words to begin. "It was not long long ago. Perhaps four month, near to the beginning of the dry season. The grass was beginning to show the sign of rest, and the bitter wind covered everything in the LRA camp with the red dust. There was talk of a group of people who were taking it upon themself to fight Kony, and Kony, he was not happy with this. He was mad mad. He could not understand how his own people would go against him when he was fighting the government that had hurt them.

"He began to suspect the children were planning to escape and join this new group that called themself the Arrow Boy." She paused and drew her knees to her side. "It was a time of great great fear for us. Many children were used as example of what would happen if anyone tried to escape. The *goyo* tree was kept busy busy, and many body were brought into the bush and fed to the hyna.

"No one dared do anything that showed they were wanting to escape. We cleared the thought from our mind so Kony could not read them. But he did read them. Many children I knew who had been brave enough and were looking for a chance to escape were killed. But I knew many other who did not have these thought and were also tied to the *goyo* tree and beaten.

"Something had to be done. The camp reeked of death, and the hyna bark filled the air for many, many night.

"Kony did not trust anyone. Not even his general. But he trusted me."

"He trusted you? Why would he trust you?" Jonasan said with a sneer. "You are a girl. You—"

"Yes, I am a girl, Jonasan, but I was always ready to do what Kony or the other commander ask. I wanted to survive. You will not understand this, and I do not expect you to. But that is what happened. Every day I was told to do this, this, and this. To kill this person, to feed this general, to be this man wife. And I did. I never questioned it. I always obeyed."

Jonasan drew his head back. He looked at Eseza with utter contempt and disgust. "You were a commander wife?"

Eseza hesitated. She could not admit she was Kony's wife. The Arrow Boys would think it was horrid enough that she was forced to share a bed with a commander. They would despise her, hate her, and treat her worse than a dog left to beg at a poor man's table. But it would be worse, much worse, if they knew she was one of Kony's wives.

She spoke slowly and chose her words carefully. "Yes, I was a wife. And I was respected in the camp. That is why I came to Kony and told him I could go to the village and find out who dared to go against him. I reasoned with him. I would be a good good cover, I said. No one would suspect a young girl with her newborn child. I would find out, and I would come back and let him know what people opposed him. I filled my mind with only these intention. I did not allow the idea of escape to enter it. I knew Kony witchcraft, and I knew it was powerful.

"I set off with Maisha, fresh from his birth, and came to Kitgum. I stayed there for a week and then footed it to Pajule. I learned nothing of the Arrow Boy. The people were too scared. Many feared even to say Kony name. You know this. I am not telling you anything you do not know already.

"But when I came to this village, the thought of escape did enter my mind. I worked hard to fight these thought every day. But the seed had been planted and the tree did start to grow. Day passed, then week, then month, and no one came to find me and bring me back to the camp. I began to think I had been forgotten. That perhaps the camp had moved and I had been left behind.

"It was a wonderful thought. And for a short time, I let my guard down and good thing began to happen. I could no longer feel Kony presence. I could no longer feel he could read my thought and know of my plan. Perhaps his spirit was becoming weak or my spirit was becoming stronger—I do not know.

"But they had not forgotten me. The evening after we met with the Arrow Boy and Ben, they found me near to the hut, and they took me. I did not resist, for it would have been of no use. They took me back to the camp, and the commander tied me to the post and left me to hang by my wrist. He did not know of this plan for me to spy out the area. He thought I had escaped. And he was right."

Eseza gathered the mango seeds and threw them into the forest then washed her hands in the bucket.

"I do not wish it upon anyone here to understand this. You would only understand if you were taken and made to be a soldier. And I do not wish that on anyone. For when you are taken by Kony, you are forced to do many horrid thing." Eseza's voice cracked. "You know this. You have heard the story from the children who have escaped and returned."

Eseza returned to her spot, sat, and laid her hand on Sam's shoulder. "We are not the same, Sam. Us, the child soldier. How could we be? We have been made to kill our own mother and father. Our own brother and sister. We have been forced to behave like wild animal, doing thing I am too ashamed to say. And who does this? Who force this evil onto other? It is only the devil himself.

"But there is something I have realized is inside all of us—the will to live and to survive. And a person will do anything if he think the next day may be the day when the evil will end.

"That is why I came here. To survive. I know I cannot ask you to forgive me for what I have done. And I cannot ask you to understand why I did this. Perhaps I should have had the courage to refuse to do the evil and to let them kill me. But I did not. And I cannot change anything. Not one thing."

The group sat in silence. Eseza gazed at each one of them. A tear rolled down Sam's face and landed on her khaki pants, making a bright green spot on the dusty fabric.

"But maybe you will consider this when you look at me. My magic showed you where the cache were. You saw that when all the bone landed in the same spot. It show that I am wanting to be on your side. It also show that the spirit are wanting me to be on your side."

"That does not prove anything." Jonasan stood and backed a few steps away from the group. "For all we know, it was a trap. You led us there because you knew there were some soldier there, guarding the cache."

"I did not know the soldier were there."

Jonasan glared. "How dare you lie! You are

possessed by the evil spirit. You are heartless. Go. You have brought more evil into our land. Go. We do not want to see you again."

Sam's eyes widened as Jonasan spoke. He hovered over Eseza, standing taller and taller as she cowered under his shadow.

"No, you have it all wrong, Jonasan," said Sam. "There's nothing evil about Eseza. I know. In the two days I've known her, I think she's probably the most courageous and kindest person I've ever met."

Jonasan scoffed. "And what do you know? As if I am going listen to you! A girl. A white girl. You know nothing of this war and the treachery that exist."

"No, I don't." Sam stood. "But I know what I saw at the LRA camp. Eseza risked her life for me—and Naboth. She snuck food to us, and water. And if she was caught, she would have been beaten. That I know."

Jonasan stared at Sam. His eyes filled with contempt. "And what does that say? That she was trying to win you over to her side. That it was only a ploy to make you think she cared for you. That she was going to use you in some way. That is all it can be. More treachery!"

"No. That's not it at all. She saved Naboth's life. He wasn't going to talk, so they were going to kill him. But she convinced them not to. She told them to tie him to a post and let the sun do the work. She was—"

"Let the sun do the work?"

"Yes, she was buying time. You know, trying to . . ."

Jonasan glared at Eseza. "You left him tied to a post, under the sun? To die?"

"No. No," Sam said. "You don't understand. If she hadn't done this, they would have killed him. Right then and there. But she knew if he was tied up, then maybe there was a chance—"

"A chance to let him die a slow, painful death?"

Eseza stood, her fists tight to her sides. "No. Do you not see that if I did not do this they would have killed him? At least by tying him to the tree he had a chance. And I could use the time to think and plan something."

"But you never did, did you? You escaped with no thought of Naboth."

Eseza hung her head. "Yes, you are right."

Jonasan walked toward the bush then stopped at the edge and cleared his throat. "Fire, or Eseza, or whatever your name is, you must leave. Go. We cannot trust you. And you, *muzungu* girl, get out. You do not belong here."

He walked into the bush. Michael Jackson and Peter followed close behind.

Chapter 24

What you help a child to love can be more
important than what you help him to learn.
~ African proverb

Sam stirred the coals and watched the smoke drift into the forest.

"So you have no idea how I can get home." Her voice was heavy with disappointment. "But you must know something about how the stones work."

Charlie thought for a moment. "No," he said. "Bruce told me it was the stone that brought him to Uganda just. That is all he said, and I did not ask anymore. It is magic." Charlie shrugged matter-of-factly. "That is all. What is there more to know? The stone brought him, and then it brought Scott, and then it brought both of them to help me again."

"Again?"

"Yes. When I first met Bruce, I had escaped from the LRA just and I was footin' my way to Lira. But Bruce and Scott came again after the LRA attacked the refugee camp and took me and some thirty boy and girl."

"But how did he leave? I mean, how did Bruce go back home? What did he have to do?"

"Eeh, what did he have to do? I do not know. Each time he left I was asleep. I woke up just and he was gone. That is all."

"You didn't see him do anything, say anything?"

"No."

"Not any spell or chant or something like that?"

"A spell?"

"Yeah, a spell. A bunch of words, a little dance or something. You know."

"No. I do not think a spell is what you are needing to go back."

Sam sighed. She was getting nowhere. "What about Scott? Were you there when he went back home?"

"Yes, but it was dark the first time he left. And I was asleep. But I saw him when he left the last time."

"You did? And was there anything he said or did before he left?"

"No, but he knew he was going soon—he said

that—and that is when he gave me the stone." Charlie paused for a moment and laughed. "But the second time Scott left, it was original!"

"Original?"

Charlie laughed. Eseza peeked out of the hut and stared. She shook her head.

"There was Scott, tied to the tree. And there were the soldier. They were looking for me when I went into the bush with the stone. But Scott, he yelled. 'Hey! Over here, you!' and the soldier, they turned and looked at him and then he vanished!"

"Vanished? Like completely disappeared before their eyes?"

"Yes, exactly like that. One moment he was there and the next he was gone, and the soldier, they ran round and round like a chicken with it head cut off. They grabbed the rope and they looked at it, and they yelled *'Jok! Jok!'*"

"Jok?"

"Yes. An evil spirit. They thought Scott was a *jok*. Imagine that."

Sam grinned. She was imagining it. "But what about Bruce and Scott? What can you tell me about them?"

"They are *bazungu*, like you just." Charlie shrugged. "Bruce was big and fat. He was well fed just." He lifted up his feet. "See my shoe? They were his, but he gave them to me after he healed my feet."

"Your feet? What was wrong with your feet?"

"When I escaped from the LRA, I ran through a field of thorn. My feet were cut and bleeding and oozing with yellow pus. But Bruce was a good angel. He saved me when the police wanted to kill me, and he lifted me up and flew away with his two big wing."

"Wings?"

"Yes, I did not see his wing when I met him first. They must have been hidden under his shirt. But when the police hurt me and I could not walk or think, Bruce lifted me in his big arm and held me tight to him as he flew away. Then he fed me manna, healed my feet, and gave me these shoe." Charlie wiggled his toes. "They do not fit, but I do not care. They keep my feet good good."

Sam took a closer look at the running shoes: blue with dark red stains, very well worn, toes that curled up from having nothing inside them. And their size? Bigger than her dad's, that was for sure.

"And what about Scott?"

Charlie paused to think. "Scott was as stupid as Bruce. He did not think. He did not think because he thought he knew it all. He tried to escape, and because of this they used a boy as example and they made us shoot at him to practice our aim."

"To practice your aim? Like target practice?"

Sam couldn't believe what she was hearing.

"Yes. To teach us. There are many lesson to learn when you are with the LRA. And the way many learn is by the other mistake. If you try to escape and you are caught, you are beaten. We are given the cane and we must whip and whip and whip, and then when our arm grow tired more children are given more cane and they whip and whip and whip. It is a powerful message. Especially if you are one of the children made to whip. You will think again if you want to escape."

Sam blinked, trying to dispel the vivid image from her mind. She didn't know what to say.

"But Scott. He was a good angel. He was sorry sorry for what he had done. He told me he was. He told me he cried when he buried the boy. And he asked me to forgive him."

Charlie thought back to that day.

"And I forgave him. I had seen much much worse. And if I could not forgive him for the boy death, then how could I expect anyone to forgive me for all I have done?"

Sam studied Charlie: small build, thin sinewy arms, quick to smile, but also quick to become silent. He was silent again. He looked into the bush, but Sam couldn't help but feel he wasn't seeing what his eyes were looking at. She had seen the evidence of the LRA's destruction; she had witnessed the grip of fear the army held over the children. And she had learned of its lust for power without any concern for the lives of the children. Children were seen only as tools, things to be used in combat, things to be traded for more weapons, things that were quickly disposed of because they could easily be replaced.

She squeezed Charlie's hand.

"And that is why I listened to Scott. He asked me to bring the last stone to Kony, so I did. He said the stone have the power to change people, and that Kony needed to change. Otherwise more and more kid would lose their life."

"The stones change people?" Sam asked.

"Yes, that is what he said. And I do believe it. When I first met Scott, I thought he was stupid, but he was not when he left. He thought more. He was not stupid anymore. It was the same with Bruce. He too was stupid. But then he learned how to think."

Sam smiled. It was funny how Charlie called Scott and Bruce stupid. "Yeah, I guess there's a lot of stupidity going around everywhere."

"Yes, sometime when I hear a person call an animal stupid I have to think. The animal, it care for it herd. But I do not see that in the human. It does not respect the herd. It kill it own kind. We are Acholi people from the Acholi tribe. Kony, he is Acholi too. But he does not respect the tribe. He does not respect the life of his brother or sister. I do not understand that."

Charlie fell silent as his thoughts turned inward.

"I do not know if the stone worked on Kony. He and the LRA are still taking the children and turning us into monster. And I do not see how it will end. But if he have the stone, then perhaps it is time just that is needed."

Sam wanted to reach out to Charlie and hold him. But would that provide any comfort? The evil needed to end. And Charlie needed to be a kid again. She couldn't do anything to change the past or anything to make a better future for him. She slid over and held his hands in hers then wrapped her arms around his small body and hugged him. Charlie laid his head on her shoulder. His body trembled.

"Apwoyo. Apwoyo matek." His voice was soft and grateful.

Eseza stepped out of the hut and placed two sacks on the ground. She tossed a pot and a couple of plates into the open sack, pulled the ends of the rope snug, and tied it tight. "Are you ready to go, big *muzungu* woman?"

Sam touched Charlie gently on the shoulder and stood. "Yeah, I guess."

Eseza turned to Charlie. "I am thinking that

265

Jonasan is planning to go to the LRA camp and
rescue Naboth. He did not say it, but I know he
would not leave him there to die. But there is
something you must know. Another group of
children are on their way to Sudan to get the tin and
the arm. It is going to be a big trade because many
many children are going. I know this because I saw
them grouping and spoke to a soldier who was
taking them."

"I will tell Jonasan."

"I do not know if he will trust the information,
but at least you will know that some have left the
camp and there will be less left behind. And I do not
know what Jonasan plan to do, but I can only think
it is all foolish. Naboth is dead. I am sure of it."

Eseza crouched and looked at Charlie intently.
"I do not know what it is you think you and the
Arrow Boy can do. They will capture you, and you
will be tied to the *goyo* tree. And you, Charlie, you
run the greatest risk of all. You have escaped, and
you want to return with other to attack the LRA?
They will be searching for me. They will be
searching along the river and into the bush. They
will have guard all around the camp. You know
this, and that make you the most foolish of
everyone."

"Yes, it is looking that way."

"I am thinking that your arm are hanging limp

to your side again. You are wanting to die. You do not value your life. Am I right?"

Charlie shrugged. "But if I do nothing, there is no hope."

"There is no hope if you do anything, Charlie."

"But there is. Look at you. You are alive. You are alive because of an angel. I am alive because of the angel. And if God give us the angel, he must be showing us there is hope."

"Here you are speaking the foolishness again. Yes, we have had good fortune on us when these people come to us and help us, but that is it. We are free. Why would we risk our life again now that we are free?"

"Because Kony has the stone now. And Scott has told me that the stone has the power to change people."

"But there has been no change. He is still taking the children. The war is still going on. And there are more and more bone that are needing the grave."

"But maybe it needs more time. Maybe Kony . . ." His voice now became more assured. "Maybe Kony is needing more time because there are great change that must happen in him."

Eseza stood and shook her head. "Perhaps. But I do not think he is a man who is able to make the change. He is set in his evil way. There is no hope for him."

"But—"

"Eeh, Charlie, do you not think I would know these thing? I shared his bed for many month."

Charlie was silent.

Eseza lifted the black sack onto her head. "Now it is my turn to leave. I am sorry for this, Charlie. I wish you well. And do not let your arm hang limp. You are worthy of life."

He smiled. "And you are too, Eseza. But maybe this is not goodbye. Maybe you will find Maisha and I will return with Naboth. Then we can have our own hut, and raise the chicken and eat the egg every day. Slowly, enjoying each and every bite."

A big tear coursed down Eseza's cheek. She offered a half smile.

"That would be beautiful and good, Charlie."

"Then when I come back with Naboth, I will go north to the refugee camp and look for you. And perhaps we will hold on to the good and there will not be a thin thin line."

Eseza steeled herself. She wiped the tears from her eyes, turned, and walked into the bush.

Sam picked up the other bag and held it to her chest as she followed Eseza. She stopped and turned. "How do you say 'thank you' in your language, Charlie?"

"Apwoyo matek."

"Oh," she said, recognizing the words he spoke to her as she hugged him. "Ah-poor-you," she said, trying to pronounce it correctly. "Ah-poor-you ma-teck, Charlie."

Charlie laughed. She turned and followed Eseza into the bush.

They took the pathway until they came to the field that surrounded the school. Without a word, Eseza turned to the right, keeping to the edge of the bush. Once they reached the bush line she turned again, this time following a pathway that ran parallel with the path they had taken away from the hut.

Finally, Sam spoke. "How far is it to the refugee camp?"

"Two day footin', I think."

"Two days?"

"Yes. Two day."

Sam shifted the bag and tried to get a better grip. The pots and dishes clanged around inside, falling to one side, making the bag lopsided and more difficult to manage. She grabbed its corners and hoisted it to her chest. A mosquito buzzed by and landed on her neck. "Git!" she said as she slapped at it. The bag slipped from her grasp and fell to the ground. She sighed as she watched Eseza follow a turn in the pathway and move out of sight. She grabbed the bag and ran.

Eseza turned and watched Sam fumbling with the sack. "Why not put the sack on your head?" she asked.

Sam lifted the huge bag on top of her head and took a few steps forward. She reached up with one hand and held the bag in place. It shifted again and dropped to the ground.

Eseza shook her head. "Here, do this," she said, taking a wrap from her waist.

She spun the cloth around and around until she created a small circle and placed it on Sam's head. She positioned the bag on the cloth and stood back, examining it. "That should do. And do not drop it again. Our food is in there."

"Sure. Thanks."

Eseza quickened her pace. "We will follow this path until we reach the main road. Once we find it, we will take it until we come to the next town. Then we will stay there for the night. It would not be safe for us to stay in the bush. And there will be plenty of night commuter we can foot it with."

"Night commuters?"

"Yes, when Kony started taking the children from their hut in the night, the children started footin' it to the town and sleeping there. They sleep on the storefront and the sidewalk. Sometime, if they are lucky, they find a business or a bus station that have it door open for the night and they stay there."

"Did you have to leave your home at night, too?"

"Yes, I did. For many month. I would take my book with me from school and sit under a light and do my work. And then I would sleep, and come the morning I would walk home again and then go to school."

Sam considered this. "It must have been very tiring for you."

"Yes, and frightening. There are other thing you must be fearing when you are alone in a town at night."

"But if you did this . . . then how were you taken?"

"At my school."

"During the day? In broad daylight?"

"Yes."

"But wasn't there anyone around to stop them? The police? The army?"

Eseza laughed. "The police? They have not the gun or the men to go against the LRA. And the government army, the UPDF? They are coward. They knew Kony army was going to the school. But what do they do? They run. They run with the tail between their leg, like a coyote from a lion." She paused and shifted the bag on her head. "But I do not put the blame on them. No. I understand their fear. There are very terrible thing the LRA children are made to do when they capture a UPDF soldier. No, I do not put the blame on them."

She stopped and looked into the distance. "There is the road now. It will be easy footin' and we will be able to go fast fast. Come, my strong and brave *muzungu* girl. It will not be long."

They stepped onto the red clay road and continued on their way.

"I think I'm getting the hang of this, Eseza. Look, no hands." Sam took her hands off the bag and took a couple of steps. The bag shifted and started to fall. Sam grabbed it just in time. "Okay, maybe I'm not that good at it yet," she muttered.

"Eeh, do not be too hard on yourself. It is an awkward load. It is full of the pot and pan and it shift much."

Sam glanced at the bag on Eseza's head. "Yours looks a lot easier to carry. Do you think we could switch?"

Eseza stopped momentarily. "No, that is not a good idea. No. It is a heavy load. I would not want you to carry it."

"What do you have in there anyway? More food?"

"No." Her tone was abrupt. "It is not the food. It is nothing. Now come, let us go. The sun is going to hide itself soon, and we must be in the town before the darkness come."

Chapter 25

Birds sing not because they have answers but because they have songs. ~ African proverb

Sam was ready to collapse on the ground and fall asleep right then and there when they entered the city of Gulu. She spotted a mess of broken red bricks next to a building, mumbled something about a taxi and giving up a year's worth of allowance, and then sat on the pile, worn out, miserable, and sore. The place reminded Sam of an Old West town she had seen in a movie. Not that it had any old wooden saloons, water troughs, or cowboys, but because everything was covered in a fine layer of red dust: the cement buildings, the signs, the trees and flowers, and even the people.

Eseza sat next to Sam, pulled out a bottle of water, and offered her a drink. Sam took a long sip, wiped her mouth, then passed it to Eseza.

"No, you drink it all. We can get more water at

the well down the way. It is not far far from here."

Sam took a couple of more gulps and poured a little into her cupped hand. She sprinkled the water over her head and rubbed her face and the back of her neck. "Thanks—ah-poor-you ma-teck."

Eseza grinned. "You are welcome. But let us go. It will be dark soon, and I want to find a place for us to sleep the night. It should not be far. I think you can foot it to there."

Eseza took Sam's hand and pulled her up. She led her down a side street, past the stores and litter-strewn roads. As they turned a corner, they met a group of women sitting on the edge of the road with piles of their spices, fruits, and vegetables lying on the ground before them. Sam stared at the perfectly round watermelons carefully arranged in front of an elderly lady.

The lady looked up at Sam, offering her a toothless grin. "They are nice nice melon, miss. Come, you take one. We talk deal now."

Sam gave a half-hearted smile. Eseza grabbed her hand and pulled her along. "I'm sorry," Sam called over her shoulder, "I don't have any money with me!"

They walked past more shops and more women selling their goods. And each time the women would call out, offering their wares for "discount prices," telling Eseza and Sam that their oranges were the juiciest and their tomatoes the tastiest. Sam could only stare and drool.

When Sam felt as though she had finally had enough of the crowded sidewalks and offers of food she couldn't buy, Eseza halted and pointed at a large building that looked something like a warehouse. "We will stay here," she said. "It look like we have come in good time. I do not see many children here yet."

They walked to the building and put the bags on the ground. Eseza found a pile of stones set up in a circle on the broken pavement. "Perfect." She rummaged through the bag Sam had carried, pulled out a pot, and placed it on the dead coals that lay in the middle of the stones. "You stay here and watch over the bag. I will get the water and we will have rice for supper." She grabbed an empty water jug from the bag, turned, and walked into the crowd.

Sam sat on the ground and leaned against the bag Eseza had carried. Something hard stuck into her back.

"Shit, what's in this thing?" she muttered, trying to smooth the lumps and bumps that protruded from the sack. She slid her hand up and down, feeling the contours of the bag, and felt something solid and heavy. She rapped her knuckles on it. A loud knock resounded. She ran her hand over the top of the bag and felt a smooth, hard surface, almost like a ball, but not quite as round and heavier—at least that's what it felt like.

"There's only one way to find out." She glanced around. Eseza was not in sight.

Sam grabbed the cord and pulled it loose, carefully noting the way the knot had been tied. She pulled the sack open and stared. She gasped and took a step back. Blinking, she shook her head and looked again. There was no denying it. The skull of a child lay on top of a pile of bones. Two empty sockets stared back at her. She glanced around, making sure no one was watching. She pulled the sack closed and yanked the cord around the top. Her hands shook as she secured the knot as it had been tied before.

"Oh, God. Oh, God. Oh, God." Sam slid to the ground and covered her face with her hands. "Why the hell is she carrying the skeleton of a child with her?" she whispered. She inhaled and let it out. She took in another, then another, expelling the air slowly, concentrating as she counted. "One, two, three—"

"Are you okay, miss?"

Sam looked up, startled. A young boy stood in front of her. He wore a ripped red T-shirt and very worn shorts held up with a rope tied around his waist. He placed his hand on Sam's shoulder and bent down, looking into her eyes. "You look very scared. Like you have seen a ghost or a *jok*. Have you? Because if you have, I can protect you. I have mighty power."

The boy reached into his pants pocket and pulled out a handmade slingshot comprised of a Y-shaped stick and a piece of tire tubing tied to both ends. Sam stared at the boy, then at the slingshot, then back at the boy. He was smiling at her, his huge brown eyes looking down at her.

"Look. I will show you." The boy picked a stone from the ground and placed it in the center of the black rubber. He pulled back farther and farther until the rubber was stretched as far as it could go. He released the rock. It flew across the street and hit a sign nailed to a street pole, resounding with a loud *thwack*.

"See, no ghost or *jok* could survive that." The boy shook his head with sincere earnestness.

"But aren't all ghosts or *jok*s invisible? What good is a stone if it will just go right through them?"

The boy looked at Sam, totally perplexed. "It has not let me down so far," he said. "And I have had to deal with many many evil *jok*."

"You have, have you?"

Eseza crossed the sidewalk and placed the water jug on the ground. "Hello, ka-boy," she said. "What is the news about Kony? Have they spotted him near to here?"

"No, they are saying he is farther to the north, that he has gone to Sudan again."

Eseza grabbed a handful of dried grass from the edge of the sidewalk and stuck it under the coals. She lit a match and placed it into the grass. The flame flickered as she blew into the base, sending its fiery fingers into the coals and setting them aglow.

"And what of the children in the village? Are they still footin' it here to stay the night?"

"Yes."

"And you are one of them?"

"Yes."

Eseza filled the pot half full of water and added some rice. She placed the lid on it and stood up, arching her back.

"Tell me, ka-boy, where are your brother and sister?"

"There are none. I am all that is left. They took my two brother and my sister long ago. I come here every night before the sun is down."

"Then you are wanting some company while you are here. You are most welcome to stay with us."

"Apwoyo." The boy bowed his head and eyed the pot on the fire.

"And I am thinking we will have enough to

share."

The boy's face lit up. "*Apwoyo matek*, miss."

"Eeh? Now where are my manner? I go by the name Ayudo Eseza, and this is my friend Sam."

"Sam?" The boy regarded Sam curiously.

"Short for Samantha, but everyone I know calls me Sam."

"That is good. Everyone I know call me Albin."

Albin picked up a piece of coal lying on the ground and added it to the fire. "Wait," he said, "I will be back quick quick."

He took off down the road, weaving in and out of the buyers and sellers, and disappeared into the crowd.

"It is not good for such a young boy to be by himself," Eseza said as she stirred the rice. "That is why I ask him to stay with us. He look okay to me. And he will offer us some protection."

"Protection? A little boy like that?" Sam looked into the crowd, waiting for Albin to return.

"Yes. He will appear to be my brother, and the men will not come by if they see we are busy with a young boy to look after."

"Oh . . . What men? Do you mean—"

"Yes. That is exactly what I mean."

Eseza rummaged through the sack and took out a piece of cloth tied up with a length of vine. She opened it and sprinkled a tiny amount of an herb into the pot. She stirred the rice. "It will be ready soon."

Sam nodded. She glanced at the black bag and then at Eseza. *Should I ask her?*

"Eseza . . . I . . ." Sam stopped. *No,* she thought. It would betray their trust. And trust was in short supply as it was. She sighed. "Never mind."

She looked up as a large group of children walked toward them, each carrying a blanket either on their head or tucked under their arms. She stared. The street was now overflowing with young boys and girls. Gradually, the sidewalks and storefront spaces filled as the children found their spots for the night. Teenagers rolled their blankets on the ground while their younger siblings scrambled to find a place to sit.

"Are these the kids who have to leave their homes at night to stay away from Kony? All of them?"

"Yes."

"But there are so many. I didn't realize—"

"Yes. And if you go to the next street, you will see the bus station full. And there is a place that a church group has set up for the night commuter too. And over toward the town center is a park where many of them also go."

"There must be hundreds and hundreds of

kids."

"Yes, it is what we do. It is what we have to do." Eseza lifted the lid off the pot and peered in. "The rice is done. Now where is the ka-boy?"

Sam searched the crowd of children. She caught a glimpse of a red shirt. "Here he comes, just in time."

Albin ambled toward them, carrying a huge melon of some sort in his arms. It was a golden-green color, covered with little pointed bumps. His tongue stuck out to one side as he struggled to carry it. When he placed it on the ground beside them, he stepped back and took a low bow.

"That thing is huge, Albin! It's gotta weigh at least twenty pounds!" Sam bent down to examine it. "What the heck is it?"

"A jackfruit. I have been keeping my eye on the tree in front of the hotel, and I say to myself, 'Albin, now is a good time to pick it. It is ripe and you have two beautiful girl to share it with. Perhaps one or both will want to marry you after they see how great a provider you are.'"

Sam laughed. Eseza shook her head and smiled.

"Oh, you're such a cute boy," Sam said. She bent down and hugged Albin.

Albin grinned. "Then you are accepting the marriage proposal?"

Sam laughed again.

Eseza placed the pot on the ground, and they sat in a circle with the rice in the middle. She lifted the lid and a puff of steam rose into the air. Sam breathed it in and closed her eyes. It was not a feast, but it felt like it.

Eseza scooped a small chunk of rice with her fingers and shoved it into her mouth. When she nodded in her direction, Sam did the same, trying her best not to drop any of the rice on the ground. Albin took his turn next, then Eseza, then Sam again. The rotation continued until the pot was empty.

Albin ran his finger around the pot, licking his fingers and smacking his lips. "Now for the jackfruit," he said, wiping his fingers on his shorts.

Eseza took a knife from the sack and handed it to him. "Your fruit. Your honor," she said.

Albin cut the golden-green fruit in half lengthwise. When he opened it, he revealed a whitish core surrounded by orange pockets containing large seeds about the size of Brazil nuts. He sliced around one of the orange pockets and lifted up a stringy, pulpy mass. Then he popped the seed out and handed the piece to Sam. "You are first, *muzungu* Sam."

Sam took the piece of fruit and sniffed it. "Mmmm, it smells delicious." She took a little bite and chewed. "This is good." She smacked her lips in satisfaction. "It tastes like . . ." She paused, thinking. "It tastes like . . . like Juicy Fruit gum! That's what it tastes like."

Albin passed a piece to Eseza and continued to cut up the fruit. As he cut the sections out from the edge, he placed the seeds in the pot lid beside him. When all of the sections were pulled out, he sliced around the inner core and removed it. He then flipped the jackfruit, pushing out its innards and revealing a mass of white and orange tentacle-like fronds. He pulled off another section and popped it into his mouth. "Eeh, I think it was worth the wait."

Sam nodded in agreement and took another piece.

"May I take the seed home with me, Eseza?" Albin asked. "My *min maa* like them. Although I do not know how she eat them with so little teeth."

"Of course. It is your fruit."

Sam took another piece and looked around her. The sidewalk along the edge of the building had now filled with children. Some sat in groups eating or talking, while others held their schoolbooks on their laps and did their best to focus on their homework.

"Now, that's dedication," Sam said as she watched a teenage boy attempting to study while a group of young boys played around him.

Eseza took a small container of oil out of her

sack and poured some over her hands. She rubbed them together and rinsed them with some water.

"Here," she said, offering some oil to Sam. "It will get rid of the stickiness."

When the pot was cleaned and the sack was tied, Eseza found an open section of lawn and sat down. "Come and sit here. The grass will be a good spot to sleep."

They sat in silence, staring at the children around them. Some children had already curled up on the ground and appeared to be fast asleep. A group of older boys and girls had found a couple of oilcan lids and were working out a beat and nodding their heads to the rhythm. The more energetic of the teens moved their bodies in unison, performing a dance that Sam surmised was traditional, since more and more of the children joined in, repeating the same jumps and twists.

Albin snuggled in closer to Sam and laid his head on her lap. She stroked his cropped hair. "Are you missing your mom right now, Albin?"

"No."

"It's all right if you do. You don't have to be a big brave boy all the time."

Albin's face scrunched up, deep in concentration. "Well, maybe a little."

"I miss my mom and dad too. Sometimes. And Eseza, I'm sure she's feeling exactly the same as you. Aren't you, Eseza?"

Eseza nodded and sighed. She drew her hands to her chin and stared into the sky, deep in thought. Sam followed her gaze into the growing darkness and watched the stars begin to show themselves.

Finally, Eseza spoke. "You know what I am missing right now, Albin?" She paused and looked at the boy with a slight grin.

"What?"

"A story. My *min maa* was the best storyteller in our whole village. Everyone would come and gather around our fire at night and listen. She had such a way in telling the tale. Maybe I will give it a try and tell one. Is there one you would like to hear?"

Albin sat and clapped his hands together. "Do you know the story of Walukaga the blacksmith?"

"Know it? It is my favorite!" Eseza clasped her hands together and put them in her lap. "Now let us see. A long long time ago there was a king in Uganda called Banzibanzi. He was a very cruel man, and a very wicked king. Every moment of his waking hour, he would think of way to trouble his people, taxing them more and more, taking their finest crop from their field, and claiming the largest of the cow and goat to be his own. For many year he rule like this until everyone in all of the many village was wretched with the fear of his control and the cruelty of his rule."

Sam smiled as she watched Eseza. Eseza's face was filled with expression; her eyes grew bigger and her voice deeper as she described the king and all of his horridness. A small group of children inched their way toward Eseza and sat beside her. The looks on their faces mirrored that of Albin's: delighted, amused, and mesmerized.

"But there was one man who did not lose his happiness to Banzibanzi wickedness. It was Walukaga, the chief of the blacksmith. It annoyed Banzibanzi to no end to see the smile on Walukaga face, and he set out to wipe it off, forever.

"One day Banzibanzi sent for Walukaga and said to him: 'You are a very intelligent man. I have seen many of your creation, but I must admit you have disappointed me. You have forged thing out of iron and steel, but you have yet to create something out of flesh and blood. I want you to make me a man. A real man who can walk and talk and do whatever a man can do. If I do not see this man, then your life will be taken.'

"Walukaga was very upset. He left the king with a great feeling of dread, for he knew he could make no such creation.

"On the way home, he met up with the village madman, dressed in rag and as thin as a bamboo tree. The madman held his arm out to Walukaga and

287

cried in a most anguished voice. 'Have pity on me! Have pity on me!' he repeated over and over.

"Now Walukaga knew he was going to die, and he decided he would try to show as much kindness as he could during his last day. He reached into his pocket and gave the madman the last of his money: two small coin. 'Take this, my dear friend, and use it to buy yourself some new clothe and some good food.'

"The madman was very happy, but he saw the sadness in Walukaga eye. 'What is troubling you so much, my dear man?' he asked. 'Do tell me and I will try to help you, for you have helped me.'

"Walukaga told the madman what the king had ordered him to do, and the madman listened with very open ear. He whispered something into Walukaga ear and then left to buy some clothe and food.

"The next day Walukaga went to see the king. When the king saw him, he asked Walukaga if he had made the man from his forge yet.

"'No,' he replied, 'but I have thought about it. This is a very difficult task, and I can only do it if I have the help of the wisest king of Uganda. I must acquire a number of item which I know only you, in your wisdom, can obtain.'

"The king gloated over Walukaga and asked, 'And what is it you require from me?'

"Walukaga replied, 'A special kind of charcoal made of human hair. I need three sack of it.'

"Banzibanzi gave the order, and all his messenger went out into the country. They ordered the people to shave their head and burn the hair and give it to the king. But when all the hair was burned, not enough charcoal was made to fill even one sack.

"The next day Walukaga went to the king with another request. 'Oh, most wise and virtuous king, before I can forge a man I must have water. But the water from the cloud or the lake or the stream will not do. I must have the tear from the people, for it take many, many tear to make a human life. Please, your greatness, may I have three water pot full of tear?'

"Once again the king sent out his many messenger throughout his land and ordered the people to weep and save their tear. But as sad and depressed as the people were, they could not collect enough tear. There was only enough to fill one water pot.

"The next day Walukaga visited the king and said, 'Sir you have given me a most difficult task. I asked you to help me by providing me with two small item. If a great king like you cannot help with such a little thing, then how can a humble blacksmith like me do the work of our Creator?'

"The king thought and thought about this. His face became hard with anger but then softened as he thought and thought some more. 'You are right, Walukaga. The task I gave you was impossible.' He gave Walukaga a present and sent him on his way.

"And that is why to this day when a person in Uganda is confused and does not know what to do, the people will tell him . . ."

The circle filled with a chorus of voices: "Find a madman and ask his advice!"

Sam looked up, startled. The circle had grown while Eseza was telling her story. Children were sitting and standing and kneeling and holding other children on their shoulders, all intently listening and watching the young storyteller. Sam had been so fixated on Eseza that she didn't notice the children gathering around them. The look on Eseza's face as she gazed around the circle showed she was equally amazed.

"Tell us another one, please, please!" one girl begged.

"Yes! Please!"

Soon the whole group joined in, making different requests.

"The story of the hippo!" shouted one boy. "Do you know that one?"

"And what about the story of the golden-crested crane? You must tell that one too," called out another.

"No, no, no, no. It is time for bed." Eseza shooed the children away. "Now go to your blanket and close your eye. Take the story with you. Perhaps it will make for the good dream tonight."

The children walked away, disappointed.

"That was a good story, Eseza!" Albin jumped up and down, holding on to her hand. "Are you sure you only want to tell one story? You can whisper one more into my ear. No one has to know you are telling another."

Eseza smiled. "No. It is late, Albin. And you have school tomorrow."

Albin stopped. All of his energy left with his smile as he stared at the ground. "Oh," he said quietly.

Eseza placed the bags at their heads and lay down on the lawn. She patted the ground beside her. "Here, Albin. You lie here in the middle. That way you can protect us."

Albin lay down. He reached into his pants pocket, pulled out his slingshot and a couple of stones, and laid them on the ground beside his head. "For protection," he said. "Just in case."

"I'll sleep well knowing I've got a brave warrior looking out for me," Sam said as she lay down. She smiled at Albin and closed her eyes.

"A man has to protect his wife, you know."

Sam and Eseza laughed.

Chapter 26

Sorrow is like a precious treasure shown
only to friends. ~ African proverb

Sam woke and stared into the sky. It was a perfect blue: bright, clear, crimson-streaked, and totally unfamiliar for a girl who was used to waking up with four blue walls and a ceiling surrounding her. She groaned.

"Our little warrior left something for you," Eseza said as she stirred a pot on the coals. She pointed to Albin's slingshot lying on the ground near where Sam had laid her head that night. "He had to leave early and did not want to wake you. He said you needed it more than he did. Said you were afraid of *jok*." Eseza chuckled. "Now what gave him that idea?"

Sam held the slingshot, pulled back the black rubber tubing, and tested its strength. "Um. Just something that happened when you went out to get the water. I saw something and it scared me."

"Really? You big *muzungu* woman are scared of something? Now what was it?"

Sam hesitated. "Nothing, really. Kind of silly now that you mention it. Let's forget it, okay?" She placed the slingshot in her pants pocket and buttoned it closed.

"Okay. I can do that." Eseza passed a cup filled with a thick brownish liquid to Sam. "Here. It is not much, but it will help us with the many mile we will be footin' today."

Sam sniffed. "Smells good. What is it?"

"It is like the oatmeal, but it is made with the wheat chop. I cook it and add the sugar to make it sweet sweet. It will give us energy for the day."

Sam took a sip. "Yeah. It's good."

"Then hurry and drink. You have missed the sunrise and we are late in leaving."

Sam gulped it down, allowing the warm liquid to take the chill from her body. She looked around. Most of the children had already left. Only a few stragglers were still there, but they were already putting their blankets on their heads and walking back down the road from which they had come.

After washing her cup, Sam placed it in the sack and Eseza helped her set it on her head.

"Is there anywhere I can use a washroom? I

really gotta go," Sam said.

"Wait until we get out of the city. The store do not like to share their washroom with the children. We will be out soon."

Sam followed Eseza until they were past the edge of the town, where the trees became more plentiful and the bush grew denser.

"Here, go in there," she said, pointing into the brush. "I will wait and watch the bag."

Sam placed her bag on the ground. "I don't suppose you have any toilet paper in that bag of yours, do you?"

"No. I am sorry, that is something I lack. You can use the leaf if you want. That is what I use."

Sam walked into the bush.

"It is a good idea to make big loud step when you go into the bush. It warn the animal and the snake you are coming. Then there is less chance of the surprise. The surprise is never good. No."

Sam stopped mid-step. She turned around. "You're kidding me, right?"

Eseza shook her head.

"No, of course you're not." Sam stomped into the bush. "Just me coming in to take a pee, okay? No reason to get upset, everyone. Get out of my way and no one will get hurt. Okay? You hear that, lions and tigers and bears?"

Eseza laughed. "We have no tiger and bear here

in Uganda."

For a second, Sam was silent. "Then that means you have lions, right?"

"Right."

"Oh, shit."

"But I do not think you have to worry. If there were any lion around, they would have gotten you by now."

"Thanks. That's good to know . . . I guess."

Sam heard the sound of an approaching truck. Its brakes squealed.

"There is someone coming, Sam. Stay in the bush."

"Yep. I'm not going anywhere for a while." She peered through a small opening in the bush to the road.

The pick-up truck pulled up beside Eseza, and a tall soldier leaned out his window. He wore camouflage army gear and a black woolen hat on his head. "You are alone, young miss? It is not good for you to be footin' it alone. The LRA are out, and you would make a beautiful wife for some commander. Even Kony himself would like a girl as lovely as you."

Sam stayed as still as she could. She cocked her ear and listened.

"Eeh? No, no sir. My father is in the bush. He is relieving himself. He will be out soon."

"You do not need to lie to me. If you are needing a ride, I can take you to where you want to go. You will be safe safe in the truck with me."

"No, that is very kind of you, sir, but I do not mind the walk. Besides, it is not much farther that I have to go. I will be going now."

Sam detected a slight quaver in Eseza's voice. She stood and pulled up her pants. She heard the truck door opening and heavy footfalls on the stony ground.

"No. I insist. It is my duty to protect the people of Uganda. That is my job."

"*Ojone*, sir." The exasperation in Eseza's voice rose. "Please, let me go!"

Sam crept toward the roadway and looked out. The man stood a few feet in front of her. He held Eseza's wrist with one hand and twisted it behind her back, forcing her toward the truck.

"Prick," Sam said under her breath. She unbuttoned her pants pocket and pulled out the slingshot Albin had left for her. *Thank you, Albin.* She looked on the ground in front of her for a stone. Nothing. She looked behind her. *Where the hell is a stone when you need one? The whole flippin' road is covered with them*. She felt the top pockets of her pants, then the side pockets near her knees. Her eyes lit up. She pulled out a smooth, round, very pink paintball and placed it in the rubber tubing.

Aiming the ball at the man's head, she pulled the rubber back, farther and farther until it couldn't be stretched anymore. She let go.

"Arghh!" The soldier yelled and turned toward the bush. He dropped Eseza's arm and rubbed the back of his neck. He looked at the bright pink paint on his fingers.

Sam reached into her pocket and pulled out another ball. She let it fly.

"Arghh!" The soldier yelled again, covering his nose. "What the?"

Sam shot a third and then a fourth ball, hitting the soldier in the face not just once but twice. He covered his eyes and screamed.

"Hop in the truck!" Sam yelled. She ran out of the bush and kicked the soldier in the groin. He fell to his knees and gasped. Sam grabbed the bags and threw them into the back. She jumped in the driver's seat, while Eseza hopped in and slammed her door. They took off, the tires spinning on the gravel road, shooting up rocks and dust as they sped away.

"Seems to me we've done this before, Eseza. I'm starting to detect a pattern here."

Eseza laughed. "Well, this will make up for all the time you wasted sleeping this morning!"

They rounded a corner and nearly collided with an oncoming truck.

"Get on the other side of the road, Sam!" Eseza yelled as she held on to a handle above the door.

"What's the jerk doing driving on the wrong side of the road?" Sam screamed. She turned her head and glared at the truck as it sped away.

"You are on the wrong side of the road! Not them!"

Sam pulled onto the left side. "Oh," she said calmly. She shifted in her seat and took a deep breath. "I didn't know that." She put her foot down and sped off.

Eseza started to giggle. And then she laughed. She laughed so hard that she held her sides and tears rolled down her face.

"What? What are you laughing about?"

"The UPDF man! You covered his face in pink! How did you do that?"

"Oh, that. Paintballs. Courtesy of my dad and Anarchy Paintball Equipment."

"Paintball? You mean ball filled with paint?"

"Yeah."

"Oh, my dear friend, you are going to have to get me some of those. I think I could make good use of them."

This time Sam laughed. "And you know what the best part is?"

"What is that?"

"I used the high-quality stuff. He ain't getting

that paint off him for a long, long time."

Eseza laughed so hard she snorted.

They came upon a group of children walking along the side of the road dressed in their school uniforms: the boys in shorts, the girls in skirts, and all wearing purple cotton shirts. Each carried their schoolbooks and a small tin can with a rope handle.

Sam slowed as they approached them. "How far is the school from here?" she asked.

"I do not know. Sometime the walk is a mile, sometime it is more."

Sam looked into the distance. There was no sign of the school, only a few huts in the fields. She pulled onto the side of the road and stepped out of the truck. "Want a ride?" she yelled.

The children looked at each other, shrugged, and then ran toward the truck. They piled into the back and sat on the edge, smiling and laughing. "*Apwoyo matek*, miss," they yelled out as Sam got back into the truck.

They continued on their way for a short distance and saw another group of children. Sam stopped. Without her saying anything, the children climbed into the truck. The laughter grew louder. Someone started to sing and the whole group joined in.

They drove another stone's throw and came upon a third group of children. Again Sam stopped, and again the children piled in. Sam looked into the rearview mirror. The box was full; children were sitting on children who were already sitting on children, but no one seemed to care. They sang even louder and waved at the children on the road as they passed by.

"You are too slow, ka-boy, ka-girl!" they yelled. "Run run or you will be late for the school and you will have to sweep the step!"

The children ran, trying to keep up with the truck. Sam drove on for another mile until Eseza pointed into the distance. "It is right here. See in the field?"

Sam slowed, pulled over to the side of the road, and stopped. The children climbed out of the truck and passed by her window. They reached in and shook her hand. Some gave her a high five, while many of the girls curtsied and gave appreciative little smiles. Sam watched them run across the field toward the school. She smiled as she pulled back onto the road and drove away.

"I am wondering now what the children are thinking," Eseza said, shaking her head. "What will they be telling their teacher? They receive a ride to school by a kind *muzungu* miss, dressed in army fatigue, driving a UPDF truck. That story will take some convincing to believe, I am thinking." Eseza laughed.

Sam smiled. "Well, anything to make their day a little brighter." She paused. "So where are we going, anyway?"

"We will take this road until it give us a choice. Then I will decide. I do not know the road that well."

"Sounds fine to me." Sam pulled the window shade down to keep the sun from shining into her eyes.

They drove on in silence past burnt huts, their grass roofs gone and the red clay walls singed black. Women were working in the fields, some with their children tied to their backs, stooped over, tilling the earth with their hoes, planting the seeds in the rich soil.

"That's gotta be hard work," Sam said.

"Yes, it is. And the women will do it all of the day, and then they will cook the meal for their husband and family. Then they will wash the dish, gather more of the water, bathe the children, and put them to bed. And then they will mend the clothing and gather the wood and . . ." Eseza sighed. "And then they will do it all again tomorrow, and the next day, and the next."

They passed by a couple of women sitting at the foot of what Sam thought looked like a miniature red mountain. One woman held a long piece of grass and pushed it into the clay mound.

Another woman stirred the coals under a blackened frying pan.

"They are capturing the termite and cooking them," Eseza explained. "They stick the stiff grass into a hole in the mound and the termite bite onto it with their sharp teeth. Then the women pull out the grass and put them in the frying pan and cook them in the oil."

"Really?" Sam's eyes grew wide. She slowed down to get a better look.

"Yes. It is what many people do when the crop are few and the tree are not giving of the fruit."

"Well, I don't know about you, but I'm getting hungry again, but not for termites, that's for sure." Sam paused. "Hey, take a look in there," she said, pointing to the glove compartment. "Maybe there's something in there we can eat or at least use to barter with in case we find a store."

Eseza pulled the door open and looked inside. She rummaged through the papers and candy wrappers. She gasped and quickly shut the door.

"What did you see?" Sam asked.

"Nothing."

"Nothing?"

"Well, there is a roll of money, but it is not our to take. Besides, we can only use it if there is a store to buy something from, and there are no store here. Not for many mile."

They rounded a curve and came to a clearing on the side of the road where several tin-roofed buildings stood. At the front of each small enclosure was a wooden shelf that opened from the front, revealing the insides of a store of some sort. And on each shelf was food. Lots of food: fruits, vegetables, breads, buns, sweets, drinks, and things the identity of which Sam could only guess at. Her mouth watered and she swallowed.

"Come on," she said. "Grab the money and we'll eat like we haven't eaten before. We'll think of it as a 'sorry' gift from the jerk who wanted to take advantage of you."

"Yes, this is a good good idea, smart *muzungu* Sam," Eseza said as she grabbed the money and stepped out of the truck.

A few minutes later they walked away from the stores carrying two very full bags of fruit and vegetables, buns, and drinks. Sam started the truck, pulled onto the road, and drove away. "Looks like an intersection up ahead," she said. "Which way do we go now?"

Eseza stared out the window. She did not respond.

"Eseza? Which way do we go?"

Sam pulled up to the intersection and stopped the truck. "Eseza?"

Eseza looked down one road and then the other.

She closed her eyes and breathed in. Her voice trembled. "I think it is best that we turn to the right." She looked away and stared out her window.

"Okay, if that's what you think is best."

"Yes . . . that is what I think is best."

Sam glanced at Eseza. She had her back turned to her and her hands over her eyes. "Are you feeling okay?"

Eseza did not respond. Sam turned the truck to the right.

They drove on in silence, past more fields and more women tilling the soil. A father and his son walked along the side of the road, guiding their two cows. Sam glanced at Eseza again. She stared straight ahead, her eyes offering no emotion, her jaw firmly set.

"I think I'm ready to eat. How 'bout you?" Sam asked.

Again there was silence.

"There's a tree up ahead. How 'bout we sit under it and enjoy some shade?"

Eseza continued to stare out the window.

Sam pulled up to the tree and parked the truck behind the large trunk, trying to keep it in the shade as much as possible. She grabbed the bags and sat under the tree. Eseza followed and sat across from her.

"Are you all right, Eseza?"

"Eeh? Yes, I am fine. I am tired, that is all."

"Well, eat first and then you can sleep. I'll keep watch this time. I still have a few paintballs left."

Eseza simply nodded and looked away.

Sam pulled out the food and set it on the ground. She grabbed Eseza's knife from the bag, cut up the tomatoes, and put the slices between some buns. "Here," she said, offering her a bun.

Eseza took a little bite and placed it on her lap. She stared down the road.

"What's bothering you? You've been quiet ever since we turned at the intersection. Come on. You can tell me."

Tears welled up in Eseza's eyes and coursed down her cheeks. She wiped them away, but they continued to flow. She sobbed.

"Hey, hey." Sam knelt beside Eseza and put her arms around her. "It's okay." Sam thought about her mom and the tears she cried after she had died. Sometimes things weren't okay and there was nothing else a person could do but cry, because nothing anyone said could make it better. She said it differently: "Okay. It isn't fine. But I'm here. Tell me what's going on. I'm a good listener."

"Not right now." Eseza stood and walked into the field and sat in the tall grass.

Sam nibbled on her bun and took a drink from her soda. She looked into the sky and watched the sun climb to its peak. Leaning against the tree, she closed her eyes for a moment and then suddenly sat up.

She looked at the sun and then at the road. "The sun rises in the east and sets in the west. So that would make this east," she said, holding out her right hand, "and that would make this way west." She held out her left. "Then this would be north and that would be south." Sam paused. "Then why are we going south? Charlie said he would meet us up north at the refugee camp, if he returned."

Sam looked at the truck. Even from the road someone would see it behind the tree.

She walked over to Eseza, knelt at her side, and tapped her on the shoulder. "Eseza, I think we'd better get going. It's not safe to be out here with the truck."

Eseza stared into the distance.

"And I think we're going the wrong way. Look, the sun's going to the west right now, so that means we're heading south. And I heard Charlie say that your son is in a refugee camp to the north."

"No," Eseza replied. "We are going the right way. We are going south."

"But the camp's in the north. Aren't we going to get your son there?"

Eseza's voice cracked. "No. We are not going to the camp, and I am not going to get my son."

"But why? What are you planning on doing? Are we going north later?"

"No. Never."

"But—"

"Did you see the look on Jonasan face when I told him I was a wife of one of the commander?" Eseza glared. "Did you see the disgust that filled his eye?"

Sam shook her head.

"Oh yes you did. You saw it. Now imagine if he or anyone was to find out that Maisha is Kony son. Can you not see what would happen to Maisha life?" Eseza's voice got louder. Her eyes widened. "He would be ostracized by everyone from every town and village. He would be labeled as the son of the man who killed many many people. He would be seen as evil and horrid, possessed by the *jok*, never to be trusted, always to be feared. Do you not see this?"

"No, I mean, I never thought about it. I mean, sure he's Kony's son, but that doesn't mean he's going to be like his father. And people should know that, shouldn't they?"

Eseza snorted. "Hmph! You have a lot to learn of the Ugandan way, *muzungu* woman."

Sam was silent. She couldn't believe what she was hearing. Eseza abandoning her child? A memory replayed itself—a scene that came to life every night before she went to bed or when she walked into the house or when she looked at her dad or when she washed the dishes or . . .

"Dad! Dad!" Sam screamed. She ran down the hallway, past the gurneys and the doctors, and through the emergency doors.

"Dad!" she screamed. "Where's Mom? Where's Mom?"

Her dad wrapped his arms around her, unable to speak.

"Dad!" she screamed. "What happened? What happened?"

He pulled her away from the door and tried to soothe her. "It's not a good time for you to see her right now. It's not—"

"Mom!" she screamed.

Sam grabbed Eseza's hands and held them tight. "But you can't just abandon him like that. Maybe you can take him away somewhere, and the two of you could live alone and you could tell people his father's dead."

"Live alone? Do you hear what you are saying? Do you even know how hard it is to survive here? I do not have a job. I do not have the schooling. I cannot raise a child by myself and work."

"But you could make it work out. I know you can. You can't leave him. You're his mother. He needs you. He needs you! A child needs his mother!"

Sam squeezed her eyes shut. The image in her mind was like a 3D movie seen from the front row.

"Mom!" she screamed.

Her dad held her tight.

"Mom!" she screamed.

He whispered into her ear. "I'm sorry. I'm sorry."

"Mom! I love you! Don't you know that? Don't you know that?"

Sam opened her eyes.

Eseza pulled her hands away. "I know a child need his mother. Do not look at me like I do not have a heart." She glared at Sam. "Do you not see that this is hard hard for me to do? Do you think I want to leave Maisha? Of course I do not. But it is for the best. Salume will raise him like he is her own, and no one will be the wiser of who he is and who is the father."

The scene in Sam's mind fast-forwarded.

"Why, Dad. Why?"

"I don't know, Sam. I don't know."

Sam had to think. She had to say something to change Eseza's mind. "But you'll know, Eseza. You'll know every day that you abandoned him. And every day you'll think of him and wonder how he is and what he looks like. No, you can't leave him. For his sake and yours."

Eseza's eyes brimmed with tears that rolled down her cheeks.

"Come on." Sam grabbed her hand and pulled her up. "Let's go back to the camp and find your son. It'll all work out. We'll make it work."

Sam led her to the truck and opened the door. Eseza crawled into the cab and sat while Sam gathered the food and put it inside. She started up the engine and turned the truck around. She drove north.

Eseza stared out the window in silence. They drove past the row of tiny stores and past the fields. The sun started to make its way across the sky. Its beams shone through Sam's window. She wiped the tiny beads of sweat from her face.

"I cannot help but think you have spoken this way to me because you have the experience in your heart, my dear Sam."

"Yes, I do."

"And why is that? Were you abandoned?"

"Yes. No. Sort of." Sam paused. "My mother abandoned me when she committed suicide. And I know it's not the same. Not really. But I feel abandoned. I feel like my mom didn't love me enough to want to live. That her love for me wasn't stronger than the depression. Otherwise she would have fought it and won."

"But I want to stay with Maisha. It is just . . . I

cannot."

"But you see, Eseza, there will come a day when Maisha will learn the truth, that the woman who's raising him isn't his mother, and he'll wonder why you left him. And all kinds of thoughts will fill his mind and he'll come up with one conclusion: my mother didn't love me." Sam paused. "And do you want Maisha to think that?"

"No."

"Then let's go to the refugee camp and find him."

Eseza glanced at Sam and stared at her hands folded on her lap. "You must think I am a horrid mother for wanting to leave Maisha."

"No. I don't. I think you were doing what you thought was right because you love him."

"Yes, I do love him. I think Maisha is what keep me strong through all this. He is what give me hope. I think the love between a mother and her child is very strong." Eseza looked up at Sam. "You agree, yes?"

Sam stared straight ahead, using the road as her distraction. "I'm not too sure about that sometimes." She paused, searching for the right words. "I mean, right now I hate my mom. I mean, I really hate her."

"Of course you do, dear Sam. It must be hard hard for you. But there must be time you love her too. There must be some good time you think about that make you feel the sun on your face and make you smile."

"Yes, of course there are."

"Then can you not accept that with the love come the dirt also?"

"The dirt?"

"Yes, the dirt. We have a saying here in Uganda. 'He who love, love you with all your dirt.'"

"Well, I sure got my share of dirt from my mom."

"Yes, you did, dear Sam. But perhaps in time you will be able to forgive her for taking her life. Perhaps you will come to understand this depression and what made your mother do this. But in the meantime you can hate her and love her." She reached over and squeezed Sam's hand.

Sam offered her a half smile. "Dirt and all, eh? I suppose I can do that. Just wish I didn't feel like I was buried up to my neck in shit, you know?"

Eseza laughed.

They drove on, past the fields, past the huts, feeling the heat of the afternoon sun on their faces. The truck began to slow, and the engine sputtered and it coasted to a stop. Sam pushed her foot on the gas, but the engine had died. She looked at the gas gauge. "Great. We're out of gas. Guess this is as far as we can go."

Eseza jumped out of the truck, grabbed the black bag from the back, and put it on her head. "Are you coming?" she called out to Sam.

"Are you coming?"

Sam sat bolt upright. She stared at the four walls around her. Faint blue, curtains, a thin green blanket, a trunk at the end of her bed.

A knock sounded at her door.

"I said, are you coming to the museum with me this morning? You told me last night you wanted to help Dr. Roget set up the displays. I'm leaving in thirty minutes if you still want to come."

Sam stared at the pieces of the wooden box on the floor, and then at the leather sack of stones by her pillow. She opened her hand. A pile of black sand lay in her palm. She looked out her bedroom window as the sunbeams crept into her room, filling it with morning light.

She was home.

Chapter 27

*Do not look where you fell, but where
you slipped. ~ African proverb*

"Sam? Sam? Are you all right?" Sam's dad
knocked on the door again. He pushed the door
open and stood in the doorway. Sam shook her head
and wiped the dust off her hands.

"I'm . . . I'm fine, Dad." Her voice shook. "Just
had a long, crazy dream, I guess. Took me a while
to wake up, that's all."

"Okay, just checking." He walked into her
bedroom. "What's this?" he asked as he bent down
and looked at the pieces of the wooden box on the
floor.

"Oh, that," Sam said, trying to clear her head.
"It was a box . . . sort of a puzzle box. I found it
with the uh, artifacts last night. I left it on the table
and wanted to show it to you 'cause it wasn't

categorized with the rest of the items, but"—Sam rubbed her hand across her face—"we got busy with the coffin. You must have put your papers on it and accidentally brought it home last night in your briefcase. And when I was looking through it for the papers you gave us last night, I found the box."

"And you broke it? Sam, that's museum property! How could you?"

"But I didn't break it. I told you, it's like a puzzle. I can put it back together."

"This is not good. Not good at all." He gathered the pieces and tried to match one piece up with the other.

"It's like this." Sam took the diagram she had drawn and showed it to her dad. "This piece here goes into this one like this, but to hold it in place you need this piece here."

He took another piece and tried to match it up.

"No, that one won't work there, Dad. You see the slot here? It's facing into the box. You need one with a slot that faces to the outside of the box, like this one." Sam fit another piece into the puzzle.

The tone in his voice changed from anxious to astonished. "You amaze me, Sam. You've got quite the brain in there, you know?"

They worked on the box together until, finally, Sam held up the completed box and passed it to her dad.

"Oh, wow," he said, turning it over and over, examining the carvings of the animals. "You know what this is, Sam? It's an ancient Egyptian puzzle box, called a loghz box. They were used as a sort of safe. The owner would keep something very valuable inside because he knew it was well protected."

"Protected? How? Anyone could smash it with a hammer and open it."

"Well, if my memory serves me correctly, they would perform some sort of a ritual that would seal the box and curse anyone who opened it."

"Guess I'm cursed then, eh Dad?"

"Yes. Quite cursed. You'll be scrubbing the floors in the museum for this one. But I want to know: was there anything in there when you opened it?"

Sam glanced at the stones on her pillow. Her dad followed her gaze.

He picked up one of the stones and examined it. "Is this what you found?"

She nodded. "They were inside the sack."

"This is amazing! You know what you have here?"

Sam hesitated. "No."

"They're talismans for an ancient Egyptian pharaoh. They believed these stones had great powers only the pharaoh was able to harness."

gz box tells me they weren't thought of as ordinary talismans. Nope, you've found something really interesting here." Her dad paused. "Come on, hurry up and get ready. We can show it to Dr. Roget. She should be arriving at the museum for the setup as soon as we get there." He took the box and stones and walked to the bedroom door. "And have a shower and get changed. You don't smell that good." He left the room.

"This is way too weird," Sam mumbled. She ran her finger over the coarse grains of sand that lay on the floor and rubbed them between her fingers. She stared at the faint rope burns on her wrists. "Way, way, way too weird."

She looked at the trunk at the end of her bed. Opening the lid, she looked inside and stroked the paintball medal that lay on top of her blanket. "Dirt and all, huh Mom? Dirt and all."

She walked into the bathroom and turned the shower on full throttle.

*   *   *   *

The warehouse in the back of the museum seemed eerily quiet and surreal. Although Sam had just been there last night—or was it a couple of days

318

ago?—it felt like it had been years. She sipped her coffee, hoping it would somehow settle her nerves, but it didn't. It was like she was in a daze, a dream, and nothing around her seemed real. She found her dad near the side counter, talking to a woman, and walked over.

"Dr. Roget, this is my daughter, Sam. She's here to help you set up the displays, if that's okay with you."

Dr. Roget shook Sam's hand. "Of course. I'd love the help." She turned to a table behind her and picked up the puzzle box Sam's dad had brought back to the museum. "This is impressive, Sam. It takes quite the skill to be able to open a loghz box. Many an archeologist has been driven mad trying to figure out how to open them. As a matter of fact, I remember a colleague of mine wanting to smash one open with the fossilized femur of an ornithopod, he was so frustrated."

Sam's dad laughed.

"But there's something else that's odd about the box, Jim. I've never seen it before, and I've worked at the museum for over twenty years now. And I didn't see it when I packed the crates either. Look"—she took the inventory sheets from a file— "there's no loghz box listed here."

"Maybe it fell in there somehow. You know, someone knocked it in there accidentally."

"But"—she pulled out her phone and showed them a message—"no one else at the museum has seen it before either. And Frank in shipping and handling said he never saw it, let alone placed it in the crate to ship here. It's like it magically appeared."

Sam caught her breath. "Yes, magically," she stammered.

"Unless . . ." Dr. Roget tapped the edge of the table with her finger. "Unless Frank threw it in there as a joke or something. Be just like him to try to mess with me. Put me on a wild goose chase, trying to figure out where it came from. He probably got an old box from a toy store, rubbed some dirt on it, threw some old stones in it from a children's rock collection, and tossed it in the crate." Dr. Roget examined the box again. "And yet, this looks pretty authentic . . . but like I said, it would be just like Frank to pull a stunt like this."

"Well, I'm taking a picture of it and putting it on the Canadian Archeological Association website. Joke or no joke, this is too good not to share. And who knows, maybe someone will have some info about it." He took the box from Dr. Roget and passed it to Sam. "Here, you hold it for the photo. You found it."

As Sam held the box, her dad emptied the four stones from the sack and placed them in her other hand.

He noticed the marks on her wrists. "What happened here, Sam?" he said as he gently touched the red abrasions.

Sam's mind raced. "Uh, probably from paintballing yesterday. I don't remember."

"Looks rough there. Make sure you keep them clean, eh?"

"Yeah," she said. "Sure."

"There, now just tilt your hands toward me so I can see everything. And smile. Try not to look so dead."

Sam forced a smile while her dad took the photo.

"Great," Dr. Roget said. "And just to play along with Frank, I'll put it in this protective case and bring it back to the museum in Toronto when I head back tonight. I'll feign total ignorance, tell him I think it's some ancient loghz box. And then, with the help of your diagram, Sam, I'll open it up. And Frank will stand there dumbfounded, wondering how the heck I did it." She rubbed her hands together. "Oh, for once I'll get him. I can't wait to see the look on his face."

Sam stared at Dr. Roget. Her breath caught in her throat.

"Could you send me the diagram you drew, Sam? Here, I'll give you my e-mail address." She took a pen from the table, wrote it on a scrap piece of paper, and handed it to Sam.

Sam took the paper and stammered, "Yeah, I can do that."

"Well, we've got work to do. Let's get going."

Sam glanced at the box on the table, then followed Dr. Roget out the door and into the museum to where the carts they had filled the night before lay waiting. Dazed, she stopped and stared at the carts. *I did this last night?* she thought. *No way—it couldn't have been only last night.* She took another long sip from her cup.

Dr. Roget picked up a falcon-headed canopic jar from the cart. "Now when you're setting up a display like this, you need to ensure that the pieces are arranged according to theme and progress from beginning to end."

Sam tried to concentrate on what Dr. Roget was saying. She felt a million cobwebs grow in her head. She felt dizzy, confused, and totally disorientated.

"The first pieces we'll display relate to Egyptian life. Items like the wall paintings you have there," she said, pointing to a cart beside the far wall, "and the stone panels over there will be part of that. The second display will focus more on death and the afterlife. That's where we'll set up the canopic jars, funerary masks, and the other items found specifically in the tombs. Then there'll be the coffins. That's set up at the end. That way we save the best 'til last."

Sam closed her eyes. An image of Eseza popped into her mind. She was telling the story about the nasty king and the blacksmith and the crazy man. The children were watching her, holding on to every word, every scowl, every fearful look or mad, crazed face. She heard the children shout, "Find a madman and ask his advice!" Her eyes opened wide and she grabbed a hold of the back of a chair. The room began to spin.

"Are you okay, Sam?"

Sam felt the blood drain from her face.

"You need to sit down."

"No. No. That's okay. I think I just need some fresh air. I'm going to sit down outside for a bit. I'll be fine." She walked out the front doors, sat on the steps, and inhaled deeply. A group of tourists was stepping out of a bus and making its way to the museum.

Crazy Bill inched his way down the stairs and put his cup out. "Need ta change. Need ta change," he said over and over again.

A couple of passersby dropped in a few coins.

"Ah po' you. Ah po' you," he called out to them, smiling.

Sam rested her head on her knees and closed

323

her eyes. She listened to the sound of more coins hitting the bottom of the metal cup and Crazy Bill's idiotic responses.

I'm going to go crazy, she thought. *If I don't figure this out, I'm going to end up like Bill saying, 'Ah po' you. Ah po' you.'* She paused. She had heard that before. *Wait. "Ah, poor you."* She shook her head. *No. There's no way, Sam. You've heard it before 'cause he says it all the time. All the friggin' time.*

She drew in another deep breath. *Okay, Sam. Let's start at the beginning.*

She replayed the whole adventure in her mind: *All right, first I was at home with the stones. Then I was in a hut in Africa . . . with Eseza. Then they tied me up.* Sam stared at the faint rope burns on her wrists. *Then there were all of the child soldiers— and Squirrel. How can I forget him? And Naboth. Oh, I wonder if he's alive. And then,* Sam thought, laughing, *that wild ride down the side of that mountain and landing in the river and floating. And the croc!* Sam felt the small of her back and flinched. *Yep, I didn't dream that, either. Then the long walk . . . shit, that was long. How many miles did we trudge on for? And then meeting Charlie and the Arrow Boys. And the walk to Gulu. And Albin. How could I forget Albin?* She felt a bump in her pants pocket and pulled the slingshot out. She ran her finger over the polished wood, smiled, and tucked it back inside. *And stealing that truck.* Sam laughed again. *But . . .* Her throat tightened and her mind filled with panic. *Eseza—where is she? Is she still on the side of the road where I left her? Is she looking for me?* Sam thought about the pile of sand left in her hand. *Is all the magic used up? Is that why I came back? Did I change?*

I know it was real, she thought. *I can't deny it, but . . . but how can you believe something's real when the sane part of you thinks you're crazy?*

Sam opened her eyes and nearly jumped out of her skin. Crazy Bill was sitting beside her with his tin cup.

He rubbed his finger over her wrists. "Ah po' you. Ah po' you." He held both of her hands in his own as tears came to his eyes. "Ah po' you. Ah po' you."

Sam was too startled to do anything. She stared at Crazy Bill, more than a little bewildered. He stood and gently placed his hand on her shoulder, then walked back to his spot.

Now that was weird. She took in a long, deep breath and let it out. *Come on, Sam. You have to get with it.* She held on to the wall as she stood, then walked back into the museum. As she pushed the door open, she met Dr. Roget.

"I was just coming out to see if you're all right.

325

Are you feeling better?"

"Yeah, I needed some fresh air. I'm fine."

"Good, because I need some help setting up the coffin. Jake is coming to help, but I need another set of strong arms to position the clear case that covers it. You up to it?"

"Yeah, no problem."

They returned to the display room and found Jake examining the paintings on the coffin. He glanced up. "Dr. Roget, I don't really know much about ancient Egypt, but just looking at these symbols and pictures, I'd say they tell a story. Perhaps the king's life story. Is that true?"

"Well, not exactly a story. More like protection. The Egyptians believed the artwork would come to life in the afterworld and help the pharaoh journey from one place to another. You see these eyes?" Dr. Roget pointed to two painted eyes at chest level on the coffin. "They helped the king see out of the coffin into the afterlife. Sort of like a window."

"And this scarab beetle, here," she said, pointing to a round insect, "is likened to the cross in the Christian religion. It's a symbol of . . ."

Sam tuned out Dr. Roget's and Jake's conversation as she walked around the coffin and examined the paintings. There were seven rows— well, sort of rows—of images. She recognized some of the figures from stories she had read as a child, ancient tales of Egyptian gods and goddesses who ruled the earth and the skies and protected—or wreaked havoc on—the people. There was Isis, the goddess of children and protector of the dead, and Nephthys, Isis's sister, another protector, and the four sons of Horus, whose heads decorated the top of the canopic jars.

Sam thought for a moment. It was interesting how ancient stories that were once held as sacred truths by the Egyptians were now labeled as myths and legends. Simple children's stories.

She looked at the next row. At the beginning of the row the king sat on his throne, looking down on a line of people, each holding something in their hands, their arms outstretched as if offering the king gifts. A man was holding what appeared to be a lion's head, another held out a headdress, another carried a crook and flail, and at the end, carrying a box, was a young boy.

Sam stopped and looked closer at the row. Each of the bronze faced men carried a gift to the pharaoh but the boy who held the box was black. Black face, black chest, black legs. She leaned in closer. Even though the box he held was small, the artist who had decorated the coffin had painstakingly painted tiny lines to show the carvings along its sides. One carving looked like an elephant, another like a lion,

and another like some sort of horned antelope or
deer.

The hairs on the back of Sam's neck began to
tingle. This was too strange. This could only be a
weird coincidence, nothing more. It couldn't
possibly be the same box.

"Sam?"

She looked up at Dr. Roget.

"Sam? I asked if you could lift the end of the
cover."

"Oh, sure. Sorry. I was just . . . Never mind,
I've got it."

Sam and Jake lifted the clear plastic cover and
placed it over the coffin. Dr. Roget locked the sides
in place.

"Thanks, Jake. I'll call you if we need any
more help. Let's get to work on the displays now,
okay, Sam?"

Sam nodded.

The rest of the morning went by quite
smoothly. They spaced out display stands on the
floor and arranged and rearranged the artifacts.
They set up exhibit cards next to the items, and all
the while Dr. Roget filled Sam's head with all sorts
of interesting pieces of information about each
piece. When lunchtime came, Sam's brain ached
with data overload.

Dr. Roget fixed up a display card and looked at

the time on her phone. "Look at that. It's noon already. Your dad invited me for lunch at a restaurant across the street from here. Are you coming with us?"

Sam arched her back and yawned. "Um, no. Thanks, though. I'll get something here."

"Are you sure?"

"Yeah, I'm pretty tired. Didn't sleep well last night. Think I'll find a pile of shipping blankets and have a little nap."

Dr. Roget laughed. "You go ahead. I'll meet you here when you're ready."

Sam walked down the hallway toward the staff room, passing the First Nations and fur trade displays, until she stood in front of the gift shop. After checking out the limited selection of chips, she chose a large bag of extra-hot jalapeno nachos and a root beer. She set her choices on the counter and reached into her pocket for some money.

"I'll be right there!" a cashier yelled out.

"Take your time!" Sam called back.

She glanced at the various baskets on the counter filled with knickknacks and souvenirs: dinosaur key chains, snowshoe refrigerator magnets, totem pole bottle openers, and polished rocks of many different sizes, shapes, and colors.

Sam dug her hand into the pile of rocks and took a closer look. There were a few deep purple ones and some of a unique mustard-yellow hue. Some were the same color as a Christmas tree—not a dark green, but the sort of green you'd see in the springtime when all of the buds opened and revealed their new growth.

Sam turned a green stone around in her fingers. A faint smile flickered across her face. She placed it on the counter and sifted through the pile of rocks again. Before the cashier came to the counter, Sam had four polished green stones hidden in the pocket of her jeans.

Best not to leave any leads, she thought. *Besides, it's just borrowing for a long time.*

The cashier rang her through. "Is that everything?"

"Yep."

Sam stuffed a handful of chips in her mouth and walked down the hall. Without missing a step, she tucked the bag under her arm, opened her soda, and took a long drink. She let out a huge belch. "Good one, Sam," she said, laughing as she pushed the supply room door open.

She glanced around the room. Everyone had gone out for lunch.

"Perfect." She pulled a chair up to the counter and stuffed another handful of chips in her mouth. She wiped her hands on her jeans, took another sip of her soda, and grabbed the protective container

Dr. Roget had placed on the counter earlier that morning. After opening it up, she pulled out the loghz box and the sack of stones, setting them on the table. She glanced at the doors and listened. It was quiet. The only sound came from the speakers that played a classical music station over the intercom.

She opened the sack and emptied the stones into the palm of her hand. She ran her fingers over their smooth surface, picked one up, and held it to the light. A faint silvery line shimmered across it. She closed her eyes and began to wrap her fingers around the stone.

"They're quite beautiful, aren't they?"

Sam jumped. She dropped the stones on the counter and turned around.

Dr. Roget walked toward her, picked up a stone, and held it to the light. "Never seen anything quite like it myself. But then again, I'm not much of a rock and gem expert. I was hoping someone from the museum could help me identify them." She set the stone down and picked up another. She enclosed it in her fist and held it for a moment.

Sam stared at Dr. Roget and then at the stone. She stifled a gasp.

"And they feel so cool to the touch, don't they?" The doctor placed the stone back in the sack.

Sam blinked. "Yeah, I noticed that myself," she

stammered.

"Your dad couldn't make it for lunch. He got called away for something. Mind if I join you here? I thought maybe you could show me how the box works." She picked it up and examined it. "Here," she said, passing it to Sam.

Sam took the box and turned it over. "See this piece here? It's the center of the whole box. Each piece connects to it in one way or another. Here, let me show you."

Sam held the center piece with one finger and then pulled at an adjoining piece with her other hand. "Now I've removed the first barrier, but if I try to pull it any farther, nothing will happen because each puzzle piece has a sort of a ridge to it that attaches to another opposing piece. See?" She held the box up so Dr. Roget could take a closer look.

"Oh, I get it," the doctor said.

"So what I need to do is pull this one while I twist this one here, and then pull this one way over here." Sam twisted and maneuvered the pieces. A piece dropped to the ground, then another and another. The whole box collapsed in Sam's hands, and she placed the pieces on the table.

"That is so amazing. How did you figure it out?"

Sam shrugged. "I don't know. Just made sense

to me. That's all."

"Do you think you could put it all back together for me?"

"Sure."

Sam found the center piece and began to put the box together.

"But how about I put the sack of stones back inside before you close it up? Then it'll be the same as when you found it."

Dr. Roget took the sack and placed the rest of the stones inside. She put the sack in the half-completed box. "There. Now if you could close it up, I'll take it to my car so I don't forget it."

Sam stared at the sack of stones and then looked up at Dr. Roget. "Are you sure? It's perfectly safe here," she said. She felt a lump growing in her throat.

"Oh, I know. But as I'm getting older, I'm getting more and more forgetful. I've learned if anything needs to be done it's best to do it now while I remember."

Sam picked up another piece of the box and inserted it. "Ah, okay. Whatever you say." She added another piece to the box and then another.

Dr. Roget hovered over her shoulder. "Ah! I get it. Now you add this piece here." She offered it to Sam.

"Yeah, that's the right one," Sam said as she

inserted the piece.

A couple of minutes later she had completed the box and placed it in its protective case.

Dr. Roget tucked the case under her arm and walked to the door. "Thanks, Sam!" she called out. "I'll meet you at the display room in a few minutes." She walked out the door.

"Ah, you're welcome." Sam dropped her head into her hands and let out a long groan. "There's got to be a plan B. There's always a plan B."

She got up, threw another handful of chips in her mouth, took a gulp of her root beer, then walked out into the hallway. Again she ambled past the First Nations display and the fur trade exhibit, then stood for a few minutes watching a couple of tourists posing with the stuffed black bear that stood on its hind legs, its mouth wide open, showing its sharp teeth.

When Sam finally entered the display room, Dr. Roget was already back at work, setting up another display case. "I'm still thinking about that loghz box, Sam. As real as it looks, I can't help but think it's Frank up to his usual tricks again. Whatever the case, I'll let you know. I can e-mail your dad as soon as I find out."

"Sure," Sam said. "That would be great."

They worked for a few more hours, and all the while Sam racked her brain, trying to come up with a plan B. But anything she thought of she quickly dismissed because, one, she assumed Dr. Roget wouldn't leave anything so valuable in an unlocked car, and two, she didn't have a clue as to how to break into a car, and three, she didn't think she'd look good in stripes and leg irons anyway.

As they were beginning to set up the last display, Dr. Roget looked deep in thought. "Hmm. I can't seem to recall how this was done." She placed a statue of a bull-headed man carrying a sun disk between his horns on a stand, moved it to another stand, and then paused. "Hey, Sam. Can you get my camera from my purse? It's under that chair. I need to see how this display was set up at our museum. I seem to have forgotten how I put it together."

Sam rummaged through her purse. *Day planner . . . change purse . . . credit card holder . . . package of gum . . . keys . . .* She stared at the keys. This was her plan B. She looked over her shoulder. Dr. Roget had her back turned to her. She grabbed the keys and put them in her jacket pocket. Then she found the camera and brought it over to Dr. Roget.

"Do you mind if I go outside for another breath of fresh air? I'm feeling a bit dizzy again."

"Sure. Go ahead. I'll be here for a while."

Sam walked out of the room, past the reception desk, and through the outside doors. She pulled the keys out of her pocket and quickly found the car key.

"Okay, *muzungu* Sam. Let's do this."

She walked up and down the rows of cars, pausing in front of each one briefly while she clicked the door-open button and listened. She didn't dare click the lock button twice and listen for a honk—that would draw too much attention. She went down one row, then another, and another until she stood in front of a light blue Toyota Corolla and heard a click. She smiled.

Glancing in the car, she saw the case sitting on the floor of the passenger side. She opened the door and slid into the driver's seat.

"Okay, plan B," she whispered.

She pulled the box out of the case and found the center piece. "Now. Take this one and pull here, and then this one, and this one, and—"

The box fell apart and landed in a heap on her lap. She grabbed the sack of stones and emptied them into her hand and pushed them into her pocket. Without missing a beat, she took the stones she had stolen from the store and put them into the pouch. She searched through the pile and found the center piece.

"Now where are you?" she mumbled as she looked for the next piece. "There you are!"

She put the two pieces together.

"And the next one . . ."

The box started to take shape.

"And . . . shit!" Sam swore under her breath. The box collapsed. Pieces fell on her lap and onto the floor.

There was a knock on the door window. Sam froze. She turned her head and stared. Crazy Bill stared back at her. He grinned a somewhat toothless grin and nodded. "Ah po' you, ah po' you," he repeated. He brought his hands up to his mouth and blew her a kiss.

Sam blinked. "You are one weird dude, Crazy Bill," she said. She turned her attention back to the box. She gathered the fallen pieces from the floor. Then she fumbled through the pile again, found the center piece, and attached the second, third, and fourth. Finally, the box was near completion. She placed the sack of stones in it and fitted the rest of the pieces. She breathed a sigh of relief.

When the box was safely tucked back inside its protective cover, she got out of the car, closed the door, and pressed the lock button. She patted her pocket, feeling the stones, and walked back to the museum.

Crazy Bill sat under the shade of the overhang, leaning against the glass wall with his knees tucked up to his chest. His head hung over his legs and he looked very much asleep. He opened one eye. "Ah po' you. Ah po' you," he said with a huge smile.

Sam glanced in his direction and paused. She shook her head. *Don't even go there, Sam. Don't even go there.* She walked into the museum and came face to face with Dr. Roget.

"Well, I'm all done, Sam. The display looks great, thanks to you."

"It was a real pleasure." Sam gave her a hug and dropped the keys into her purse. "And thanks for coming all the way out here to help us. Be sure to let me know about the loghz box and the stones."

"Will do, Sam."

Sam held the door open. Dr. Roget walked out of the museum and went straight to her car. Sam turned and walked back into the museum.

"Sam!"

Her heart raced. "Oh shit. You are so caught, Sam," she muttered.

She turned around as her dad called out to her from the reception desk. "Come and see this."

She leaned over the counter.

"Remember that photo I posted of you and the box on the Canadian Archeological Association website? Well, we've already got some responses. Look," he said, pointing to the screen. "Here's one who says he believes the stones are an unusual form of green apatite found only in Mozambique. And here's another one who says he's seen a very similar box in a museum in Botswana. And then there's . . ."

Sam skimmed over the various comments listed below her picture with the headline, LONDON GIRL SAM WALLACE FINDS LOGHZ BOX AND RARE STONES. "What a great find . . ." "Fascinating . . ." "I believe the wood used to make the box is a rare type of mahogany . . ." Finally, she came to one that made her stop short. She gasped and held her hand to her mouth.

"How's Charlie?" it said.

It was signed "Scott."

Chapter 28

The friends of our friends are our friends.
~ Congolese proverb

It was the third time that day that Sam had sat on the museum steps, and it was the third time she felt she was really going crazy. She stared at Crazy Bill and a shudder went down her spine. "Great, I'm going to be sitting beside Bill any day now, with my very own tin cup." Crazy Bill looked back at her, then turned his gaze to two teenage boys walking up the stairs. One, tall, broad shouldered, and with cropped black hair, wore an old AC/DC shirt. The other, who had a smaller build, ran his fingers through his blond hair. Crazy Bill smiled at them.

They paused, looked at Sam, then at each other, shrugged, and continued up the stairs. When they were a couple of steps away from her, they stopped and stared at her.

After an awkward silence the boy with the blond hair cleared his throat. "Are you Sam? Sam Wallace?" he asked as he glanced at her hands.

Sam pulled her sleeves over her rope burns. "Yeah, I am. Who wants to know?"

The teen continued. "You're the one in the photo. With the stones, right?"

Sam shook her head. "Photo? What?" At last she realized what he was talking about. "Yeah. That's me. Who wants to know?"

"I'm Scott. Scott Romo. I saw your photo on the Canadian Archeological Association website this morning. You were holding a box and four green stones."

Sam did a double take. "Scott? As in 'How's Charlie?' Scott?"

"Yeah, that's me."

Sam inhaled sharply. She blinked. "Holy shit. This cannot be happening. This cannot be happening."

Scott continued. "We were wondering. Well, not really wondering. We . . . well—"

"Get to the point, Scotty. There's four stones in the photo, and she has rope burns around her wrists. It couldn't be more obvious." He stared down at Sam. "I'm Bruce. And—"

"Oh, my God. Bruce. The angel. You're the one who helped Charlie."

Bruce laughed.

She turned to Scott. "And you're the one who gave Charlie the stone to give to Kony. Charlie told me all about you."

Scott looked relieved. "Yes. That's us."

Bruce nodded. "Okay. So everyone knows each other. Let's get on with it. Tell us, how's Charlie?"

Sam looked around. "I don't know. It's been a couple of days since I saw him. But let's go somewhere private where we can talk. I need you to explain some things to me. About the stones, that is. And I can tell you everything I know."

"Yeah," Scott said while Bruce nodded.

Sam led the way into the museum, then into the empty staff room, and closed the door behind them. "You first," she said as she sat down. "Right from the beginning."

Bruce and Scott each took a seat across from her.

Scott told the story of the stones, starting from where he had found them in the hands of a skeleton to the very end when he had given Charlie the final stone and disappeared. He also told the story Blandine had shared with him that night, when he saw the same stones on her necklace at the hotel; about the woman who wept over a fire and a spirit who gave her and her two children each a set of stones. When Scott didn't know certain details, Bruce added the necessary information. All the while Sam listened intently, interrupting with only an occasional "Oh, my!" or "You have got to be kidding!" or "Now that makes sense."

After telling the story, Scott and Bruce leaned back in their chairs and grinned.

"Kinda weird, eh?" Bruce said.

"Yeah. Real weird." Sam nodded. "But how did you know the stones in my box were the same as the stones in your sack?"

"Wasn't hard," Scott replied. "I just did a close-up of the photo on the website and noticed a thin line of silver over the green polished surface. And we saw the marks on your wrists and figured they probably came from a rope, tied tight. LRA style. You know. Pretty easy to figure it out, especially with there being only four stones in your hand."

"Yeah, good thinking," Sam said. "But what were you doing on the Canadian Archeological Association website?"

"My dad's an archeologist and, well, I like checking things out on there now and then."

"Oh."

"So we told our parents we were staying at each other's house for the night, hopped on the next

Greyhound bus from Toronto to London, took a city bus, and here we are. Now tell us, what happened when the stone took you to Uganda?"

Sam told her story. She began with her discovery of the box and the stones, and then told Scott and Bruce about finding herself in a mud hut with Eseza tied to a pole. She recalled the fear she had felt when a commander said she would be given as a "gift" to a general in Sudan, and she spoke of watching Naboth being tied to a tree, beaten and bloodied and unable to move. Sam wondered aloud if he was still alive. When she described the moment she and Eseza escaped in the truck and the encounter with the crocodile on the river, Scott and Bruce shook their heads in amazement.

"You are one tough woman, Sam," Bruce said with a smile.

A hint of red came to Sam's cheeks. She continued. "We walked and walked on through the day and into the night, and that's when I met Charlie. He told me all about you guys, and he called you"—she tilted her head toward Bruce—"his 'angel'."

Bruce chuckled.

Scott smiled. "Some angel," he said.

"But he couldn't tell me much about the stones. I wanted to know how they worked so I could figure out a way to get back, but he couldn't tell me anything—just that one time, Scott, you knew you were going to leave and you told Charlie to give the last stone to Kony. And he also—"

"And did he?" Bruce said. "Did he give the stone to Kony?"

"Yeah. He said he did. He said that the stones had the power to change people. That they changed you, Scott. He said . . . he said you were 'stupid' at first, and that while you were in Uganda you learned how to think and weren't stupid anymore."

"Really?" Scott said. "He really said that?"

"Yeah."

Bruce laughed.

"And he said the same thing about you, too."

Bruce stopped laughing. The boys stared at each other and shrugged.

"But that was all I could learn about the stones. I had to leave with Eseza 'cause the Arrow Boys had banned her from the community. They said she couldn't be trusted since she had lied to them and had been sent to spy on them by Kony."

"Arrow Boys?" Bruce asked.

"A group that's fighting Kony. From what I could see, they were mainly teenage boys. There was Peter, and then Jonasan—he was the leader. I think so, anyway. And Michael Jackson."

"Michael Jackson? Like the singer?" Scott asked.

345

"Yeah, same name, different guy. And they were heading out to the LRA camp that night, the night Eseza and I left, and they were going to rescue their friend Naboth, the boy I told you was tied to the tree."

"But"—Bruce's brow furrowed in concern—"how many were going?"

"I don't know. Eseza told him he was foolish to go. She believed Naboth was dead by then, and there was no use in going to the camp. And she warned Charlie they didn't have a chance against a whole army, but he wouldn't listen."

Scott and Bruce stared at each other. Both shared the same anxious look.

"But what about weapons? Do they have anything? Guns? Bows and arrows? Anything?" Bruce asked.

"They had bows and arrows, but no, the only guns I saw were at the LRA camp. Mainly AK-47s, a few old rifles, maybe stuff left over from the cold war. You know, stuff like that."

Scott and Bruce exchanged curious glances.

"How do you—?" Bruce asked.

"You mean how would I know anything about guns? It comes from paintballing. My dad and I go out a lot and, well, I sort of developed this interest in guns. That's all."

Bruce stood. "I don't know about you, but I

346

think we need to go back there now. We've got Charlie and these Arrow Boys heading off to the LRA camp, and the Arrow Boys obviously don't know what they're up against. Either that, or they have some sorta kamikaze mission going on. But if Charlie's going on it, he must have a good reason. It's not like Charlie to be stupid like that. That was our job."

Scott laughed. "But there's one thing that's bugging me about all of this," he said. "You said Charlie gave Kony the stone. What's happened to Kony? He's still out there. He's still taking kids. He hasn't changed."

The room was silent. Sam cleared her throat. "You know how the older adults get, the harder it is to get them to change?"

Bruce and Scott nodded.

"I had a grandpa who always insisted that the only way to write to someone was the old-fashioned snail mail way. Even when I showed him how easy it was to use a computer and e-mail people and get a response right away, he still insisted on writing letters by hand and spending money on stamps. It absolutely bugged me. Anyway, the point I'm trying to make is that adults don't change. Well, not as easily, anyway. And Kony's an adult, right?"

"In other words, you're saying we can't rely on the stones to change Kony," Scott said.

"Exactly."

"Then it was all for nothing—Charlie giving the stone to Kony, I mean. It couldn't have been all that easy, you know?"

"But what she says makes sense," Bruce said. "That woman, the one in the museum with the necklace. I often wondered about that. She's had the stones for years and she's gotta have held one at least once, but she's obviously never gone anywhere 'cause all five stones are there, right?"

"Good point," said Sam. "It was the same with Dr. Roget, this woman who came to set up the Egyptian displays today. I saw her hold a stone, wrap her fingers around it and everything, but nothing happened."

"But that happened to me, too," Scott said. "I held the stones over and over again when I came back from Uganda with my dad, and nothing happened. It wasn't until later, after you came back, Bruce, that they took me to Uganda—again."

"Then maybe they only work when . . . never mind. I have no idea how they work," Sam said.

"I don't think it matters if we figure out how they work or not," Bruce said. "The point is, Charlie's going back to the LRA camp, and if he gets caught again, he's dead. And I don't mean a-bullet-in-the-head dead. I mean they'll tie him to a tree and torture him for hours until he's dead. They do that to the kids there, you know?"

Sam closed her eyes. The image of Naboth lying on the ground as the child soldier beat him relentlessly filled her mind. The sound of the stick as it flew through the air and landed with a loud whack resounded in her brain again and again. She pushed the image out of her head. "I know."

"But we need a plan before we go, right?" Scott asked.

"But what's to plan?" Sam said. "We don't know where anyone is, so we don't know where we'll land, do we? And we don't even know what Charlie's doing right now. It would be horrible to land right in the middle of an escape and foul it all up. The only thing I can be a little sure about is where Eseza is, and that's the camp for the people who have escaped from Kony. She went there to get her son. And even then, I can't be a hundred percent sure."

"You're right," Bruce said. "This time we don't plan anything. But we go and we go as soon as possible, okay?"

"Yep, you're right," Scott nodded.

"You got the stones?" Bruce asked.

"Yeah," Sam said. "I almost lost them, but I've got them now. But that's another story." She reached into her pocket and pulled out three stones. She passed one to Bruce and one to Scott. They held them in their outstretched hands.

"I miss the guy," Bruce said, smiling. "But I'm gonna have a word or two with him for calling me stupid."

"Yeah, me too," Scott said.

"I miss Eseza too. I hope she's okay and she found her son. And I hope things are gonna be better for her. Maybe they won't be as bad as she thinks they'll be."

"Well, at least when we get there, things will be a bit better," Scott said.

"Better?" asked Bruce.

"Yeah, there'll be the three of us and we'll be together."

"Shall we get going?" Sam asked.

Bruce clutched his stone. "See you there," he said. He closed his eyes and vanished.

Scott and Sam stared at each other. "That is so cool," Sam whispered.

Scott held his stone tightly in his fist. "Good luck," he said. He smiled, and just like Bruce, he vanished before Sam's eyes.

She took a deep breath. "Well, what have you got to lose, big *muzungu* Sam?" She wrapped her hand around the stone and the room disappeared. She was back in Uganda.

Chapter 29

Many hands make light work.
~ Tanzanian proverb

Bruce opened his eyes and looked around. A cool wind blew across his face. The moon brought a surreal glow to the bush that surrounded him. He cocked his head and heard the faint rustle of leaves. He leaned forward, not daring to move his feet. The faint outline of a boy running into the bush came into focus until the boy was hidden by the trees. A bare back. Running shoes.

"Charlie?" Bruce whispered.

He looked behind and stared into the darkness.

"Scott? Sam?" he called out quietly. "Where are you?"

*   *   *   *

Scott looked from one side of the moonlit clearing to the other. He knelt and surveyed his surroundings. A small mud hut stood to the left of him, a tattered sheet hanging from its door, moving slightly with the breeze that blew across his face. Straight ahead was a vague outline of an opening to a pathway. Scott listened to the breeze as it rustled the leaves. He held his breath. He heard a faint moan and turned his head.

A young boy, about his age, was tied to a tree that stood beside him. His legs were sprawled out before him, while his arms were firmly fastened to his side. His head hung down and his chin rested on his chest. His face was swollen, and his shirt was ripped and stained with blood. Scott wrinkled his nose as he caught the scent of dried blood and something else that emitted a fetid smell. He looked behind him.

"Bruce? Sam?" he whispered. "Where are you?"

*   *   *   *

Sam stared into the darkness. A modest fire, contained within a circle of rocks, glowed in front of her. Above her a sliver of the moon lit the scene. A girl in a long white dress sat crouched on the ground holding a baby tightly to her chest. She rocked back and forth. A slow, mournful moan came from her lips.

Sam walked to her and crouched down. She lifted the girl's chin and stared into her eyes. "It's okay, Eseza. We can get through this."

Sam held her and stared into the surrounding bush. She looked from one part of the clearing to the other. "Bruce? Scott?" she called out. "I'm right here! Where are you?"

She waited for a response. She called out again. The only sound she heard was Eseza's sobs and the rustle of the leaves. She held on to her a little tighter.

"Maybe we won't be together, Scott. Kinda looks like we're on our own."

AUTHOR'S NOTE:

Shortly after I returned from Uganda in 2008, I visited with a friend who had volunteered at the World Vision/UNICEF recovery center for former child soldiers in Gulu. He told me about Florence, a woman he knew from the center who had worked as a counselor shortly after her fifteen-year-old daughter, Angela, had been abducted by Joseph Kony and the LRA. Florence worked there for years, hoping each day that when one of the government army trucks pulled into the compound, carrying children who had managed to escape from the army, that her daughter would be on one of them.

She waited nine years.

Then one day while my friend was there, Florence's daughter was found by the UPDF and reunited with her mother.

He said the whole center erupted in praise. The drums were brought out, people sang and danced and clapped and shouted and then a huge parade started and went from one end of the compound to the other and back again. He said the people on the other side of the barricaded cement walls must have thought it was the second coming. And then he showed me a picture of Florence and Angela hugging, and I cried.

And so, when I returned to Uganda in 2015, it should have come as no surprise when I walked into the Gulu Recovery Center that Angela came out to greet me, her arms extended in the traditional Ugandan way: You are most welcome. She was now head counselor at the center.

I said, "I know you. You're Angela. I know your story."

As it turned out, I only knew a very small part of it.

And so, I dedicate this book to Angela. A wondrous and courageous and strong strong woman.

If you enjoyed this book, please leave a review online at Amazon.com, Amazon.ca and Goodreads. Even if you didn't enjoy it, your feedback is appreciated!

To receive notice of the next release in the Stones Trilogy go to:
www.donnawhitebooks.com.
To join in the conversation:
www.facebook.com/donnawhitebooks

Glossary

As in the first book of the trilogy, I made great efforts to include common words and phrases of the Acholi tribe in their native Luo language. Sometimes, however, I used a type of street slang known as Uglish, a cross between Luganda and English. In other cases, I used Kiswahili, because it was more suitable for that word or phrase at that moment. Sometimes it was difficult to find a suitable word because the word in Luo did not exist, and if it did, the meaning was lost in translation. While the dialects of the people of Uganda vary widely from region to region and class to class, the dialect that is portrayed in this novel is an assembling of different styles of speech from various regions and various classes of the people of Uganda. If I have made any mistakes, I apologize, again. I am, after all, a muzungu just.

Glossary of Acholi (Luo) words

acel, ariyo, adek, angwen, abic: one, two, three, four, five

ajiji: Literally translated means "to see again", flashback, Post Traumatic Stress Disorder (PTSD)

Anansi: famous spider trickster god

apwoyo matek: thank you very much

bolingo, and kakopi kakopi: popular games children play in Uganda and other parts of Africa

cawa marac: bedtime

cet: shit

goyo: beat

gu: large. For example: gu-rock is large rock

gway: hey

gweye: here

hyna: hyena. In Uganda the people do not say the middle e sound, so the word is pronounced high-na

hujambo: hello - Swahili

itye nining: greeting, "How are you?"

jela: jail

jok: evil spirit

ka: little. For example: ka-boy is little boy

kapere: Uglish for nobody

kit kwo ma gang: life at home

kit kwo ma ilum: life in the bush

konyi pee: dirt

kwaro: grandfather

latin gunya: child gorilla

latunge ki remo: brown noser

lajok: witch doctor - believed to possess great and evil power

maa: mother

min maa: grandmother

machet: machete. In Uganda the people do not say the final "e" sound, so the word is pronounced ma-shet.

muzungu: Literally translated it means "someone who roams around" or wanderer. Word used to describe first Europeans who came to Africa and appeared to be wandering or lost. Plural: bazungu.

ojone: please

opego: pig

romo: sheep

simsim: sesame seed or any sweet made using sesame seed and honey

sufuria au moto: Fire or pan - Swahili

tin: ammunition - slang

wora: father

Author's Thanks

No man is an island and no book is written solo. Well, this one wasn't anyways.

To my beta readers/editors: Jeannie Pendziwol, brother Dave, sister Sandra, Susan Rogers, and Caroline Kaiser: Thank you. I could not have done this without your expertise, support and encouragement, and all of those lovely things you said about the book to keep me going. Your confidence in this story has been the foundation for my perseverance and I thank you immensely. And to Amy, Katherine, and Zachary, my testers, thank you for your feedback. You helped me bring it up a notch or two or three.

To Heather, my cover designer extraordinaire. Chip Kidd says, "A book cover is a distillation. It is a Haiku of the story." Yep. You are one fine poet.

To Angela, Janet, Florence, Agnes, Margaret, Christine and all of the wonderful people who work at Watye Ki Gen, the Gulu recovery project for former child soldiers, I thank you. You have restored my faith in mankind. If you ruled the world there would be peace in abundance everywhere.

And to all of the men, women and children who shared their stories with me at the center I cannot thank you enough. You revisited your past and brought me face to face with your most horrid memories. I listened, we cried, we covered our faces in dismay, we prayed and you taught me: while there are many stones in our lives, we have the ability to plant the seeds and see the flowers grow.

To Peter, our driver and translator while in Uganda: thank you for taking us on the roads less traveled, to huts hidden and places haunted with sad sad memories. You kept us safe, and for that I am thankful.

To Ben and Penny at Great Lakes Safaris, thank you for the wondrous days of exploring the savannah and visiting places where your majestic animals roam free. Your knowledge of the plant and wildlife in northern Uganda, Ben, was a huge asset to this book. And meeting up with the lions and the black mamba was pretty cool too. Thank you.

To Jason, my friend and fellow World Vision volunteer, thank you for accompanying us on this trip. You are a rock and I think you know what I mean by that.

To Colleen and all of the World Vision staff in Canada and Uganda who made our trip possible, thank you. I could not have done this without you.

To Eben, thank you for sharing your story

about the sun and the shadows. It completes the story just fine.

To my family: Gary, Kira and Karl, I've put you through so much and feel that I've neglected you greatly. But I'm hoping as I learned more and shared more with you that you became more compassionate and understanding, if that was possible being the wonderful family you already are.

And to God. Yes, you amaze me. Putting people on my path, directing me and helping me to persevere. You told me again and again: tell Charlie's story, it needs to be heard, it needs to be heard. Thank you for giving me the means to tell it. Thank you.

And to all of the people who said, "That was a great book, when is the second one coming out?" thank you. You made me believe in Charlie's story. You made me believe in myself as a writer and a story teller. A teller of Charlie's story.

ABOUT THE AUTHOR

Donna White is a teacher and author of the *Stones* trilogy. She resides in Canada with her husband and children. Visit the author's website at **www.donnawhitebooks.com** to find photo galleries, teaching resources, and much more.

A percentage of the proceeds from this novel will be given to World Vision Canada programs to help former child soldiers receive medical support, counseling, education and, when possible, reunite them with their loved ones.

If you wish to make a donation to help these children, go to:

https://catalogue.worldvision.ca/products/2501

For more information about child soldiers go to

www.donnawhitebooks.com

Now you know. Do something about it.